D1442276

COURAGE STOUT

Center Point
Large Print

Also by William MacLeod Raine and
available from Center Point Large Print:

Desert Feud
Border Breed

**This Large Print Book carries the
Seal of Approval of N.A.V.H.**

COURAGE STOUT

STOUT

WILLIAM MacLeod RAINE

CENTER POINT LARGE PRINT
THORNDIKE, MAINE

The text of this Large Print edition is unabridged.
In other aspects, this book may vary from the original edition.
Printed in the United States of America on permanent paper.
Set in 16-point Times New Roman type.

ISBN: 978-1-62899-346-2

Library of Congress Cataloging-in-Publication Data

Raine, William MacLeod, 1871–1954.
  Courage stout / William MacLeod Raine. —
    Center Point Large Print edition.
  pages ; cm
  Summary: "Neil MacGowan, owner of the K-B Ranch sees both good
and bad on both sides of the struggle between the cattlemen and the
others—homesteaders and rustlers. When the struggle starts to escalate,
it will be up to him to find a solution"—Provided by publisher.
  ISBN 978-1-62899-346-2 (hardcover : alk. paper) —
  ISBN 978-1-62899-353-0 (pbk. : alk. paper)
  1. Large type books. I. Title.
  PS3535.A385C68 2014
  813′.52—dc23
                                                    2014028582

Cowards fear to die; but courage stout,
Rather than live in snuff, will be put out.

SIR WALTER RALEIGH

CONTENTS

CHAPTER I

Austin Reynolds says thanks

Austin Reynolds tied his horse in the cotton-wood grove that ran up to the draw at the foot of the hill. He could tell by the number of mounts there that most of those coming to the funeral must already have arrived. As he read the brands on some of the cowponies he smiled grimly. They belonged to gentlemen who had come a long way to pay their respects to the memory of Stuart Lane, much farther than they would have come to see him if he had been alive.

He followed the path up the hill, taking the ascent with an easy stride. His strong figure moved with a confident assurance, none the less because he knew he would not be welcome here.

The Lane family stood alone at one side of the grave. Janet was going-on-eighteen. Now she would have to be the head of the house. Already she seemed to be schooling herself for the part. Her slender figure was rigid and there were no tears in her unhappy eyes. The little girl clinging to her hand was crying. Harry, a weedy boy thirteen years old, gulped down the sobs that kept rising to his throat. Once Janet put an arm around his shoulders to comfort him, but she did not let it stay long for fear of hurting his pride.

With the exception of three women the rest of those present were men. Reynolds let his gaze drift coolly over them as Finn Wood read selections from the Scriptures. They were brown hardbitten sons of the saddle, wearing Levis or chaps, spurs attached to their dusty boots. Each held a big wide-brimmed hat in one hand. They were grouped together, well back from the coffin, in their manner a shy grave respect for the young mourners. When the eyes of any of them met those of Reynolds, the owner of the Triangle R read in them a fierce hatred, an angry resentment of his audacity in attending the funeral. Stuart Lane had been shot down from ambush, and the general opinion was that the killer was some assassin hired by the big cattlemen because the settler had homesteaded a quarter section along a stream Reynolds and other large ranchers wanted to dam in order to irrigate alfalfa fields for their stock.

Finn Wood was not a preacher, but he had been a Christian many years. He spoke very simply about the dead homesteader they were here to bury. Stuart Lane was a God-fearing man, he told them, with no ill will in his heart for anybody. When he came to this new land it had been with the hope of making a home for his motherless children. The ways of God were not always clear to men. None of them knew why this good man, so greatly needed by his family, was called from them now. Somewhere in their community was an unknown man with the brand of Cain on him. He might think he had escaped, but this was not so. God had his eye on him, and to the day of his death and afterward he would have to pay for his evil deed.

As soon as the services were ended Finn Wood and his wife drove the Lanes home in their wagon. The men drifted down by twos and threes to the cottonwood grove where the saddled horses were tied. On the path back of Reynolds walked a group who took occasion to talk at but not to him.

'I reckon he came to make sure his killer got Lane,' a heavy voice sneered bitterly.

The owner of the Triangle R did not look round. It was not necessary. Jess Blackburn was talking, a huge hulk of a fellow with little pig eyes set in a beefy face. He had been out of circulation lately, except to a few cronies who nested with him far up in the hills among the deep cañons. The law wanted to talk with him about a train robbery in New Mexico.

Reynolds recognized the next voice as that of Allan Dunn. He knew it well, for Allan had worked as a rider for the Triangle R before he slipped across the line and became a rustler.

'Hush yore mouth, fellow,' it jeered. 'Don't you know you are talkin' about one of the big moguls of this Flood River country? You're liable to get yore name on the black list if you don't watch out.'

The third man of the group tittered. He was Luke Fox, a person of no account, not expert even in his own lawless specialty of branding other men's calves.

Austin Reynolds strode down the path, paying no apparent attention to those behind him. They could read whatever answer they liked in the flat straight back and the head poised arrogantly on broad muscular shoulders. He knew already what these hill men thought of him and nothing they said would affect the course he followed.

A dozen men were in the cottonwoods, some moving toward their mounts and others in the saddle. Their gazes focused on Reynolds as if he had been a magnet for them. The owner of the Triangle R felt their rage beat on him as tangibly as gusts of wind.

He faced them almost disdainfully, though he knew he had walked into a situation that might at any moment become perilous. These men were not all scoundrels, though they were united in a common resentment of the dominance of the big cattle outfits. Some were homesteaders, decent enough citizens, even if they might at times eat slow elk[1] under the pressure of hunger. One was a storekeeper from Sundog patronized largely by

[1] Rustled beef was known as slow elk in the cattle country.

the nesters, and another ran a saloon in the same town. In the background, a cynical but interested observer, stood Neal MacGowan, a cattleman with a big spread but one ostracized by the other stockmen of the district. In the entire group the searching gaze of Reynolds could not find a friendly face.

Blackburn put the feeling into words. 'Take a good look at him, boys—the fellow who laid Stuart Lane in that wooden box and has come to gloat over what he has done.'

There was a chorus of furious assent.

A smooth-faced lad on a pinto horse ripped out an oath. 'What harm had Lane ever done him, outside of taking up a homestead he had a right to locate?' he demanded.

'What's eatin' you, Russ?' Dunn asked with scornful irony. 'Are you claimin' any nester has a right to his own water holes when Mr. Big here wants them?'

Reynolds pulled the slip knot that tied the bridle reins of his cowpony to the limb of a cottonwood. He stood beside the horse, his right hand on the saddlehorn. The hard steady eyes of the cattleman took in Dunn's lanky frame and came to rest on his face.

'Any more than I have a right to my calves when Mr. Little wants them,' he replied hardily.

Dunn took a threatening step toward him. 'If you're claimin' I take yore calves—'

'I'm claiming nothing just now, except that I do not know who killed Stuart Lane or why he did it,' Reynolds interrupted.

'That sounds to me!' Blackburn cried, and moved closer. 'Who wanted that stretch of water Lane homesteaded? Whose cattle did he aim to keep off it by fencing?'

Reynolds's voice was dry and scornful. 'Lane was not a rustler. Do you think I was starting to rub out every settler nesting round the Triangle R?'

Dunn answered that. 'Starting with Lane. Why not? He was in yore way more than the others. You figured you needed that stretch of water, and the others might scare and light out after you had bumped him off. Don't try to pull the wool over our eyes. We know yore high and mighty crowd. You used to pay us five bucks apiece to put the Triangle R on maverick calves, but when we burned our own brands on 'em we were rustlers, by God. You made the laws to suit yoreselves, and we were only a bunch of slaves working for you.'

The cattleman sensed a rising tide of hatred that might sweep over and destroy him. He had thought his reasons good for coming to this funeral, but he realized he had made a mistake. His cold gaze swept the circle of hostile eyes fixed on him, and he was reminded of a wolf pack ready for the kill. Presently a leader would make a move. He saw the hunger for revenge in Dunn's harsh bitter face. The man had missed going to the penitentiary by the narrowest squeak on evidence gathered by Reynolds. From Blackburn's animal countenance the same eagerness leaped out. He too had a debt to pay. There were others here who had private reasons for disliking him, since both officially and as an individual he had been the leader of his group in the fight to hold the range.

For an instant his glance fell on Neal MacGowan, who was taking in the scene with detached and sardonic amusement, the bridle of his chestnut cowpony held negligently in one hand.

'That's right,' a cowboy growled. 'Slaves working our heads off for thirty dollars a month.'

A mounted man with a face as leathery as his chaps rapped out the suggestion simmering as a floating thought in the minds of several. 'He came to this graveyard without invitation to see poor Lane buried. Nobody asked him here, but since he's so interested in funerals—'

He left the sentence unfinished, but Reynolds's glance picked up the response to it in the circle of shining eyes surrounding him. It was time for him to be gone, if not already too late. No motion of his body betrayed his intention of shifting hands on the pommel and vaulting to the saddle. No muscle of his brown face, no expression in his steely eyes, showed his awareness of imminent peril.

'You're a bunch of half-witted fools,' he said contemptuously, 'believing what you want to believe with no evidence to back it.'

The man who had been standing with an arm resting on the neck of the chestnut gelding laughed lightly and sauntered forward. He had a dark good-looking reckless face and was as lithe and graceful as a cat.

Reynolds took advantage of his approach to turn toward him, changing hands on the horn as he did so. In a land of big men such as Wyoming Neal MacGowan was considered small. He stood five foot eight and scaled one hundred and forty-seven pounds. But he was built beautifully, and it was said that he could whip his weight in wildcats.

'Mr. Reynolds isn't going to like having me on his side, but for once I agree with him,' the black-haired young man said. 'There aren't going to be any fireworks, boys. That would be heap bad medicine. We don't know who killed Stuart Lane. Why pick on the first big cattleman who happens to be handy? One of these days you'll know the right man, and it probably won't be Austin Reynolds.'

'Thanks for this support,' the owner of the Triangle R told MacGowan ironically. 'Of course I understand you would have a lot of influence with—with gentlemen like these present.'

'Meaning what?' Blackburn demanded.

The ranchman looked at him, with cool steady insolence.

'Meaning that you may write your own ticket. Call yourselves what you like. We all know what you are.'

'And we know what you are,' the bandit countered. 'The man who hired a killer to murder Stuart Lane.' He added, in a burst of heat, 'We ought to rub the fellow out now, boys—right damn now.'

'Why not?' Reynolds asked with cold disdain. 'You're only fifteen or sixteen to one.'

MacGowan moved forward to face Blackburn. His steady gaze challenged the pig-eyed ruffian. 'For a stranger, making us a short visit, aren't you talking a little loud?' he drawled. 'You couldn't have a personal reason for objecting to Reynolds, could you?'

The dark blood poured angrily into the beefy face of the bandit. The high spots of his unsavory record were known to all present. Turbulent cowboy, range bully, mavericker, calf thief, killer, outlaw. Swiftly he had gone from bad to worse, until even those with whom he associated avoided him when they could, both from individual dislike and the feeling that the evil in him was dangerous. MacGowan had put his finger on a sore spot, one that had been sensitive for years. In the days when Reynolds had been sheriff, elected through the influence of his fellow cattlemen, he had curtly served notice on Blackburn to get out or be killed, and the bad man had elected to make a shift of residence to Montana.

'You can't tell me what to say and how to say it, MacGowan,' the outlaw answered thickly. 'I don't have to take that from you.'

'But you're taking it.' MacGowan spoke almost gently, yet the brown eyes in the lean sun-tanned face were hard as granite and as unwavering.

The shifty gaze of Luke Fox slid from Blackburn to MacGowan and back again. 'Let's not have any trouble, boys,' he interposed hurriedly. 'We all aim to be reasonable, I reckon. Maybe Jess went a mite too far. 'Course we're all excited about poor Stuart Lane, but we want to keep our heads and not push on the reins.'

A touch of whimsical mirth twitched at the lips of MacGowan. 'That's fine, Luke,' he said. 'Here we are, standing shoulder to shoulder, you and Reynolds and I, one for all and all for one.'

Dunn scowled at MacGowan. He spoke with the forced patience of one who is annoyed but determined not to give offense. 'Do you have to buy chips in this game, Neal? Reynolds is no friend of yours. He couldn't have any kick if you swung to the saddle and hit the trail, leaving us to talk this over with him.'

Neal shook his head. 'No, Allan. I'm sitting in. When I leave Reynolds is going with me.'

A hard-faced man in store clothes seconded the cattleman. He was Brick Carson, a saloonkeeper from Sundog. 'Neal is right, boys. We want to make sure we've got the right man before we settle his hash.'

'I expect, Brick, that you and Neal and Luke will be sleeping under the same tarp with Reynolds soon,' Dunn flung out, with a harsh bitter laugh. 'Well, boys, I don't know what you other fellows are doing, but I'm hittin' the trail.'

He swung to the saddle and rode out of the cottonwoods. The others followed, most of them relieved that the crisis had been averted. Reynolds and MacGowan were the last to go.

'You make your friends toe the line,' Reynolds commented icily. 'Must make you proud that you have them trained so well.'

MacGowan did not pick up the scornful charge hurled at him, the implication that he was the leader of the thieves and outlaws who did their night riding from the hill pockets to which the gorges back of his ranch led. That he was regarded as a renegade by the other cattlemen he knew. His withdrawal from the Association a few months earlier had brought no protests from the other members. They felt that they were fighting to maintain the way of life the stockmen had followed for years, to hold against incoming settlers the grazing land and water holes necessary for their herds. After the Indians had been driven to reservations they were the first comers. This was cattle and not farming country, and they claimed a priority right to it regardless of the laws written at Washington by men who did not understand frontier conditions.

To the managers and the owners of the big ranches Neal MacGowan was a traitor, a pill more bitter to swallow than the nesters and the rustlers, small fry they often succeeded in weeding out one way or another. For Neal was a cattleman himself, and he walked among them gay and debonair in spite of their disapproval. His ranch was the gateway to Rustlers' Gap, yet he did not lift a hand to stop the shadowy night riders who rode across his range in the dark of the moon on their nefarious errands. Those who ran the big outfits could not prove that MacGowan was in league with the thieves or that to hold his friendliness the rustlers burned the K-B brand on other men's stock, but they believed he was at least on the borderline, if not a thief himself one who winked at lawlessness in others.

A warm sun beat down on the barren sage hill. From the heels of the two horsemen a cloud of dust rose as they followed the long brown undulating road ribbon.

Reynolds knew that Neal MacGowan had rescued him from imminent peril and that he rode with him now as a protection against ambush. This irritated him. He was annoyed at himself for having let such a situation arise, and at MacGowan (unreasonably, he realized) for being the means of his escape.

'I have to thank you for your help,' he said stiffly.

Neal waved the obligation aside carelessly, with a sardonic grin. 'If I'm the boss of Rustlers' Gap I have to crack a whip once in a while to let the boys know it.'

The sound of a rifle shot whipped across the shoulder of the hill behind them. Reynolds glanced down at his hat lying in the dusty road and swung swiftly from the saddle. He dragged a Winchester from its boot beside the horse. MacGowan had instantly lifted his chestnut cowpony to a gallop. He was heading straight for the clump of cottonwoods at the mouth of a draw from which a puff of smoke was rising. There was a clatter of hoofs, a glimpse of a roan horse disappearing up the winding gulch. When Neal reached the trees, the rifleman had gone.

He rode back to the road. Reynolds looked down grimly at two holes in the crown of his hat. 'You ought to teach your scoundrels to shoot straighter,' he said curtly.

'Looks like hell has broke loose in Georgia,' MacGowan drawled.

A hundred yards ahead they came to a parting of the road and separated.

CHAPTER II

Neal drops in on a neighbor

From the door Janet called cheerfully to the children, 'Dinner is ready.'

It was three days after the funeral, and whenever she thought of her father a lump still came to her throat. How quickly the violent grief of the children had worn itself out surprised her. Already they were accommodating their lives to his absence. After breakfast they had fussed with each other about feeding the pigs. A few minutes ago she had heard them laughing over the strutting pride of a hen with one chick.

Now they came shouting to the house, clamoring to know whether there was pudding or pie for dessert. This was the way it should be with the young, Janet thought. Sorrow with them ought to be only for a day. Life had to go on, for her as well as for these half-growns. For years she had been a little mother to them. From this time she must be father too.

They were eating the last crumbs of their dried apple pie when a voice outside shouted, 'Hello the house!'

Harry scuttled to the door and called back joyfully, 'It's Neal MacGowan.' Mary slipped from her chair and joined her brother. 'Can I ride Keno, Neal?' she shouted. Janet looked in the glass and patted down her soft wavy brown hair. Stuart Lane had not approved of MacGowan, nor did his elder daughter. He was a wild and reckless young man about whom evil stories were whispered. Sarah Wood had warned her not to be too friendly with him, since he consorted with outlaws and might be one himself. But in spite of her better judgment Janet had a liking for the ranchman. He was kind to the children and sometimes tossed them candy when he came back from Sundog. Also, he had a cheerful disposition and brought gaiety into a house which did not have enough of it.

MacGowan's excuse for dropping in was that he had shot a turkey on the creek and did not want to bother taking it home. Janet started to tell him a little primly that they had plenty of meat, but he forestalled a refusal by saying casually, 'Oh, that's all right, feed it to the hogs.'

Just like him, Janet thought. He was a man hard to discourage. During the two years since Lane had taken up this homestead he had done them a dozen helpful favors and made nothing of them. Though he must have sensed the new settler's aloofness, due to Lane's determination not to let himself become associated with the nomadic night riders infesting the bad lands back of the K-B Ranch, MacGowan had ignored the older man's rebuffs.

'What are you going to do about a man,' Lane once asked his daughter ruefully, 'who without any by-your-leave shows up with a score of riders, half of them wanted by the law, and builds a good barn for you out of logs he has cut and snaked out of the woods?'

In appraising Neal MacGowan it was hard for Janet to leave out of account all the attributes that made him such a likable person. He was a superb rider, one of the best in the state. From tales she heard about him she gathered that he went into danger as gaily as a lover goes to meet his sweetheart. No doubt the eyes she had seen so often lit with mirth could mirror the explosive violence that was in him, but she had never seen any evidence of it. Though he made no claims to education, she knew he liked books. He had surprised her by flashing out with a quotation from Keats.

The custom of the country was that anybody coming to a house at meal time must be invited to eat. Janet set a plate for their guest, but he told her he had dined at the Wood place.

'If you don't mind, I'll take a piece of that apple pie,' he added. 'It looks good, and pie is one thing I can't resist.'

Janet cut him a wedge. 'I hear that Mr. Reynolds had some trouble at the cemetery,' she said, not looking at him.

He was not surprised she knew. News travels fast in a frontier land with few settlers.

'I wouldn't call it trouble,' he corrected. 'Some of the boys had ideas for a minute or two, but they changed their minds.'

'With your help,' she suggested. 'How did it start?'

'Easy to get a fuss going these days. Some loose talk.'

She said, her face tight to hold back emotion, 'They accused him of having Father shot, didn't they?'

'Yes. Without any evidence.'

'Do you think he did it?'

'No. Reynolds is a hard tough man, but I think if he had any killing to do it would be done in the open.'

'*Somebody* . . . murdered him,' she replied in a low voice, her eyes on the table.

Neal looked through the door at the two youngsters admiring his horse. He asked gently, 'Have you anything at all to go on—any suspicions?'

She lifted her eyes to his. 'Only that his homestead was interfering with Austin Reynolds's plans for a dam.'

He nodded. 'And Reynolds wouldn't like that. He's an autocratic fellow. But what I had in mind was something else. Had your father made any personal enemies? Did he seem to be troubled about anything?'

'No enemies of that sort. Father did not make

any. He was always just and fair.' She frowned out at the children for a minute, considering MacGowan's second question. 'I think he did have something on his mind, but he did not tell me what it was. He had been up Squaw Creek to cut a box elder for smoking the hams. That was the day before he was . . . shot. All evening he was unusually quiet, as if he was thinking something out. Even after Harry and Mary went to bed I didn't ask any questions, for I knew that when he wanted to tell me he would. I wish now I had made him tell me.'

'He didn't give you any hint?'

'No. He did mention meeting Mr. Reynolds. Of course he may have been worrying because things weren't going too well with us some ways.'

'Did he do much worrying about that?'

'No. Usually he was very optimistic and cheerful. He was building up a home, and he felt there were more important things than making money.'

Neal drummed on the table with his fingertips, eyes narrowed in thought. The explanation of Lane's absorption offered by his daughter did not satisfy the ranchman. He wished he knew just where the homesteader's wagon had gone and whom he had met in addition to Reynolds. He might have heard or seen something that led to his death later.

'There are no box elders on the creek,'

MacGowan said. 'He would have to go back into the hills to find one. I don't suppose he told you where he cut this one.'

Janet shook her head. 'But there isn't anybody up in the hills would want to hurt him. What reason could they have?'

MacGowan knew of none, but he thought he would ride up Squaw Creek and scout a little. Not many wagons went up that road. He might find tracks telling him where Lane had turned off to find a box elder. To Janet he said nothing of this. The sooner she stopped brooding about her father's death the better.

As she walked beside him to his horse he felt a warm sympathy for her loneliness. She had gone such a little way in life, and already it was robbing her of the carefree girlhood to which she was entitled. Her dress was a cheap print from which the pattern had almost faded, but it could not conceal the loveliness of her young slender lines. A faint color bloomed in her soft cheeks. In spite of the responsibilities that had turned her into a grave young virgin mother there lingered in her, he thought, a shy and fawnlike innocence. Janet Lane had none of the bouncing good looks he saw at dances where the buxom daughters of the small ranchmen romped with the cowboys. Her beauty was more rare and fugitive.

From the first meeting Neal had been attracted by the serious poised maturity that went so oddly with her slim and fluent youth. It had pleased him when something he said brought laughter into the overly anxious eyes. Too much care rested on her young shoulders. It would do her good to be awakened to love. He guessed that some day thoughts of a man would send the hot blood beating through that clear skin. But not of Neal MacGowan. A very different kind of young woman held the center of his meditations, a long-limbed young sylph whose provocative and mocking glances courted excitement and adventure. All he wished was to make life easier for Janet, regardless of the fact that she had weighed him in the balance of her judgment and found him wanting.

CHAPTER III

Rustlers' Gap

Neal MacGowan rode through the knee-high blue-stem grass to the creek and followed its sinuous bank into the hills. There had been no rain since Stuart Lane had driven a wagon up the little-used road, and in places the wheel tracks were still plain. The rider picked them out twenty times in the first five miles. As he got deeper into the foothills it became more difficult to read sign on a path getting continuously more rocky.

More than once he lost the tracks, but at each draw where Lane might have left the creek Neal swung from the saddle and made a careful examination of the ground. At the third attempt he found the place where the homesteader had swung to the left into a small mountain park skirted by a rim rock. Here Lane had evidently left the wagon and had ridden up a steep slope. The torn sage showed where later the trunk of the box elder had been snaked down to the wagon by the horse.

He rode up the shoulder and reached the summit by way of a break in the rim rock. A plateau stretched before him upon which a few cattle were grazing. From the farther edge of the plateau the terrain rose to the rocky defile known as Rustlers' Gap. Back of this, in the far distance, he could see the tips of a few of the peaks in the range, blue and hazy against the foreground of the brown ridge just beyond the Gap.

Since he was a cattleman Neal rode close enough to the grazing stock to read the K-B branded on their flanks. The spring rains had helped the grass and the cows looked plump and sleek. Not far from them his glance fell on the stump of the box elder Stuart Lane had chopped. It had to be the same one, since here and there signs showed where the trunk had been dragged along the ground recently.

MacGowan cut other sign, the tracks of four horses heading for Rustlers' Gap. He looked at the hoofmarks a long time, his thoughts sweeping over possibilities. The Sheridan stage had been held up and the shotgun messenger killed the day before the murder of Lane. Either four or five men had been in the robbery according to the two passengers and Hank Baldwin, the driver. These might be the tracks left by the bandits on their way back to hole up in the hills. If so, they must have been passing pretty close to the time when the homesteader was snaking the box elder back to his wagon. He might have seen and recognized them.

But even so, there would be nothing incriminating in meeting a group of men riding fifty miles or so distant from the locale of a holdup, no reason for them to rub out later a man who had seen too much. Why go all round Robin Hood's barn to find another cause for the death of Lane when the logical one stood out like a sore thumb? Detectives of the Cattlemen's Association had within a few months shot down two rustlers and left pinned to their breasts papers upon which the words 'Cow Thieves Beware' had been roughly printed. On Stuart Lane's coat the same warning had been found. The homesteader was of course no rustler, but he was more in the way of two or three of the big ranches than any brand-blotter.

Neal hesitated for several minutes. He was not a manhunter, and there was no sense in his looking for trouble. But in the end he turned and followed the prints toward the Gap. He had not lost any stage robbers, but he was determined to clear up if possible the killing of Lane.

Before he had ridden a quarter of a mile he made a discovery. One of the riders had been chewing tobacco. Twice Neal saw the dried juice spattered on flat rocks.

'If the gent is traveling on an iniquitous errand he oughtn't to sign his name all along the way, Keno,' he drawled to his horse.

The Gap was a narrow pass strewn with boulders through which horses could pass only in single file. In front of it was a table-shaped crag that completely concealed the opening. From the summit of the defile Neal looked down on a panorama so rough and torn that few travelers ventured into it. Hills piled up one behind another, a huddle of them, some bare and some with pine forests marching up the slopes, and hidden in these were scores of ravines, gorges, little mountain parks, and streams flowing down from the snowclad range.

MacGowan guessed where the tracks led. He wound down to a cañon which brought him to a pocket almost hidden by a thick growth of aspen. A path led through the young growth to a grassy flat upon which horses grazed. Close to the high rock wall inclosing the little park nestled a one-room log cabin.

He hailed the house and a man showed in the doorway with a rifle in his hands. Neal rode forward and dismounted.

' 'Lo, Dunn,' he said. 'Been checking up on some strays.'

'Expect to find them here?' Dunn asked, suspicion in his narrowed pale blue eyes.

The K-B man shook his head smilingly. 'Not here. But since I was close to the Gap—'

'You figured you would drop in and say hello,' the lanky rustler jeered.

Jesse Blackburn's bulky body joined Dunn in the doorway. Together they blocked it. Neal wondered if there was something in the cabin they did not want him to see. Blandly he explained his presence.

'I wanted to ask you a question. The day before he was killed Stuart Lane drove up Squaw Creek to cut a box elder to use in his smokehouse. He mentioned to his daughter that he had met Reynolds. I'm wondering if they had some kind of a quarrel. Any of you happen to see Reynolds or Lane that day?'

Blackburn had been chewing tobacco steadily. Now his jaws stopped moving. The man's small pig eyes fixed themselves on MacGowan, in them a wary startled expression.

'What made you think we might have seen them?' Dunn inquired, a bristle of hostility stiffening his lank frame.

'I didn't say I thought so,' MacGowan replied mildly. 'I asked if you did.'

Blackburn's gaze found a flat rock about three yards from the door and he spattered it with tobacco juice. 'So Lane told the girl he met Reynolds and had a row with him,' he said. 'What else did he tell her?'

The cattleman brought his eyes back from the fouled boulder. 'He did not mention any trouble. I guessed they might have had some.'

'Where did they meet?'

'I don't know. Maybe on Squaw Creek. Does it matter where?'

The big outlaw slid a look at his lean swarthy companion. 'Not to us, it don't. Far as I know none of the boys were out of the Gap that day.'

33

Neal had reason to know that was a lie but did not say so.

An irritable voice from the cabin called querulously, 'If that's the doc don't keep him gabbin' out there.'

Awkwardly Blackburn swung his heavy body round. 'Keep yore shirt on, Nels. It's MacGowan.'

'Nels sick?' asked the owner of the K-B.

Sulkily Blackburn gave information. 'Got throwed from a bronc and busted an ankle.'

MacGowan shrugged his shoulders with a grin and quoted a bit of range doggerel:

Never was a horse that couldn't be rode,
Never was a rider that couldn't be throwed.

Dunn added detail. 'The damned broomtail put its foot in a gopher hole and had to be shot.'

'I've seen that happen two–three times,' the ranchman admitted. 'I reckon Nels wasn't too unlucky at that. He might have been put out of business instead of the horse. Well, so long, boys. Be seeing you in Sunday School.'

After he had mounted, Jess Blackburn walked beside the horse for a few yards. He wanted to add something to what had been said but found it difficult to begin.

'If you get anything more on Reynolds be sure to let us know,' he blurted out. 'I'll join a party any time to rub out that fellow.'

'We haven't anything on him yet except suspicion,' MacGowan answered. 'I don't believe he had a thing to do with Lane's death.'

'Well, I do,' Blackburn differed harshly. 'He was in it up to the neck. . . . Sure Lane didn't tell that girl of his anything about what happened that day except just that he met Reynolds?'

MacGowan's eyes met the beady ones of the big man very directly. 'Not a thing. He had something on his mind, but he did not say what it was. She wishes now she had made him talk more.'

The brutal face of the bad man showed relief, his visitor thought. He laid a big hand on the mane of the horse and spoke confidentially. 'Depend on it, Neal. That scoundrel Reynolds had trouble with Lane when they met. Probably he served notice on him to get out of his house before sun-up. That's the way these high and mighty cattlemen treat settlers. When Lane didn't light out, Reynolds gave the word to his killer and the poor fellow turned up his toes to the daisies.'

From his seat in the saddle MacGowan looked down on the villainous face upturned to his. He shook his head. 'Don't think so, Jess. I know Reynolds pretty well. He's not an assassin.'

'Who killed Thorne and Norwood?' Blackburn demanded bluntly.

'I don't know.'

'You know damned well that some detective of the stock association bumped them off, probably that fellow Brock who roosts up on the Bar A B range.'

'I don't *know* it. Do you? That's merely our opinion. And even if we're right, it doesn't follow that Reynolds was a party to it. I've thought of Brock, but Reynolds may not be involved at all.'

'They elected him sheriff, didn't they, before we put in Cullen this time? He's one of the head men of their crowd. They don't pull off a thing he doesn't know about. You can't tell me. I know him well as you do.'

MacGowan did not argue it any further. He rode out of the park into the cañon, and up it to the defile which let him from the Gap. What had been only a flight of fancy in his mind, a bare possibility, had grown into a strange suspicion. Blackburn had been one of the riders whose tracks he had cut while tracing Lane's movements. The tobacco splash on the rocks had told him that. In itself this might not mean anything. But why had the two men barred him from entering the cabin if they had nothing to conceal? Nelson Gurley was lying on a bunk inside it expecting a doctor. If he had broken an ankle from a fall there was no need of keeping Neal from seeing him. There was something fishy about that story.

When he had asked them whether they had seen Lane or Reynolds, both had shown alarm or at least disturbance. Because Blackburn had still been afraid their visitor was not convinced, and because he had to make sure that Lane had told his daughter nothing about him or his men, he had held Neal a minute longer to insist on the guilt of his enemy. All of this had a sinister look. But MacGowan did not see what Lane could have discovered that would make trouble for this bunch of miscreants.

Reynolds had been somewhere in the neighborhood that afternoon. It might be a good idea to ride over and see him. This was a happy thought, since it would be a pleasure as well as a duty. For he would no doubt meet Eleanor, and any day in the week he would be glad to take a fifteen-mile ride if she was at the end of it.

CHAPTER IV

An uninvited visitor

The Triangle R ranch-house was famous in the Flood River country. It had been built some years before by a young Englishman regardless of expense. That had been in the boom days when anybody with money could make a paper fortune in cattle. The original owner held the ranch about four years. Overgrazing, rustling, and the blizzard winter of '86–'87 had wiped him out, as they did scores of other outfits which had been run on the theory that stock-raising in the West was a bonanza and not a business.

Austin Reynolds bought the Triangle R for a fraction of its value. He already owned an adjoining ranch and he threw the two together, running them as one. Reynolds belonged to the new order of cowmen. He bred up his stock, raised alfalfa for winter feed, and was careful not to deplete the range by crowding it with too many cattle. From the first he had been successful. An aggressive man, keen to assert his rights, he had fought hard against the thieves who shot his cows and stole his calves. Nobody in the county had more enemies than he. His unpopularity did not disturb him at all, though he knew that some day he might be shot in the back.

He sat on the porch steps cleaning a gun. Except for a wrangler greasing a wagon the yard was deserted. In an hour or two the men would come loping in eager for supper.

The sound of gay voices drifted to him. He looked up, to see his sister and young Muir riding down the lane. The man had dismounted to open the gate, but she waved him aside, put her horse at it, and sailed over as gracefully as a deer. Muir opened the gate, led his mount through, and closed it again. Fifty yards back of them another rider jogged down the lane. He too went over the barrier without taking the trouble to clear the way. Neal MacGowan, Austin identified with no enthusiasm.

Eleanor Reynolds stopped beside the wrangler and drew from the shirt pocket of the man a sack of smoking tobacco and a book of wrappers. He grinned at her, admiration of her audacity in his surprised eyes, and watched her roll a cigarette and light it with a match borrowed from Muir.

MacGowan joined them. He had never seen a young woman smoke until now, except those in dance halls and brothels, but if she was trying to shock him no evidence of success showed in his amused gaze. It was Muir who murmured protestingly, 'Oh, I say, Nell.'

The riders moved forward to the porch and

dismounted. Reynolds looked at the girl, anger in his eyes. His sister was ten years younger than he, and he found her a handful.

Eleanor slanted a glance at him. 'Austin does not approve of me. He thinks I'm not a lady.'

'I don't approve of your folly,' he answered stiffly. 'There's probably not another decent girl in Wyoming would smoke, at least in public.'

'Somebody has to do the pioneering,' she told him lightly.

'And what d'you suppose Slim thinks of you? I won't have you be so free with the men.'

'Does it matter what he thinks?' she asked negligently. To Neal she said, over her shoulder as she left: 'Wait till I get out of these togs. I want to ask you how your friends in Rustlers' Gap are doing. And whether you have punished the one who missed killing Austin and only ventilated his hat.'

Neal chuckled at her insolence. 'I'll be here,' he promised.

The eyes of both MacGowan and the Scotchman Muir followed the girl. She was tall and slenderly full, in her movements a supple sensuous grace. She walked as if life, the mere living, sang a song in her blood. To these young men her beauty and high spirits justified adventures into the unconventional. The outrageous things she did and said they would have condemned in another, but Eleanor made her own laws. Moreover, beneath her brittle showmanship, they sensed a spirit sweet and gallant.

Reynolds waited for MacGowan to explain his visit. He had not been to the Triangle R for a good many months. The owner of the ranch could not tell him he was not welcome, in view of what he had done the other day after the funeral.

'I was talking with Janet Lane today,' Neal said. 'She told me that while her father was up Squaw Creek to get a box elder the day before his death you met him.'

'That is correct,' Reynolds replied coldly.

'I gathered from her something that may possibly throw light on her father's death. She thinks he was worried when he came home. He did not talk much—acted as if there was something on his mind. He was mulling over a problem. What I am wondering is whether it could have had any relation to any event that may have happened during the day.'

'Such as what?'

'I don't know. What time of day did you meet him?'

'Shortly after noon. On his way up, about four miles from his homestead. Why?' The back of the Triangle R owner was as straight as a ramrod. He did not know what this questioning was leading to, but he resented it none the less.

'I cut the tracks of some horsemen heading into Rustlers' Gap. You didn't meet the men?'

'No, I didn't. What are you driving at, MacGowan? Are you trying to pin this killing on me?'

Neal shook his head. 'Maybe it is a crazy notion, but this is what's in my nut. These riders might have been coming back from the holdup of the Sheridan stage. Say Lane met them and discovered something implicating the fellows. Later they may have talked it over among themselves and decided it was better to rub out a dangerous witness. I don't say it was that way. Still, it might be so. To divert suspicion they would leave the "Cow Thieves Beware" warning on the body.'

Robert Muir spoke for the first time. 'Man, you may be right, but even so you'll never be able to prove it now Lane is dead.'

'We have no evidence to prove they shot Lane. That is true. But if men from the Gap were in the stage robbery we might be able to prove that.'

'I thought they were friends of yours,' Reynolds said bluntly.

'I'm particular who my friends are,' MacGowan retorted curtly. 'Among them I don't include killers, regardless of whether they are outlaws or big cattlemen.'

'By Jove, you know, you shouldn't say that,' Muir protested.

Reynolds bristled. 'If you're referring to me—'

'I don't think I am,' Neal cut in coolly. 'But I have some of yore friends in mind. The

Cattlemen's Association paid to have Norwood and Thorne assassinated. That's the opinion of this country. Lane was my neighbor, a good upstanding citizen. The Association is getting the blame for this murder too. I want to know who is guilty.'

'Thorne and Norwood were proved thieves,' Reynolds returned, anger beating into his face. 'Your rustler juries would not convict them. We warned the fellows again and again. I don't know who killed them, but I will say that they deserved what they got. Lane was an honest man as far as I know. That is why I attended the funeral. Not for a moment have I believed that any of my friends had anything to do with this murder.'

'Then you want Lane's death cleared up, just as I do. I came to you because I thought you might have met the fellows riding to the Gap. But since you didn't you can't help me.'

'Afraid not,' Reynolds agreed, the hostility ironing out of his face. 'But I would if I could. The chances are about three to one that some gang from the Gap pulled off the stage robbery.'

Muir raised an objection. 'I don't see how you can prove anything by the tracks, since you don't know what day they were made.'

'But I do,' MacGowan differed. 'It rained the night before the holdup and hasn't rained since. So the tracks couldn't have been made before that time. When Lane was dragging the tree down to his wagon he cut across the sign left by the horsemen. The riders must have passed that day, maybe within a few minutes of the time he did.'

'By Jove, you've got something there!' Muir cried. 'But of course you don't know who they were.'

Neal knew who one of them was, but he did not want to tell all he knew. For if word of this got back to a certain tobacco-chewing ruffian he might not live long.

'Hank Baldwin was driving the stage,' Reynolds mentioned. 'Cole Tracy took a crack at one of the road agents before they killed him. Hank is pretty sure Cole hit the fellow because he let out a yelp. If I were still sheriff I would be looking for a wounded man.'

MacGowan stared at Reynolds in surprise. 'News to me. I hadn't heard one of them was hit.'

'Hank may have been wrong. He's a pretty reliable old-timer, but naturally he was busy trying to control the frightened horses.'

Neal was sure that Hank had not been wrong. There jumped to his mind the picture of two men sedulously screening with their bodies the doorway of a cabin in which Nels Gurley lay disabled. He recalled Blackburn's words, 'He got throwed from a horse and busted an ankle,' and Dunn's added detail that the horse had broken a leg and had to be shot. At the time there had seemed something queer about this, in view of their determination not to let him see Gurley. Now he knew it was false. Cole Tracy had shot the fellow during the holdup. This opinion too Neal kept to himself.

He came to another reason he had for paying a visit to the Triangle R. 'The Lanes are going to have a hard time of it this winter,' he mentioned. 'Miss Janet is too proud to accept charity. She has spoken to Finn Wood about teaching the school. She is not too young and she has been well educated. Finn will support her. If you can see your way to vote for her that will make a majority of the board.'

Reynolds thought for a moment. 'That might be arranged,' he agreed. 'I'll talk with her and find whether she is competent. If she is, I don't know any reason why she shouldn't have it.'

Eleanor reappeared presently in a flower-printed challis, very neat and trim. Muir excused himself, to return to the Blue Bell, a Scotch-owned ranch twenty miles away of which he was assistant manager. A wrangler summoned Reynolds to look at a horse which had been rather badly cut on a barb-wire fence.

'I'm losing all my men,' Eleanor told Neal. 'Come into the house where you will be surrounded by four walls and can't escape so easily.'

'You're quite sure Reynolds won't have me thrown out,' he said, and followed her into the big comfortable living-room.

During the tenancy of the original owner this had been a man's den, filled with guns and fishing rods and hunting trophies mounted on the wall. Eleanor had modified the character of the room without entirely changing it. At one end there was a piano, and a bookcase had been built into the wall beside the big open fireplace. The lounge and its pillows were of the new régime, but the moose and elk heads still remained. What really transformed the room was Eleanor herself.

Neal watched her sink indolently into the pillowed lounge and curl herself up. To him she was a discovery in women. He had never seen one like her before. The late afternoon sun burnished her reddish hair and gave it a golden bronze tint electric with life. Amber lights shone in the soft brown eyes of the piquant provocative face. She was vivid and enticing, a glamorous girl to dream about in the darkness of the night.

'I hear you heaped coals of fire on Austin's head by saving him from your friends,' she began.

'From my friends?' he repeated, making a question of the words.

'Followers, then. When you tell the honest folk of Rustlers' Gap to behave they wear at once their nice Sunday manners, I'm told.' She flashed small white teeth in an impudent grin. 'It's fascinating to know a modern Robin Hood. You don't need a Maid Marian in the band, do you?'

'I'll file your application,' he said.

'Were you in the Sheridan stage robbery yourself? Or do you just send your men out on raids while you stay at home and count the loot you've taken in?'

'Before I give myself away I'll have to know whether you are lined up with me or the enemy.'

Looking into his lean, sun-tanned sardonic face, she thought that it would be easy to let herself go and be on his side. She liked his hard whipcord body so lithe and graceful, and the supple play of muscles when he moved. There was a fluid poised balance in his stance, a repose that somehow suggested the possibility of explosive violence. Moreover, he was an individual who owned himself. He lived gaily and cheerfully on a pattern of his own design. The first time she had seen him was at a rodeo. He had been astride a wild outlaw horse and had ridden it superbly. Breathlessly she had watched his ride, and she had made it her business to meet him afterward. From the point of view of her friends he was beyond the pale, so she had seen him not more than four or five times since. But each time she had felt the same disturbing flutter of the blood. It was queer that a man and a woman could look into each other's eyes and know that some strong tug was drawing them together though all they did and said denied it.

Reynolds rejoined them, and MacGowan rose to go.

'You'll not forget about Janet Lane,' Neal reminded his host.

'I'll not forget,' Austin replied.

'What about her?' Eleanor asked.

'She wants to teach the school this fall.'

Her gaze shifted to MacGowan. 'They say she is very pretty.'

'Pretty isn't quite the word,' he replied. 'She's too thin, and she is a very grave young person. Carries too many worries. But there is a shy loveliness about her.'

'I think I'll go see her,' Eleanor said.

'You'd better come with me,' her brother suggested. 'I want to have a talk with her.'

'I wish you would,' Neal urged the young woman. 'She needs a girl friend.'

Eleanor laughed. 'I can teach her to blow her troubles away in smoke.'

CHAPTER V

MacGowan makes a deduction

Neal MacGowan's high-heeled boots clicked a staccato beat on the wooden sidewalk of Trail's End Street. He walked lightly, broad-rimmed hat tilted jauntily on his head, moving with a smooth-muscled coordination unusual in the cow country, where spurred cowboys clumped awkwardly when they traveled afoot.

It was evening, and Sundog's gambling-houses and dance halls had awakened to activity. The singsong voice of the quadrille caller, the sawing of fiddles, shuffling of feet, and rattling of chips, with the occasional shout of an excited puncher, drifted to the street along which men in chaps, Levis, and store clothes moved to and fro in their search for amusement.

Among the cattlemen Sundog was known as a rustlers' town. The sneer was not entirely just. It was true that when thieves came down from the hills to see the elephant, as they sometimes phrased it, Sundog was their Mecca. But it was no less true that most of the residents were honest people, though their sympathies were with the nesters and even with the less flagrant of the calf thieves rather than with the big outfits.

A dozen men greeted MacGowan as he passed. He was liked because of his devil-may-care camaraderie. They approved of him as a liberal spender, a bold plunger at faro and poker, and for the casual good will that ran at times to generosity. His reckless courage found an echo in the hearts of most of these frontiersmen, who respected him too for the independence with which he had cut loose from the other cattlemen. They realized that he was unpredictable, usually gentle, occasionally violent, but they were aware in him of a charity toward the underdog that gave poor settlers the benefit of the doubt even when they stepped a little outside the law.

Neither faro nor poker held any temptation for Neal this night. He turned from Trail's End to a side street and stopped before an adobe one-story building which bore the sign in the window,

DOCTOR ALPHEUS SENECA
Physician and Surgeon

There was a light in the room and he knocked on the door. Answering the invitation to enter, he walked into an office where a plump red-faced man sat with his feet on a desk pretending to read the *Sundog Sentinel*. Back of a pile of medical books Neal glimpsed an imperfectly hidden glass containing whiskey.

Seneca was usually a cheerful optimist, but he

looked at his visitor with no evidence of being glad to see him. 'If you've come to get me to go out to the K-B to set a broken leg for one of your dumb riders—' he began.

'I haven't,' Neal interrupted. He drew up a chair, and his boots joined those of the doctor on the desk. 'You needn't bother hiding that glass, doc. I saw a man take a drink once before.'

The doctor drew the glass forward and took a bottle from a drawer in the desk.

'It's these W.C.T.U. women,' he complained. 'They claim I drink too much, and they're always busting in here with a kid who has to have a tooth pulled or a boil lanced.'

'They're probably dead right about you drinking too much,' Neal said with a grin, 'but I hasten to announce it's none of my business.'

'Nor theirs either, long as I give satisfactory service,' Seneca growled. 'I haven't been drunk since seven years ago Christmas. After a fellow has ridden forty miles, about half the way over rough trails, he's entitled to take a drink or two when he gets back.'

'It's quite a trip to Rustlers' Gap,' Neal murmured innocently.

Seneca had been getting another glass from the drawer, but he stopped to glare at his guest with surprised suspicion. 'Who said anything about Rustlers' Gap?' he demanded.

'Why, I did. Wasn't that where you were

today—looking after Nels Gurley's gunshot wound?'

'Where did you get that crazy idea?' the doctor rasped irritably.

'If you'll ask the high moguls of the Cattlemen's Association they'll tell you that I'm the big boss of the Gap,' Neal explained amiably. 'I'm supposed to know everything that goes on there.'

'Hmp! Fine business. I'm to keep my trap shut, or it will be too damned bad for me. But they can shout it all over Wyoming. I don't like any part of this, MacGowan. They took me up there to look after a man who had broken his ankle. So they said. And it turns out he's been shot. Who plugged him? I don't know, but I can guess. I'm an honest man, but it's to be curtains for me if I let out a peep. Fact is, I don't like your friends.'

'Third time today I've been told Blackburn's crowd are my friends,' Neal said. 'Jess himself did not mention it to me when I saw him. Maybe he has a different idea about it. You've sure enough got your tail in a crack, doc. What you would like to do is tell the sheriff of your suspicions. Don't do it. Cullen wouldn't lift a hand against the Rustlers' Gap outfit. That wouldn't be good politics. But he would certainly let them know what you had told him. Sit tight, and be a clam. It might be that somebody else would open the door and let your tail out.'

'Who?' Seneca wanted to know. 'If Sheriff Cullen won't do his duty—'

'Some doggoned idiot might butt in and do the job for him,' Neal said with a wry sardonic smile. 'The world is full of guys who can't mind their own business. I wouldn't worry if I were you, doc.'

The doctor looked hard at the lean bronzed clean-cut face of MacGowan. He liked this young man in spite of his reputation. Seneca had friends in both factions. He did not need to be told that the big cattle outfits thought Neal too friendly with the thieves preying on their stock, in fact too sympathetic toward outlaws in general— and certainly a great deal too insolent. Careful mothers felt he was too wild to know their daughters except casually, though their husbands chuckled over the scrapes he had been in and out of. In their gossip the matrons admitted that he was always very polite and respectful to them, but the imps of mischief dancing in his brown eyes suggested to some of them that there was a mocking irony back of his courtesy. He understood very well their distrust of him.

The doctor's gesture was in the nature of an apology. He shoved the bottle and a glass at his guest. 'Have a drink,' he said. 'And talk more about this doggoned idiot who is going to get my tail out of the crack. How does he aim to do it?'

'You're better off without knowing that.' Neal

looked at Seneca with level inquiring eyes. 'Can you answer a question and forget that I ever asked it?'

'Maybe so. I live under my own hat mostly.'

'What sort of a wound has Gurley?' the cattleman queried.

The eyes of the two men locked in a long silence. Doctor Seneca was trying to puzzle out what was back of this. If he told the truth he knew he was putting his life in this man's hands.

'Six buckshot from a shotgun in his shoulder,' he said at last, reluctantly.

'And Cole Tracy, the treasure guard, carried a sawed-off shotgun loaded with buckshot,' Neal added.

'I told you a fact,' the doctor replied. 'You're making the deduction.'

'I've forgotten you told me.' Neal rose, then hesitated for a long time, drumming with his fingertips on the desk. 'I'm going to give you some advice, doctor, after telling you something you ought to know. My opinion is that the stage robbers shot Stuart Lane because he knew too much—found out what he knew by chance. *But he didn't know as much as you do about this business.* What man in town do you trust most?'

'Lance Arneill, the banker.'

Neal nodded. 'You can tie to him. My advice to you is to write out a plain account of what has taken place—of how you came to go to the

Gap and what you saw and did there. Seal this in an envelope, and write on the outside that the envelope is to be opened and the contents read only in the event of your death. Give it to Arneill. Are you going up to the Gap again?'

'Once more, to see that the wound is getting along all right.'

'That's fine. Look Blackburn right in the eye and tell him what you have done but without telling him to whom you have given the envelope. Be bold and blunt. Let him see you are protecting yourself, and at the same time make it plain that you are doing no talking. You'll have him in a cleft stick. It's the only way you can make yourself safe unless you light out of the country.'

'I won't do that,' Seneca said quickly. 'This is my home. I'm going to stay. But I think you're right, MacGowan. They might shoot me down on the way home if I don't throw a fear into them.'

'If you like I'll go into the Gap with you,' Neal offered.

The doctor thought that over. 'No, I'll go alone.' Anger rode for a moment his rubicund face. 'I'll not let those villains bluff me. I'll let them know I have the whip hand.'

Neal shook hands with him. 'That's the way to talk, doc. If I went along they would think it a frame-up. But with you playing a lone hand they will figure you were smart enough to protect yourself from a shot in the back. You'll be as safe from Blackburn's gang as if you were in God's pocket.'

The doctor looked at MacGowan sourly. 'So you say. But I'm the man who knows too much and has to take a chance. All the way down I'll be expecting a bullet in the small of my back.'

'It won't be that way,' Neal promised.

He nodded good-bye and walked out of the office.

CHAPTER VI

Neal cuts sign

Neal dropped into the Round Up. The bar was lined with patrons and a dozen others stood around the roulette table. Near the back door a poker game was going, most of the players in their shirtsleeves. He had no intention of taking a whirl at the wheel or trying his luck at faro. An invitation to join those at draw met a smiling shake of the head. MacGowan was looking for a K-B rider. Two or three of them were in town tonight. He did not care which one he found.

His eye picked up Tim Owen at the roulette table. The redheaded cowboy was in the second row and did not appear to be playing. Neal drifted through the crowd and presently touched the boy on the shoulder. Tim slewed his head, grinned, and said, ' 'Lo, Neal.'

MacGowan drew him to one side and gave instructions. 'I want you to take my horse home when you go, Tim. It's at the hitch-rack in front of the Silver Dollar. Rope and saddle Denver soon as you have had breakfast tomorrow. Be at Three Pines, on the Sheridan stage road, by two o'clock in the afternoon. And don't do any talking about where you are going.'

'You meeting me at Three Pines?' the cowboy asked.

'Yes. If I'm not there wait for me.'

The boss of the K-B slept and breakfasted at the hotel, after which he took the Sheridan stage. Hank Baldwin was driving. Neal took the seat beside him.

Hank was a small wrinkled man with washed-out blue eyes. He had driven stage for twenty years on different parts of the frontier from Texas to Montana and had been held up a good many times by road agents. An easygoing garrulous man, he told all about the latest one to MacGowan. They had been going through the cut at Three Pines when the order came to pull up.

'Only one thing to do when the guy behind the mask yells "Hands up!" ' Hank said dogmatically. 'That's to reach for the sky *prontito*. The bird has got the drop on you. I'll bet I've told that to Cole twenty times. But he raises that scatter-gun of his and blazes away. About two seconds later he tumbled down from his seat dead as a stuck shote.'

'Know any of the holdups?' Neal asked with offhand carelessness.

Hank's bleak eyes met his. 'No, sir,' he replied with emphasis. 'Not none of them. They was all masked.'

'Did they mask their clothes and their horses?' MacGowan inquired genially.

'I couldn't swear to a-one of them,' the driver returned promptly.

'Probably they were just about average size, not fat, not thin, not tall, not short,' Neal laughed. 'Don't blame you a bit, Hank. You're paid to drive the stage rather than to identify outlaws who can drill a man through the heart the way they did Cole.'

'I didn't know 'em,' Hank answered. 'That's short and sweet. And like you say, if I did have ideas I wouldn't shoot them off, seeing I don't want to sleep in smoke.'

It was past noon when they came to the pass at Three Pines. The road ran through a deep cut strewn with boulders, flanked on both sides by rocky walls about twenty feet high. Hank pulled up and pointed with his whip to where the bandits had stood. Two had come out from the boulders and stood one on each side of the stage. Another had appeared on the rock wall to the left of the coach and had done all the talking. The tracks examined later showed a fourth had remained with the mounts out of sight. There might have been a fifth. Hank was not sure. One of the passengers had insisted that there was.

Neal stepped down from his seat. 'Here's where I leave you, Hank,' he said.

The driver stared at him. 'You aim to walk to town?' he asked.

'I'll get there somehow. Don't worry about me.'

'I ain't worryin' about you none,' Baldwin snapped. 'But I don't git yore play. Two sheriffs have been all over the ground and messed up any sign the holdups left.'

'I want to look the ground over so that I'll know how to pull off a stage robbery when the time comes,' Neal explained airily.

'Okay with me,' Hank said. He released the brake, swung the whip, and went clattering through the cut. For more than a week he gossiped about MacGowan's fool trick of stopping at Three Pines without even a horse to get him home. After that time there was no need to guess why he had done it.

Neal quartered all over the ground on both sides of the cut. There were plenty of tracks, too many of them; for two posses had been here since the robbery. It was impossible to make sure which tracks had been made by the bandits and their horses.

One thing he discovered that was informing, a splash of dried tobacco juice on a rock near where the mounts of the robbers had been tied. Jess Blackburn had left his signature.

Taking for granted that the robbers were from Rustlers' Gap, Neal felt sure they would make for home as directly as possible by cutting across country and avoiding roads. His guess was that they would ride to Lame Cow Creek and travel up the bed of it for several miles in order to leave no tracks for the pursuers to follow.

As soon as Tim Owen arrived Neal mounted and the two men started. There was a well-defined trail to the creek, for both posses had cut sign of the robbers to that point and there lost the trail. MacGowan thought he understood the reason for that. The sheriff of Big Horn County was a comparative newcomer to the West and knew nothing about picking up and staying with a trail. Cullen had been in charge of the other posse, and as soon as he suspected the bandits were heading for Rustlers' Gap he was willing to find a reasonable excuse for being thrown off the track.

Neal took one side of the creek and Tim Owen the other. It meandered through sage flats, moving in a leisurely fashion toward the distant hills. The men traveled for an hour before MacGowan called across to his companion, 'They pulled out from the creek here.'

The marks left by the horses as they emerged from the water were still plain. The bandits had struck across the sage flats toward a cleft in the hills.

'It would be close to dark before they got here,' Tim said. 'Bet you they camped for the night on Deer Creek below Bryan Jennings' place.'

That was probably a good guess, Neal thought. Riding hard, they would reach the creek long after dark and would feel safe from immediate pursuit. The mounts of the outlaws would be jaded. Long before daylight they could start again and be safely in the foothills before sun-up.

Night had fallen before the two K-B men topped a rise and looked down into a valley that gave the impression of a deep gulf of darkness out of which rose vaguely small islands. From one of these a light shone. The riders let their horses pick a way down the loose rubble to a path leading to the ranch.

At their call Jennings came to the door. He was a tall dark man, rough and unshaven, no longer young. As a matter of course he invited them into the house.

'The woman will fix you-all up some supper,' he said.

Mrs. Jennings began making preparations at once. She was a thin dried-up woman in the thirties, but all the youth had long since been parched out of her by hard work and desert winds and poverty. The family had come from Arkansas a few years since. Until that time they had always been renters.

'We sure hate to trouble you, Mrs. Jennings, to fix up supper for a pair of guys ridin' the chuck line,' Tim told her. The freckle-faced redheaded puncher was a likable friendly youth who treated all respectable women with a deferential courtesy. 'I wouldn't blame yore husband if he would like to cuss us out for drappin' in so late. Don't you go to much trouble, ma'am.'

The nester's wife took one swift look at his curly head and homely face. She had a son of her own about two years younger than Tim.

'I don't mind,' she said. 'We live here at the yonder end of nowhere. Folks never come by. Hardly ever. I kinda like to see another face than the old man's. A man did hello the house one night last week plumb late. Must of been near midnight.'

Jennings cut in gruffly. 'What they want is grub and not gab, Sal.'

His wife looked at him a little resentfully. 'Land's sake! I'm workin' while I talk. I haven't had a chance to speak to anybody but you for weeks. Can't I say a word?'

'It's not considerate of us to show up so late,' Neal apologized. 'I suppose this other fellow wanted supper too.'

'No.' Their hostess measured Arbuckle's coffee into a pot. 'He wanted some clean rags and a kettle of hot water. He was one of a party of cow hunters camped down the creek a ways. One of them had broke his laig. His horse had stepped in a gopher hole and threw him.'

'Sounds like it might have been some of Jim Hart's riders,' MacGowan suggested carelessly.

Jennings looked uneasy. 'Sal doesn't know who they were any more than I do. The man was a stranger.' Abruptly he changed the subject. 'Do you reckon the Democrats will win the election?'

For supper they had corn bread, beefsteak, and coffee without milk or sugar. Neal wondered whether he was eating his own beef, but he ate without asking questions.

Though he knew the nesters must be very poor, he could not offer to pay for the meal without insulting them. Before leaving he did fling out a friendly line.

'You're a long way from supplies here, Mr. Jennings,' he said. 'If the snows hem you in, don't hesitate to kill a K-B steer when you run short.'

The woman threw a quick startled look at her husband. The man glanced at MacGowan suspiciously, then his eyes slid away.

'Much obliged,' he said awkwardly.

The K-B men camped on the creek that night and reached Sundog in the morning. Here they parted, Owen to take the horses back to the ranch, MacGowan to buy a ticket on the stage to Cheyenne. Neal had some new business there that could not wait.

CHAPTER VII

An olive branch rejected

Austin Reynolds and his sister rode through the stem grass to the wire fence surrounding the homesteader's cabin on Squaw Creek. He opened the poor man's gate,[1] let the horses through, and closed the gap behind them. They moved forward to the two-room log cabin. Eleanor observed that there was a commodious barn and a dugout root cellar sunk into the side of a hill. The house itself had a sod roof and mud-chinked walls.

Evidently Janet had seen them approach. She stood in the doorway and watched the girl dismount. Her visitor was in riding breeches, and she swung from the saddle light and trim. That this bareheaded young woman with the glorious hair must be Eleanor Reynolds, Janet knew. When settlers of the Flood River Valley and the hill country back of it met to gossip, they had a good deal to say of the Triangle R girl's beauty, boldness, gaiety, and surprising clothes. While herding stock Janet herself sat astride the saddle in Levis for safety, but these ultramodern mannish

[1]A poor man's gate consisted of three strands of wire with supporting sticks at each end and in the middle.

breeches were something different. She had never looked at a pair before. They were immodest but fascinating.

A pulse of angry excitement throbbed in Janet's throat. She resented this call of the Reynolds, and particularly on the part of the young woman. Stories were current of her flippant tongue, her disregard for the feelings of others. Though Janet was not ashamed of her poverty, she did not care to have it inspected by this young woman.

With some embarrassment Reynolds introduced his sister. He was doubtful of their welcome, since he did not know whether the girl believed him guilty of complicity in the murder of her father.

'We wanted to call on you,' he explained. 'Neighbors ought to see each other sometimes and be of help when they can.'

Janet stood aside to let them enter the house, her small head proudly erect. They had never come while her father was alive. She did not want them here now. If they meant to be kind to the poor orphans on Squaw Creek, she would have none of their patronage.

Eleanor's quick eyes took note of the home-made stools and bench, of the puncheon floor covered by a rag carpet. There was a Home Comfort range, and against the wall a cupboard for dishes made of two drygoods boxes fitted with shelves. Through the open bedroom door she saw a tripod pie-crust table with molded rim that looked like a genuine Chippendale, and beside it a walnut case filled with books. This hapless family which had come pioneering into the raw frontier had known better days. One glance at Janet had been enough to tell her she was no poke-bonneted daughter of a Tennessee sharecropper.

'Neal MacGowan has talked to me about you,' Eleanor said. 'He liked your father very much and'—the white teeth flashed in a smile—'admires the courage of his daughter.'

A faint color streamed into the younger girl's cheeks. She was annoyed that Neal had discussed her with this stranger. 'Mr. MacGowan has been very kind,' she answered primly.

'*We* haven't,' Eleanor admitted. 'But if you'll forgive us we'll do better in the future. In a land so sparsely settled we two girls ought to know each other better. I hope that soon you and the children can come and stay a few days at the ranch.'

Austin looked at his sister, surprised and pleased at this unexpected invitation. He was no more surprised than she was to hear herself giving it. A minute earlier nothing had been farther from her thoughts.

'Thank you,' Janet replied stiffly. 'That wouldn't be possible. We couldn't leave the place and the stock.'

'If we can help you move when you make your plans to go, it will be a pleasure,' Reynolds said.

Janet's dark eyes met his steadily. 'Thank you very much, but we are not going to move.'

'I mean, after you have sold the homestead.'

'We are not going to sell it.'

Reynolds knew she could not handle the place without the help of a man. The mere physical labor would make that impossible. But the finality of her answer made advice from him impertinent. He could see that she had shut the door against them. His suggestion had been an indiscreet one, since it was to his interest to get hold of the place. Very likely she shared the general opinion that the big cattlemen had contrived the death of Stuart Lane to secure the water rights along the creek. She resented this visit, as the hillmen had his presence at the funeral services. There was nothing to do but accept her refusal of their friendliness.

He shifted the reason for this call to a business one.

'MacGowan told me you might be willing to teach our district school this fall, Miss Lane,' he told her dryly. 'It is hard to get a good teacher at the price we can pay. If you are interested we should be glad to get your application.'

She met his change of attitude with quiet businesslike directness. 'Mr. Wood thinks I could do it. I haven't a teacher's certificate, but I can get one. Ought I to make a written application? I graduated from a Cleveland high school.'

'I think you had better, giving qualifications and references.'

Though rebuffed, Eleanor held no ill will. 'Don't worry about the school,' she said. 'Of course you can have it. The district will be lucky to get you.'

'That is true,' her brother agreed.

Again Janet said 'Thank you' in a voice drained of expression.

They had come to an impasse. Eleanor still wanted to break through the cold hostility of this girl who though still so young had been buffeted by the tragedy of life, but she knew that words could not mend the situation. Her gesture of good will had been rejected. She nodded a good-bye and walked out of the house.

Janet followed to the door, noting how rhythmically the long legs of the young woman moved. It was no wonder, she thought, that Neal MacGowan was wild about this golden girl.

Eleanor swung to the saddle and waited for her brother to mount.

The crack of a rifle sounded. A bullet whipped past Janet and plowed into a log of the house a foot from her head.

Startled, Eleanor looked at her brother. 'Who is shooting?' she asked, unaware of where the lead had struck.

'Get into the house—both of you,' Austin ordered. He was drawing from its boot beside the saddle the rifle he carried.

Another puff of smoke rose from the brush across the creek several hundred yards away. Janet staggered back against the door jamb. Eleanor slid from the horse and ran to the doorway.

'You're hurt!' she cried, and slipped a supporting arm around Janet's waist.

As they moved into the house she heard the roar of her brother's Winchester. Before they had reached the bed he too was inside, the door slammed behind him. He drew together the window curtains in the inner room.

'She's hit—in the arm,' Eleanor said.

Janet sat on the bed, very pale, and looked at the red stain on the sleeve of her dress. She was very much frightened.

'I don't understand,' she murmured. 'Why—why—?'

'Forget that now,' Austin told her. 'You're safe. I'll see to that. Lie down and let us take care of the wound.'

'Maybe . . . maybe he'll come—'

'No,' the man answered confidently. 'I know the breed. He's lighting out hell-for-leather to get away and not be discovered.'

None the less Austin took a long careful survey of the rolling terrain on the other side of the river. He saw a thin line of dust above the bushes evidently flung up by the hoofs of a galloping horse. His guess had been a correct one.

Reynolds had had considerable experience with broken bones and gunshot wounds. One could not run a large ranch in the days of the open range without frequent accidents to the reckless cowboys. He examined Janet's arm and assured her she was lucky. The bullet had ripped through the flesh below the elbow without striking a bone or cutting an artery. His quiet matter-of-fact manner and the skill with which he took care of and bandaged the wound allayed her fears.

'I'm in luck you were here,' she said, and smiled faintly.

The cattleman agreed. She was in double luck, though he did not say so. For if she had been alone, the would-be killer would have finished the job. The fellow had not used his brains. He could have waited ten minutes and got the girl when she was alone. Perhaps he had thought she was going to ride away too. Or perhaps, at that distance, he had mistaken Reynolds for Harry Lane.

Austin could not understand any more than Janet could why anybody should attempt her life. Whoever it was must have known she was the head of the family with two small children dependent on her. The callous cruelty of the attack appalled him.

CHAPTER VIII

Neal talks turkey to Janet

From the window Austin Reynolds watched two horsemen ride into the yard. One was Neal MacGowan and the other Tim Owen. Neal swung from the saddle and walked to the house.

'Hello, Mary!' he called. 'Come a-running. I've got something for you.'

Eleanor opened the door. 'Come in,' she invited. 'The children aren't here. They are spending the day at Finn Wood's. But I'm glad you've come. Janet has been shot.'

Neal stared at her. 'Shot?' he echoed.

'By somebody from the brush across the creek. Austin says it's only a flesh wound and ought to heal nicely.'

He put down on the kitchen table a box containing a doll that he had bought for Mary in Cheyenne. What he had just been told shocked him. His mind was trying to adjust itself to the facts, to the presence of the Reynolds here and to the attack on Janet.

'Tell me about it,' he said.

She told him, in a few sentences. 'Maybe it was somebody shooting at Austin,' she added, and corrected the guess at once. 'But that couldn't be.

He was twenty feet from the door where Janet stood.'

MacGowan followed her into the bedroom. At sight of his face the wounded girl spoke comfort to him.

'I'll be all right,' she told him, and mustered a little smile. 'Mr. Reynolds says so.'

'Of course you will.' He looked down at her, touched by the wistful loveliness of the thin troubled face. 'You've been working too hard. The rest will do you good.'

'She is going home with us,' Eleanor said with crisp decision. 'We're only ten miles from Sundog, and Doctor Seneca can come out every day to see her.'

'No,' Janet objected. 'I couldn't think of troubling you.'

'We nearly always have guests at the ranch, and you are going to be one.'

'I can't leave the children.'

Eleanor tossed that off airily. 'Oh, they're coming too.'

'It's good of you, Miss Reynolds, but—'

Janet shook her head, not finishing the sentence.

'I won't have it that way.' Eleanor sat on the bed and took the hand of the unwounded arm. 'Let's be friendly enemies,' she smiled. 'Austin and I are not really ogres. Be generous and let us help.'

'We'd be all right here,' Janet insisted. 'I can't

burden you. Besides, there is the stock to look after.'

'Let me talk turkey to this obstinate girl,' Neal interrupted cheerfully, and took from Eleanor the small hand she had been holding. 'Now see here, Janet Lane, you will be a good patient and do as you're told. One of my men will look after your stock. Just now it is not safe for you and the children to stay here, and anyhow it would be much more convenient to have you close to a doctor and where you can be nursed. So you're going to say, "Thank you, Miss Reynolds," and go for a visit to the Triangle R.'

Janet forgot that she disapproved of this young man. He was her dear friend, and when his kind eyes looked down into hers something choked up inside her.

'You know I can't go,' she answered, in a whisper.

'Yes, you can,' he assured her firmly. 'I've been busy this week. I know who killed your father—and why. The big cattlemen are as innocent as I am.'

Her dark eyes dilated. 'You know?' she repeated.

'Positively. But I'm not going to talk about that now. I'll come to the Triangle R and tell you all about it after you are better.'

It was queer, but Janet trusted him absolutely. The dark head on the pillow turned to the other girl. Janet did not see her very well for the tears in her eyes. 'I'm sorry, Miss Reynolds. I'll come. It's you who have been generous, not I.'

Neal sent Tim Owen to the K-B to bring back a wagon with the bed full of hay. Another of the ranch boys was to ride into Sundog and ask Doctor Seneca to get out to the Triangle R as quickly as he could. A third was to cut across the spur trail to Finn Wood's place and arrange for the children to go to the Reynolds ranch next day.

In a telescope grip Eleanor packed the wounded girl's clothes and changes for the children. The stockings had been darned and the underwear patched, but everything was immaculately clean.

Meanwhile Reynolds stayed with the two girls while MacGowan walked through the stem grass to the creek and crossed it on the bridge Stuart Lane had built. From the Triangle R man he had learned approximately where the ambusher had been crouched when he fired the shots. He moved through the sage over the rolling terrain to a rock scarp which offered a chance for concealment. Above the slope, back of the summit, he found where the man's horse had been tied.

Carefully he retraced his steps through the boulder field, examining the ground back of the outcroppings which might have given the fellow cover. A gleam of reflected sunshine caught his eye. He picked up an empty rifle cartridge. Not ten feet from it he saw a tobacco splash on the tilted side of a rock.

Ropelike muscles stood out on the clenched jaw of the cattleman and his eyes grew steely. He stared at the splattered boulder, resolution hardening in him.

Jess Blackburn had not believed that Stuart Lane had died without telling his daughter what he had seen on the hill back of Squaw Creek. He had come to make certain that she would do no talking.

Neal returned to the cabin. Rifle in hand, Reynolds came as far as the stable to meet him. Austin waited silently for a report.

'Jess Blackburn,' Neal said. 'I'm going up to drag him from his hole.'

'How do you know it was Blackburn?' Reynolds asked, astonished at the certainty of the other.

MacGowan told him how he knew.

'I'll go with you,' the Triangle R man volunteered. 'I think Muir would like to go with us. He's a good man. How many do we want?'

'Can't take you,' Neal answered. 'Sorry. If you and Muir went, Rustlers' Gap would consider it an invasion of the enemy. I'm going to take Tim Owen with me. We are going to bring back Blackburn with us, and nobody else.'

'I don't quite see what's to prevent Muir and me going if we want to go,' Reynolds replied coldly. 'This isn't a private war of yours against this murderer.'

Neal turned back the flap of his coat and showed

a star. 'I'm a deputy United States marshal. Went to Cheyenne and got the appointment this week. I choose my own posse. Don't get me wrong, Reynolds. You and I aren't friends. Just the same I don't know a man I would rather have side me in a jam than you. Muir is all right too. But if I took you it would make trouble.'

'Do you expect to bring Jess Blackburn back without trouble?' Reynolds asked. 'A man known as a desperado and a killer, living in a nest of lawless scoundrels?'

'I think I can get the others to keep out of it. Even rustlers don't approve of shooting at a girl. They won't lift a hand for him, once they feel he is guilty.'

'You're taking nobody except Owen?'

'That's all. I'll take care of Blackburn. If it's necessary to warn back some of his gang, Owen can do that.'

'I judge from your interest in protecting the honest men of Rustlers' Gap that you are going to make a valuable United States marshal,' Reynolds said ironically.

Neal ignored the sneer. He understood the point of view held by the Triangle R and other big outfits. Their position was that the time had come to decide whether the state should be controlled by thieves or honest men. Rustlers could be arrested, proved guilty, and yet escape conviction in the courts. Juries made a travesty of justice.

Cattlemen had to present a solid front in fight or go under.

As Neal saw it, this was true but not the whole truth. The little man had rights too, and while they had been in the saddle the large ranches were arbitrary and unfair. They had fenced open range belonging to the government. Homesteaders had been driven from the claims they had lawfully located, cowboys discharged when they took up land for themselves. It had been so difficult to make a living that settlers felt forced in order to feed their families to kill calves they did not own.

All his life Neal had revolted against living on a conventional pattern. He was not only an individualist. There was in him a strong sympathy for the underdog. With Reynolds he agreed that this was a stock country and could not profitably be farmed, but he did not find it easy to blot out of mind the struggles of covered-wagon immigrants to get a foothold in this wide-open West supposed to be free to all. Of the calf thieves, a fair percentage were men fundamentally not criminal.

CHAPTER IX

In the high hills

Neal MacGowan and Tim Owen rode through the Gap and looked down on a country so rough that few ever attempted to enter the gateway. In these huddled hills were many crooked paths which crooked men followed. Walled cañons cut into the ranges. Chasms inclosed roaring rivers. In the hidden mountain pockets and the forests a wary nomadic population found safety. Here they skulked, frequently shifting camp for greater security, occasionally riding out from their retreats on swift night raids that would not bear investigation.

Tim whacked the packhorse with a quirt. 'Git up, Rusty,' he urged, and added, apropos of what had gone before: 'If I was a thief or a killer wanted by the law I would figure this was heaven. All the game and fish a guy wants. Nothing to do but chew over old times and swap windies. No forty-dollar job to keep a fellow hustling from dark till dark, eatin' dust and ridin' out blizzards. And no sheriffs close enough to ride herd on them. I'm blamed if the slit-eyed sons-of-guns don't have the best of us two-bit punchers.'

Neal shook his head. 'I wouldn't say so. You've

homesteaded a nice piece of land with water on it. You're building up a little herd of cows, and after you marry Nellie a redheaded family of kids will be yelping "Poppa" at you. You can look anybody in the eye and tell him to go jump in a lake. No, Tim, you're too full of vinegar to roost up here and like it, even if you didn't have one big draw-back, that of being honest.'

'I reckon so,' agreed Tim. 'When a bird starts taking a short cut to get rich, like as not he ends with a rope round his neck.'

They dropped down a cañon to the pocket where MacGowan had seen Blackburn and Dunn a week earlier. The K-B men were not surprised to find that the cabin was empty. Evidently the outlaws had been disturbed by Neal's visit and had left for another hiding place.

'Where do we go from here?' Tim asked with a grin.

He did not care where they went. They had with them food enough to last for a week. Traveling in the high hills was a lot more pleasant than chasing cows through the dust, and there was a spice of danger in it that sent a fillip through the blood. Jess Blackburn had the reputation of being a bad man. He probably was, but Tim was ready to put his money on Neal any day against him.

'We'll call on Cad Clemson,' MacGowan answered. 'He usually hangs out above Owl Gulch.'

'You know the Gap pretty well,' Tim said.

'Not too well, but I've had dealings with Cad.'

'He's supposed to be the brains of the bunch that nest up here, isn't he?'

'He has a lot of influence with them. Cad is a cold-blooded killer, but he is shrewd. Not the kind to run his head into a stone wall.'

Heavily wooded slopes pushed down from the high hills. Below were small green valleys from which ran draws and gorges by which horsemen could travel into the wilder back-lands. Neal had been only once to Clemson's holdout. It had been several years ago, and he was not sure he could find the small mountain park where he had been taken to meet the man.

Every mile took them deeper into the tangle of hills and gulches. Darkness found them by a small brook racing down over stones and waterfalls to a larger stream below. They made camp, and after eating sat for a time beside their fire, the glow of which pushed back for a few yards the darkness increased by the shadows from the ridge pressing closely in on them.

Tim was a healthy youth without much imagination, but the black night made him shiver. There was something eerie about it. A hundred times he had heard the wind in the pines by lonely campfires, but tonight it seemed to carry the wail of lost souls.

He grinned apologetically at his companion. 'I

ain't so sure now about this country being a heaven for bad men,' he said. 'It kinda gets my goat. Now if I was a killer instead of a one-gallus brushhopper, when I heard that wind sobbing I'd start thinking about the poor devils I'd sent to kingdom come.'

'That's where a killer differs from you and me, Tim. He starts with a conscience, I reckon, but he gets rid of it soon as he can. By and by he doesn't have any regrets at shooting down a man.' Neal rose and stretched. 'I'm going to roll up now.'

Both of them were asleep inside of five minutes. They did not wake until daybreak. They made breakfast, ate, and packed. Before they started the sun showed over a hill crotch.

A wooded prong led them to a ledge. From the summit a shale slope descended to a small green valley, at one end of which was a clump of pines. Out of the grove rose a thin trail of smoke.

The riders let their mounts pick a way down to the meadow.

Neal gave one last word of counsel. 'Remember, Tim, we don't want to get on the prod. If we start trouble there will probably be two graves in the nearest gulch covered with rocks. Yours and mine. This is a peaceable conference between two parties who don't trust each other any farther than they can throw a bull by the tail.'

'Suits me,' Tim answered. 'You do the talking.'

A man with a rifle in his hands watched them

ride across the valley to the house hidden in the trees. Tim hoped he did not have a nervous trigger finger.

'Lookin' for someone?' a voice called.

Neal drew up and put his hands on the horn of the saddle. 'Like to have a pow-wow with Cad,' he said amiably.

'Cad isn't here.' The owner of the voice was a giant in boots, butternut jeans, and a blue shirt checked with white. His leathery face terminated in a heavy bulldog jaw.

The owner of the K-B smiled pleasantly. 'I reckon he isn't far away, Dave. He'll see me.' Neal swung from the saddle with the confident manner of one who had no doubts.

'Stay where you're at,' Dave Dagwell ordered. 'I'll find out if he's here."

He called, and a smooth-faced lad with ruddy cheeks appeared in the doorway. 'What's doing?' he asked, his eyes on the strangers.

'Find out if Cad's around and if he wants to see MacGowan, Russ,' he snapped.

Russ vanished into the house. Neal had last seen these two men at the Lane funeral. He mentioned this to Dagwell. The giant in butternut jean trousers had a bitter comment to make as to that.

'If you hadn't butted in, the boys would have rubbed out that high-flyin' buzzard Reynolds,' he growled.

'That would have been fine for you boys,' Neal

retorted. 'A half-dozen posses would have come in to clean up the Gap and there would have been war.'

'Which would suit me down to the ground,' Dagwell flung back.

Presently Russ reappeared in the doorway. 'Cad says for them to come in.'

Clemson limped forward to meet them. One of his legs was shorter than the other due to a fall many years before from a bucking horse. He wore an unctuous smile on his sly and evil face. The smile did not reach the cold malignant eyes. Though a small man, he was not one anybody could look at and be likely to underestimate.

'Sure good to see you, boys,' he said with a heartiness as obviously false as his smile. 'Come right in and rest yore weary bones.' To Russ he gave an order. 'There's a bottle in that cupboard, son.'

The K-B men both declined the drink. Neal knew they were not welcome but gave no sign of it. He saw the man's gaze watching him, head tilted at a slanting angle.

The visitors took the offered chairs. 'It's been quite some time since we last met, Cad,' mentioned Neal easily. 'You don't get down much, do you?'

'Not much. This busted leg of mine makes riding hard. Take a man or a horse, either one: when he gets stove up he ain't what he used to be.'

Neal agreed that might be so. Both of them were marking time. Clemson knew they had not come for the pleasure of seeing him.

'The boys tell me you got as far as the old cabin the other day,' the lame man carried on. 'I was right peeved you didn't get this far. Checking up on Reynolds, the boys said. That's good. He oughtn't to be let get away with killing a man like Lane.'

'Not if he did it,' Neal agreed.

'He did it all right. Him or his crowd.'

'I don't think so.'

The hooded hawk eyes of Clemson searched the cattleman's face. 'Who do you think did it?' he asked, his voice low and smooth.

'Can I talk with you alone?'

'Anything you want to say to me you can say to the boys,' Clemson replied. 'But if you want to be mysterious that's all right too.'

He looked at Dagwell, who left the room with Russ.

'Shoot,' the outlaw suggested.

Neal leaned forward and spoke in a low voice. 'I think Jess Blackburn killed him and shot Lane's daughter yesterday afternoon.'

Either this last was news to Clemson or he was a good actor. He repeated what had been told him, making of the words a question.

'Shot her from the brush across the creek from her house,' Neal said.

'What would Jess kill her for?'

'I didn't say he killed her.' Neal stretched the truth. 'He wounded the girl. She's not dead yet.'

'Sure was a crazy thing to do. Who saw him shoot her?'

Neal gave his reasons for accusing Blackburn, aware that the other would not accept them.

'You're crazy,' Clemson cried. 'That's no evidence at all.'

'It satisfies me, till I can get more.'

'Why, I'll bet Jess has an alibi.'

Neal's smile was sarcastic. 'I'll bet he has. Probably he was playing cards with three pals right here in the Gap when Miss Lane was shot.'

'If the boys say so, that would let him out. Cullen would accept it as a good alibi.'

'Cullen isn't in this,' Neal told him. He turned back the lapel of his coat and showed the star. 'You're up against Uncle Sam this time.'

The hard eyes of the outlaw narrowed. 'So that's yore game,' he said venomously. 'You've been against us all the time, playing us for suckers and pretending you had quarreled with the big outfits.'

'Reynolds wouldn't agree with you about that,' MacGowan differed. 'But get me right, Cad. If I haven't lifted a hand against anybody in the Gap, the reason was that I wasn't hired to run down criminals. I'm a cattleman. But this is a horse of another color. Lane was my neighbor, a quiet man attending to his own affairs. I don't propose to see him murdered and do nothing about it. So I got myself appointed a special United States deputy marshal. Now the killer has struck again—at a woman. I came up here to drag the scoundrel out to justice.'

'That's supposed to be dangerous,' Clemson said softly, and smiled.

'Meaning what?' Neal demanded bluntly.

'Meaning only that they claim Jess is a holy terror with a gun. I wouldn't know.'

'You would keep your hands off?'

'Of course.' There was a hint of a chuckle in his voice. 'It's up to you, Mr. Marshal. I don't think Blackburn is guilty. But that is your business. Take him out if you like.'

'Where can I find him?'

Clemson lifted his hands in a gesture that disclaimed any part in this. 'I haven't the least notion where he is.'

Neal rose. He spoke gently, as if to himself. 'That's too bad. No use hunting for him without a posse. I'll go out and bring back twenty-five or thirty special deputies. If we don't find Blackburn we'll pick up several others wanted by the law.'

The Rustlers' Gap man did not stop him until he had reached the door. 'Wait a minute, MacGowan. No use flying off the handle. I'll have to think this out.'

'I would, Cad.' Neal's smile was confident and sure.

Clemson faced a dilemma. He had meant to send Blackburn word to go into hiding until MacGowan was out of the Gap, but the deputy had forestalled that. It would not do to let him come back with a big posse to comb the place and perhaps drag out half a dozen fugitives. Why not let him take Blackburn out? The fellow had not been here more than a few weeks, and already his overbearing ways had made him unpopular. Moreover, if he had killed a woman they could not protect him. Public opinion would be too strong. There was always the chance too that Jess would kill MacGowan. Clemson could see no objection to that.

'All right,' he said. 'You can have Blackburn. He's giving the Gap a bad name anyhow. I won't help you take him, but I won't stand in yore way.'

'I thought you would see this right,' Neal said blandly. 'I'll want a guide.'

'I didn't promise to run him down for you,' Clemson complained sourly. 'But I'm a law-abiding citizen. I'll give you Russ.'

That suited Neal very well.

CHAPTER X

Blackburn weakens

Russ Miller was in the lead, his pinto pony climbing like a cat up a steep gulch trail. From the rear Tim put a question to his chief.

'You talked mighty brash to Cad,' he said cheerfully. 'How did you know he wouldn't figure out that the best way wasn't to give orders to have us drygulched?'

Neal turned, his hand on the back of the saddle. 'He thought of that. But after he had looked the idea over carefully he saw it would be a mistake. He was afraid if I disappeared the U.S. Government might get too inquisitive.'

Tim laughed. 'That's what you hope he thought. He may right now be putting a couple of killers on our trail.'

'Yes,' Neal agreed. 'But not likely. He's a wily bird. Blackburn doesn't mean a whole lot to him.'

They reached the top of the gulch and looked down on a mountain meadow through which a small stream ran. Miller gave him instructions.

'All you gotta do is follow the crick for about a mile—mebbe a mile 'n a half. You'll come to another cañon, a kinda box one with straight-up walls. On the left there's a break in the wall.

Follow that draw and you can't miss the house. It's a log cabin.'

'Much obliged, Russ,' Tim said.

'And no matter what happens keep yore mouths shut about me bringing you here,' Miller insisted. Already he had spoken of that three times. He did not want Blackburn to know that he had guided MacGowan to his hole-up.

'That's a promise,' Neal assured him. 'And think over what I told you, Russ. Come down to the K-B and there's a job waiting for you.'

The boyish face of the red-cheeked rustler took on a dogged look. 'I can make a lot more on my own,' he answered. 'What's forty dollars a month?'

'You can make more rustling another man's beef—for a time,' Neal conceded. 'But this isn't going on long. Law is coming to this country. You know what will happen then. Cow thieves will be swept into the penitentiary, or they will be blotted out. I'm not threatening. I'm just telling you. The time for you to turn over a new leaf is now.'

'Easy for you to talk thataway,' the lad growled. 'You've got a fine well-stocked ranch.'

'I started from scratch,' Neal replied patiently. 'Look at Tim here. Three years ago he came in here riding the chuck line. Now he has a nice homestead, a brand of his own, and a small bunch of cows. He is building a little log house. Soon he will be married, and on his way up. In ten years

Tim will be one of the responsible ranchmen of the Flood River country.'

'If he's lucky,' Miller assented. 'I aim to be one myself some day.'

'You won't be the way you're starting out. Don't be a lunkhead and do Cad Clemson's dirty work for him.' Neal's smile was warm and friendly. 'If you have the guts to take it the hard way, you'll get a lot more out of life, Russ.'

'I'm satisfied,' the youngster flung back at him. He waved a hand at them and headed for Clemson's place.

Tim shook his head. 'He's got hell-in-the-neck, like so many kids. Won't listen to reason.'

'He says he is satisfied but he isn't,' Neal commented. 'Some day we may see him riding in to the K-B for a job. I hate to see a boy like that go wrong.'

They used the little stream for a guide. It took them into a box cañon and they passed through the rock break up the draw Russ had mentioned. In a grove of pines a log house was half-hidden. When they came to the first trees they tied their horses and went forward on foot. No sign of life showed except the smoke drift from the chimney. The K-B men reached the door undiscovered.

The sneering triumphant voice of Blackburn came to them. 'High, low, jack, and the game,' it taunted. 'Why don't you tinhorns learn how to play before you tackle a top hand?'

They were playing cards at a table, four of them—Blackburn, Dunn, Fox, and a stranger unknown to Neal. Dunn was the first to see the visitors.

'Look who's with us, boys,' he drawled, his pale blue eyes hard as obsidian.

Blackburn jumped to his feet with a startled curse.

With chill malice Neal gave him ironic advice. 'Why be so goosey, Jess? A top hand oughtn't to scare so easy.'

'What are you doing here?' the big ruffian demanded. Truculently he added: 'And don't you tell me I'm scared of you or anybody else.'

'I'm lookin' for a scoundrel who shot a girl yesterday,' Neal answered evenly, his gaze fastened to the pig eyes in the flushed beefy face. 'D'you know who he is?'

The stranger at the table spoke. One had only to look at his fierce lupine countenance, lined by the ravages of many years of vice, to guess that he was here in hiding.

'If someone would give me a knockdown to these gents I might know where we were at,' he suggested.

'Sure,' Dunn obliged, a harsh sarcasm in his tone. 'Meet Mr. Neal MacGowan, a good friend of us honest settlers in the Gap. And meet Tim Owen, the bird with the red topknot. Mr. Owen and Mr. MacGowan, meet Cass Purdy, a gent who has come to build up his health in our salubrious air.' At Neal he flung a sharp question: 'What's this about someone shooting a girl?'

'Ask Blackburn,' the cattleman replied, a challenge in his low clear words. 'He can tell you all about it.'

'That's a lie!' Blackburn cried. 'I don't know a thing about it.'

'Ask him where he was yesterday afternoon at two o'clock,' Neal continued.

The lanky rustler glared at Blackburn. 'All right. Where were you, Jess?'

'Why, I was right here playin' seven up with Luke and Cass,' the accused man floundered.

'What girl was shot?' Dunn demanded of MacGowan.

'Janet Lane.'

Again Dunn's appraising gaze rested on Blackburn. Watching the flurry of fear in the pig eyes darting from one to another of them, Allan Dunn felt the fellow was guilty. He knew too that the man was as dangerous as a cornered wolf.

'Better fix a better alibi than that, Jess,' the tall calf thief said contemptuously. 'At two o'clock Luke was over at my place.'

'That's right,' Blackburn corrected. 'It was Lee Daly, not Luke. Cass will tell you I was right here.'

Purdy came to scratch. 'Sure he was here, sitting at this table. I won eight dollars from him.'

'Or maybe it was nine,' Neal amended, politely skeptical.

'Say, what is this bird doing here?' Purdy wanted to know, bristling up. 'Is it any of his business where Jess was?'

Tim Owen gave information. 'Neal is a deputy United States marshal.'

This was startling news. All four of the card players looked at MacGowan. Each of them was wondering how much this affected him if at all.

Dunn was the first to speak. 'So you've thrown in with our enemies,' he cried angrily.

'No,' Neal denied. 'But I won't have my good neighbors shot down from ambush. And when I knew you in the old days, Allan, before you moved up here, you wouldn't have stood for it either.'

'I won't stand for it now any more than I would then,' Dunn retorted hotly. 'But I want more evidence than your say-so.'

Neal did not want to go too closely into the evidence, since this led back to the stage robbery in which Dunn probably had been involved. He said, stretching a point, 'Blackburn was recognized.'

'Another lie,' the killer screamed. 'I wasn't outa the Gap.'

'Who saw him?' Dunn asked.

MacGowan shook his head. 'Can't tell you that,

Allan. Same thing might happen to him that did to Lane and his daughter.'

'Whoever says he saw me shoot the Lane girl is lying,' Blackburn broke out, beads of perspiration on his forehead.

'Since you are innocent, you won't mind going down with me to meet yore accuser,' Neal said.

Blackburn pounded the table with a hamlike fist. 'I won't go a foot of the way!' he roared. 'If I went I'd be arrested on some other trumped-up charge. The big ranches have got it in for me.'

'Sounds reasonable,' Dunn agreed. 'If it wasn't one thing it would be another.'

The lank rustler was in a quandary. He did not want to protect a cold-blooded assassin. Once or twice he had suspected that Blackburn had killed Stuart Lane, and he had rejected the thought because he did not want to believe it. Now he was almost convinced. Moreover, he knew that the fellow had been out of the Gap yesterday, and he could see a sick fear sticking out of all his protests. For Blackburn knew that this country would run down ruthlessly the murderer of a girl. But Dunn's past misdeeds tied him to the ruffian. He had been in the Sheridan stage holdup and had seen Cole Tracy shot from his seat. Allan guessed that if crowded Blackburn would try to buy immunity by betraying his companions. He made a temporary decision to keep his hands off and let Neal and Blackburn settle this themselves.

'Saddle a horse for Blackburn to ride, Fox,' MacGowan ordered quietly. 'He's going with us.'

Neal was not sure whether any of Blackburn's companions would fight for him or not, but he knew that he was going to find out in a very short time.

'Now, looky here, Mr. MacGowan, we don't want to go off half-cocked,' Luke Fox began to whine.

The officer cut him off sharply. 'Saddle that horse.'

Blackburn appealed to Dunn. 'He's got another fellow with him. You wouldn't let him pull a dirty trick like this on me, would you, Allan?'

Dunn looked at him in sour distaste. 'How do I know whether you did or didn't shoot Miss Lane? You've lied ever since Neal came into the room. You were outa the Gap yesterday. I met you coming across from Squaw Creek. Settle this with him yoreself. I'm not in it.'

As Fox slid out of the room, glad to escape from a place where guns might soon start smoking, Blackburn yelled after him, 'Don't you saddle that horse, Luke, for I won't be using it.'

'Step outside and see he slaps a saddle on a bronc, Tim,' his employer said.

Owen had his eyes on Blackburn, who had fallen back from the table to one of the bunks ranged along the wall. Tim could see the butt of a revolver sticking out from under the edge of a blanket. He was not sure Neal from his position could tell the weapon was there.

'I see you sleep with a gun under the blanket beside you, Jess,' he said, with intent to convey the news to his friend. 'I'd be scared to do that for fear I'd roll over it and shoot myself.'

Neal laughed. 'Much obliged, Tim. I see the gun. You mustn't put notions in Mr. Blackburn's head. He never kills when the other fellow is looking.'

The pale blue eyes of Dunn rested on the cornered bad man. He was curious to see what the fellow would do. The man had an evil reputation as a killer, but that did not necessarily imply courage. There was a type of gunman who always set the stage for his murders, and Dunn suspected that Blackburn belonged to it. In a few seconds he would know about that. For MacGowan had flung at Jess a contemptuous challenge.

That the big ruffian had meant to snatch up the revolver lying so close to his fingertips and send lead crashing into Neal's body all of them in the cabin were aware. The marshal had not moved his hand a fraction of an inch nearer the forty-five suspended from his hip, but the poised wariness of his stance, the steadiness of the watchful, brown eyes, were warning enough that he would get into action lightning-fast. Dunn knew what thoughts were sifting through the desperado's mind. Since the gun beside him was already in the open, he would have a thin fraction of a second's advantage in the draw. But even if he shot MacGowan through the heart, as he very likely would, the officer might still kill him. For all gunfighters knew that there was a moment of time before even a deadly wound paralyzed the muscles. Moreover, Tim Owen had to be taken into account.

Slowly Jess Blackburn's hand drew back from the weapon on the bunk. There was a creeping reluctance about the gesture, as if the fingers were obeying an order from the brain against their will.

'I don't want trouble with you, MacGowan,' he said thickly. 'All I'm askin' is for you to let me alone.'

Neal said to Tim, not lifting his gaze from the outlaw, not raising his voice, 'Better get a move on you and see Fox is saddling the horse.'

Tim's glance swept the room. It was plain that Dunn did not intend to take a hand in this. Blackburn had not been able to bring his nerve to the sticking point. The stranger Purdy probably would follow the example of Allan and not help a quitter.

The K-B cowboy said, 'Okay, boss' and walked out of the room.

CHAPTER XI

One saddled horse not needed

Still doubtful about leaving his chief alone in that den of wolves, Tim Owen hesitated at the door and looked back into the room. Blackburn still stood in front of the bunk, black sullen anger in his face. Rage simmered in his heart. He knew he had lost caste. MacGowan had forced him to choose, and his decision had been not to fight.

Dunn looked at the whipped bully, a cynical smile on his scornful lips. 'Jess has changed his mind, Neal,' he said. 'A bucked-out bronc ain't any more peaceful than he is.'

'There's two of them to one,' Blackburn complained unhappily, to bolster a lost reputation.

'Better move forward to the table,' Neal suggested.

Blackburn did as he was told, his feet dragging.

'I'll see about the horse,' Tim called in, and started for the corral.

He could see horses milling around the inclosure. Luke Fox had roped one and was saddling it, a flea-bitten sorrel owned by himself. Owen leaned on the fence and volunteered information to the little man.

'I guess you're hard of hearing, Luke,' he said.

'Neal told you to get a horse ready for Jess, not one for yoreself. You're not the guy we want—yet.'

Fox slid an angry look at the cowboy. 'I'm gettin' outa here *muy pronto*,' he announced, and tightened a cinch. 'I got to see a fellow.'

'You do yore chores first,' Tim drawled. 'You've been subpoenaed by the law, as you might say.'

'What's the matter with you saddling the horse,' Fox snapped. 'You're able-bodied—got two hands and two feet.'

'Not my job. Get busy, Luke. Neal is kinda on the prod today.'

Fox glared resentfully at him and picked up a rope. He stepped toward the remuda, and as the horses raced past him, threw and missed. Pulling in the rope dragging in the dust, he rewound it and made another throw. The loop dropped over the head of a dark brown gelding.

'You're doing fine, Luke,' Tim told him.

The commandeered wrangler took the captive horse to the stable and saddled it. He led it toward the house, Tim by his side.

Allan Dunn stepped out of the doorway. 'Here's yore bronc, Jess,' he called back into the house.

Purdy appeared, and after him Blackburn with Neal at his heels.

'You'll have a fine ride down,' Dunn continued, sarcasm heavy in his voice. 'It's a real nice day.'

'You might bring our horses, Tim,' Neal said.

The prisoner started to cut across back of Purdy to his horse.

'Wait just a minute,' his captor advised. 'It will be more friendly if we all leave together, those of us that are going.'

The trapped desperado turned, rage and hatred burning in his eyes. He was standing to the right and a little back of Purdy.

'Lay off me, Mac,' he said, the words whistling through tight lips. 'I'm not going. You got no right to take me.'

'You're going,' Neal answered, not raising his voice, but keeping it strong and clear. Then swiftly, he flung out a warning, for he saw what the man was going to do.

'Don't you!' he cried.

It was too late.

Blackburn snatched the revolver from Purdy's holster and fired from the hip. The crash of Neal's forty-five was scarcely an eyebeat later. Again the sound of the guns whipped through the trees. The outlaw's knees gave way. His big body sank forward, at first slowly. It pitched heavily to the ground, turning over before it struck. The trigger finger twitched, then became still.

There was a long silence after the booming of the guns had died. Dunn looked down at the prone lax figure. 'He sure asked for it,' was his comment. He added, as if to himself: 'I never liked him. He was poison to any outfit he trailed with.'

For a moment Neal stood motionless, watching the man his bullets had cut down. He set his face, so that it would not show the horror that filled him. He had never killed a man before. A slack sickness ran through him and had to be fought down.

'I call you all to witness that he fired first,' he said in a low voice.

Purdy's wolfish face knotted angrily. 'You drove him to it,' he spat at MacGowan.

Neal moved two steps closer to the man, his eyes bleak and bitter. They dominated a face of fine bony confirmation, setting the mood for laughter or for sternness. There was no mirth in it now.

'You killed him, Purdy. I didn't get it in time to interfere. But I know now. You gave him the sign to grab yore gun out and stood where he could reach it easy. You expected him to kill me, but it didn't work out that way.'

Purdy's shifty eyes narrowed. 'You're crazy with the heat, fellow. I didn't have any idea of what he was aiming to do.' His manner was blunt and stiff, but he fell back as MacGowan advanced. He had let himself be stripped of his revolver. That had been a mistake.

The cool gaze of Dunn shifted from one to the other and back again. He was interested, as he always was in a situation where men acted under stress, but he did not intend to lift a hand now any more than he had before. So far he was satisfied with what had taken place. Blackburn had become a menace to his safety. It suited him to have the fellow dead.

'Listen, you damn buzzard head,' Purdy shouted, still backing. 'I'm not in this, I tell you.'

Neal's arm lifted and came down hard. It broke through the arm flung up as protection and the barrel of his forty-five skidded from the side of the outlaw's head. Purdy groaned as he staggered back to lean against the horse Fox had saddled for Blackburn.

The incident was finished. Neal turned to his friend.

'We'll get going, Tim, if you'll bring the horses,' he said.

On Dunn's sardonic face there was the flicker of a smile.

'You're thorough, Mac,' he said dryly. 'Are you satisfied with me? Or do I get my come-uppings too?'

Neal did not answer. He looked down at the huge barrel-chested body of the dead man and started through the trees toward the horses.

CHAPTER XII

'Some of Cad Clemson's slick work'

The K-B men were careful not to show any signs of hurry, but they did not lose any time in getting under way. They wanted to be out of the Gap before the story of what Neal had done reached any more of the outlaws skulking in its hidden pockets. There were probably a dozen men in this refuge for desperadoes who would ask no questions before drygulching them if an opportunity occurred.

As soon as they were out of sight they quickened their pace. When they dropped into the cañon through the break in the wall Tim's glance swept the boulder-strewn floor anxiously.

'Ever see a better place for sharpshooters to pick us off?' he asked with a wry grin.

'It would be easy as shooting tame ducks in a pond,' MacGowan agreed. 'But I reckon Cad isn't quite ready to rub out a United States marshal yet. That might start a lot of trouble for him.'

'Hope you're right.' Tim looked across at his chief, a boyish admiration in his blue eyes. 'I never saw yore beat. Once I heard about a guy who crawled into a grizzly's den. He got clawed up some. That wasn't a circumstance to what you did. Bet you there isn't another fellow in the Flood River country crazy enough to come up here without a big posse and try to arrest a bad killer like Blackburn. And then get away with it —mebbe.'

'I had a responsible man siding me,' Neal mentioned.

'The responsible man is plumb goosey right now,' Tim admitted.

They came out of the box cañon to the mountain park below and traveled along the creek to the top of the gulch where Russ Miller had left them. It was late in the afternoon when they cut sign of their own tracks made earlier in the day. This was the point where they had ridden across to drop down into the valley where Clemson lived.

'We'll have to hurry to get out of the Gap before night,' Neal said. 'We had better camp on Squaw Creek if we can make it.'

The miles seemed interminable as they wound through the tangle of hills, gorges, and wooded parks. The sun had set before they climbed to the cut that was the entrance to Rustlers' Gap. Dusk had fallen, but there was still light in the sky, though darkness was near.

Neal was in the lead when they stopped for a moment at the summit to breathe their horses. His companion looked back into the wild country through which they had just come.

'Sure seems to be filled with absentees,' Tim commented. 'Betcha a regiment of men could hole up there and not a dozen of them be found in a week.'

MacGowan gave his mount the signal and moved forward. Before the horse had gone twenty yards, a great boulder crashed down from one of the walls and struck not three feet in front of him. The horse reared wildly and Neal was flung sprawling to the ground. He clung to the rein and scrambled to his feet.

'Get going, Tim!' he cried, and vaulted into the saddle.

Owen's horse brushed past him and jumped to a gallop. From the gathering darkness above a rifle cracked. Neal pounded after the cowboy, crouched low in the saddle. Another bullet zipped against a rock.

Tim pulled his pony up hard. 'All right, Neal?' he cried.

'All right,' MacGowan answered. 'Light a shuck out of here, boy.'

The Winchester sounded again, but the bad light favored them. In another minute they were out of range. They drew up presently, and the packhorse came clattering up to join its mates.

Though they were probably safe in the growing darkness, the K-B men kept going. They did not stop again until they struck the headwaters of the north branch of Squaw Creek. If there had been any pursuit, it apparently had long since been given up.

They ate a cold supper without a fire, and after they had eaten put another five miles between them and the Gap before they stopped on the creek bank for sleep. They chose a spot well surrounded by brush. The horses they picketed.

Before rolling up in their blankets they smoked a last pipe.

'Some of Cad Clemson's slick work,' Neal said after a long silence, referring to the ambush in the cut.

'Why Clemson rather than Purdy, say?' Tim wanted to know.

'Purdy would have waited in the brush for a shot. He would not have bothered with fixing up a boulder to throw down on us. Cad wanted it to look like I had been killed by accident.'

At dawn they made coffee, fried ham, and cooked flapjacks. Tim headed for the K-B with the packhorse and Neal cut across country to Sundog.

It was a day of pleasant sunshine, and Neal did not hurry. The morning was well advanced by the time he rode down Trail's End Street. The little town lay somnolent, as drowsy as the straddled horses tied to the hitch-rack in front of Brick Carson's saloon. He caught a glimpse from the bridge of a barefoot boy fishing at the bend of the small river and guessed the youngster was playing hooky from school. A woman with a market basket over her arm disappeared into Doyle's grocery. Two chair-warmers lounged in front of the saddler's shop. No other sign of life showed on the street.

Neal turned out of Trail's End and drew up at the one-room office occupied by Doctor Alpheus Seneca. A horse and buggy were standing there, a line tied to a post.

'How are you this glad morning, Doctor Alpheus?' Neal asked cheerfully.

Seneca was busy drawing on a boot and did not answer until he had finished. 'Don't you call me that fool name,' he grunted.

'Got a hangover,' Neal murmured, as if to himself.

'I haven't either.' The doctor changed the subject. 'Now you're a government manhunter I reckon you think you can pester anybody. Or haven't you started yet?'

'Started and finished,' Neal replied. 'I don't like any part of it.'

Under his shaggy brows the doctor looked a question. 'Tell me more,' he said.

'You talk first,' Neal evaded. 'How did you come out on yore last trip to the Gap?'

'All right. I did like you advised, left a letter with Lance, to be opened only if anything happened to me. Soon as I saw Blackburn I told him I had left such a letter with a party unknown. He threw a fit—wanted to know if I didn't trust him and the boys. I said sure, but one of them might get a wrong idea and I thought it better to take out a little insurance. He's a black-hearted scoundrel. I could see he was half a mind to torture me so as to find out where I'd left the letter. Dunn put his foot on that. He said he was a white man and not an Apache, and he wouldn't stand for any of that business.'

'You fixed up Nels Gurley's wound and rode home?'

'Yes. Dunn went with me far as Squaw Creek. Looked like he didn't trust friend Blackburn too far. That fellow may try to bushwhack me yet.'

'No,' Neal told him. 'How is yore patient out at the Triangle R ranch?'

'Doing fine, and the two kids are having the time of their lives there. I had the wrong idea about Miss Reynolds. She's all right. What d'you mean no, about Blackburn shooting at me from the brush? He's a muddle-headed fool. You can't tell what he'll do if he gets sore enough.'

'He has done all the meanness he'll ever do, doctor. I killed him yesterday in the Gap while he was resisting arrest.'

The plump red-faced man stared at him in astonishment. 'You—killed him?'

'After he had shot at me. I went in with Tim Owen to drag him down. He killed Stuart Lane and wounded his daughter.'

'You know that?'

109

'Practically. The alibi he gave as to where he was at the time of Janet's shooting couldn't stand up. Allan Dunn told him he was a liar.'

'Then he decided to fight it out and said for you to come a-shootin'?'

'Not exactly,' Neal corrected dryly. 'He surrendered, and just before we started down grabbed a gun from another fellow's holster and took a crack at me. He missed. I didn't.'

'Bully for you!' Seneca cried. 'I'm glad he's dead. I feel a lot safer.'

'I'm not glad I was the one had to kill him,' said the marshal.

'No, I reckon not. Just the same it is a good thing for this country. They ought to give you a medal.'

Neal changed the subject. 'How long are the Lanes going to stay at the Triangle R?'

'Not much longer. Miss Janet worries about being a trouble to the Reynolds, and she says she can't stay there and let your boys look after the homestead.'

'Tell her to forget that. It's no trouble. They take care of her stock when they're over that way anyhow.'

'Tell her yourself.' Doctor Seneca looked at him sharply. 'What's the matter with you young squirts nowadays? Here are two young ladies, both pretty as painted wagons, noways hostile to you, and you haven't enough pep and vinegar to go see 'em. Hell, you'll never be young but once.'

'That's true,' Neal agreed. 'I'll drop in on them tomorrow.'

'Hmp! You act like it was a favor to them.'

MacGowan laughed. 'You're an eligible bachelor. What's the matter with you cutting a few capers before them?'

'I've got some sense left,' Seneca grunted. 'I'm old enough to be the father of either one of them.'

MacGowan dropped into Brick Carson's place to leave a message for any of his riders who might come in there. Dunn and Fox were at the bar. The lanky rustler was telling a story to which the few men in the room were listening with intent interest. At Neal's entrance he broke off his narrative. Everybody present stared at the cattleman. Dunn was the first to break the silence.

'Damn if he isn't here himself to finish the story for you, boys,' he said.

Neal waved the suggestion aside. 'Go ahead, Allan. Don't let me interrupt you.'

He knew the eyes drilling into his were asking questions. It was known by all that he had been sympathetic to the nesters and the homesteaders and had stood up against the arbitrary arrogance of the other cattlemen. Though he had not approved rustling, he had held that the practices of the big ranches had been in part to blame for it, or at least had given the thieves a sense of justification. What the men watching him now wanted to know was whether he had gone over to the side of the large outfits and deserted their cause.

Brick Carson crossed his arms on the bar. 'Seems you are a United States marshal, Neal,' he said pointedly.

'A deputy,' the K-B man amended.

'That means you go out and bring in all the fellows wanted by the Association.'

'No, Brick,' Neal corrected. 'I'm not working for the Cattlemen's Association. I was appointed a special deputy U.S. marshal at my own request because I wanted to find out who killed Stuart Lane and then arrest him. I found out. Blackburn did it. Tim and I went up to arrest him. He tried a quick draw on me after he had given up to us. His bullet missed me and mine hit him. I'm not on regular pay, and the government doesn't expect to send me out to arrest other criminals.'

'Then I reckon you'll resign now yore job is done,' Dunn said, his bleak gaze on MacGowan.

'Not yet, Allan,' answered Neal quietly. 'I'll wait awhile and see how things go. When Tim and I were coming through the pass Cad Clemson tried to murder us. Tell him from me that I'm still a deputy and if he wants trouble he can have it. He can be dragged out from the Gap just as Black-burn would have been if he hadn't chosen instead to be killed. I never was a friend of miscreants, and I am not now.'

'They say you and Austin Reynolds have made up and are friends,' Fox put in, rubbing his unshaven chin.

MacGowan's scornful eyes rested on the sly little scoundrel. 'Reynolds doesn't say it, does he? And get this, Luke. If we are, that's my business.'

Brick stopped polishing the top of the bar with a cloth. 'I don't reckon this country will miss Jess Blackburn any,' he said, with intent to avoid a breach. 'He was a bad citizen—mean, ornery, and vicious. If he killed Stuart Lane he deserved what he got.'

Neal gave his reasons for thinking Blackburn guilty, omitting one or two of them. Unexpectedly, Dunn supported him. Two or three little things had made him suspect Jess, he said. The fellow had been out of the Gap half a day and wouldn't tell where he had been. Also, he had dropped some boastful hints his associates did not understand at the time.

A man sitting at a table playing solitaire asked why he had killed Lane.

Brick Carson turned to the cattleman. 'Why did he?'

'Stuart knew too much,' Neal replied curtly.

'What did he know?' Dunn asked, his cold light eyes on the K-B man.

MacGowan returned the challenging look, with a sarcastic smile.

'I don't know any more than you do, Allan, what

Stuart had got onto that was dangerous to Blackburn.'

If there was a double meaning in the answer, Dunn decided not to look for the less obvious one. He said, in an offhand way, 'Then I reckon neither of us knows.'

To lessen the strain Carson suggested a drink on the house. Before raising his glass Dunn looked down a long time at the liquor. 'I'm a plain-spoken geezer, Neal,' he blurted out. 'You claim to be some kind of a special marshal. I dunno what that means. Let's say some guy above you sent orders to bring in some ordinary fellow, not a black-hearted scoundrel like Blackburn. Take me, for instance. You would have to gather me in, wouldn't you?'

Neal's cool eyes rested on the swarthy cowboy. 'Does the government want you, Allan?' he inquired.

Dunn flushed angrily. 'No, sir. But this bird at Cheyenne I mentioned, sitting with his feet on a desk, might think different if some of yore cattlemen friends got at him.'

Probably Dunn was in the stage holdup, MacGowan reflected, and robbing the mails was a government offense. Yet he had no proof of it. The man had sided with Blackburn to keep him from seeing the wounded bandit Gurley. But he and Nels Gurley were close friends. Allan might want to protect him from motives of loyalty.

'Far as I know you might be a Sunday School superintendent, Allan,' Neal said. 'I haven't any evidence against you at all. I've a notion I'm through manhunting anyhow. I certainly hope so.'

The lanky rustler hoped so too, for both their sakes. But he was far from sure of it.

CHAPTER XIII

Eleanor and Neal exchange amenities

At sight of Neal riding into the Triangle R yard Mary Lane slid from the bare back of a fat old mare and ran shouting to him. He dismounted and waited for the little pigtailed girl with long thin legs who was so eager to hurl herself into his arms. She was in a pair of overalls patched in the seat with a piece of bed ticking.

'Neal,' she shrieked, clinging to him. 'Baby Bunting is the most wunnerful doll. She opens her eyes, and they are the *bluest.*'

He unpeeled her from his legs, and hand in hand they walked together to the house. A young woman stood on the porch and watched them approach, a quick hot interest in her eyes. When she saw this man something wild and primitive fluttered in her heart. Her brother was as steady and reliable as tested steel. She knew what he would say and think on most subjects. But Neal MacGowan was of more fluid stuff. Not forty-eight hours ago he had killed a man. Now he was talking gaily with a child who skipped happily beside him because her dearest friend had just come.

What Eleanor said had no relation to what she was thinking. 'Janet will be glad to see you,' she told him.

His reply too was only words. 'I hope she is better.'

The racing thoughts that whipped through his brain were not for her to know. *Some man will walk beside her lovely youth. Time will stand still for them, and beauty will fill their lives. But I shall not be that man.*

She led him into the big room that was the center of life in the house. Janet lay propped up on a lounge. Her gaze followed his progress across the room. A pulse of excitement beat in her throat. What he had done made a tie between them—and opened a gulf.

He took her hand in his and smiled down at her. 'You're looking bully. Seems to me the Triangle R has been treating you well.'

'They have been lovely to me,' Janet answered. 'Eleanor has nursed me and fed me and treated me like a baby. It has been so nice to lie here and rest. But I'm all right now and ready to go home.'

'The doctor does not think so,' Eleanor differed. 'Neither do Austin and I. We love having the children here too.'

'And my boys are taking care of your stock,' Neal added. 'What's the big hurry?'

'I'm making myself a burden to all of you.'

'Sheer nonsense.' Eleanor turned to Doctor

Seneca, who had just walked into the room. 'Tell this obstinate girl she can't go home yet.'

'If she behaves herself and keeps on improving as she has, she can go home a week from today,' Seneca announced with decision.

He shooed Neal out of the room, to dress the wound. As the young man was leaving, Janet said in a low voice, a wave of pink beating faintly into her cheeks, 'I'd like to see you . . . to thank you . . . before you go.'

Neal wandered out to the porch and down to the corral. Presently Eleanor came out of the house, looked around, and found him. She came toward him, straight and of a slender fullness, her knees modeling the skirt at every light-footed step.

'I'm going down to the road for the mail,' she called to him. 'Since you are a cowboy, I don't suppose you can walk that far.'

He joined her. 'I can try. If I can't make it I'll lean on you.'

They struck out down the lane.

She glanced at his bronzed face, the eyes gay and reckless, and she liked what she saw. 'Wasn't it a little . . . careless . . . of you to go into Rustlers' Gap to arrest that villain when he had all his men around him?'

'Just a little,' he assented. 'But if you're thinking of the danger, there is always less when you walk right up to it.'

'Did you expect him to come out with you quietly, making no trouble?'

'He almost did. At the last moment one of his friends put temptation in his way.'

'And if he had shot straight you would never have left there alive.'

'If you had been fording Bear Creek last spring at the time of that cloudburst you would have been drowned,' he suggested.

'Not a parallel case. You deliberately invited this. Why?'

'Do you expect the men of this country to sit by and let murderers kill women?'

'What about Sheriff Cullen? Isn't he paid to attend to that?'

'Cullen is a lump of putty,' Neal said. 'Stuart Lane was my neighbor. I liked him. It seemed to be my job when this killer tried to assassinate his daughter.'

'I can understand that.' Her lips were parted and tiny amber flecks were shining in her eyes. 'Janet is a dear girl, one in a thousand.'

'Yes.' There was a whimsical lift to his left eyebrow. 'She doesn't approve of me.'

'Not always. That's the Puritan in her. She's very grateful to you, and at the same time she is shocked at what you have done. You see, she remembers her Bible, "Thou shalt not kill." There's a battle going on inside of her. She admires you tremendously. You're the kind of man she would have to get a thrill from watching.'

'What do you mean by that?' he demanded suspiciously.

'You can be gay and reckless and violent. I can feel the excitement in her when she talks about you. But you haven't a good reputation, Mr. MacGowan.' She gave him a tilted impudent smile. 'You're a wild young man. You don't give a hoot what anybody thinks of you. I'm afraid you gamble a great deal. And they say you will fight at the drop of a hat, whatever that means. It's distressing to be in love with a man who tugs you two ways. So poor Janet is at war with herself.'

He pulled up and frowned at her. 'Stop talking crazy nonsense,' he ordered. 'Janet is a nice girl. She has too much sense to have any interest of that kind in a fellow like me. Maybe she would like to reform me. That's all right. Women are that way. But don't go to confusing that feeling with—with anything else.'

'I won't.' A slow smile lit her face. 'And don't you forget that a girl, a man, and propinquity sometimes make dynamite when you mix them together. Not that I'm warning you off. Janet would be very good for you, if her conscience would let her accept you. Whether you would be good for her is something else again.'

'Listen,' he urged. 'Get that foolishness out of yore head. Janet is the finest girl I know. Far too good for me. She never gave me a thought that way. What sense is there in making up stuff like that?'

'I suppose she has told you all her thoughts,' Eleanor mocked.

'She and I aren't cut from the same kind of pattern. Your brother would be more her style.'

'He's beginning to think so too,' the girl said, and her eyes crinkled to mirth. 'I never saw him take an interest in a woman before. They talk together about cattle and grass and winter feed. Maybe that's his way of making love.'

'It wouldn't be yours,' he remarked.

She was a little startled, and greatly interested. 'What would my way be, kind sir?' she asked.

'There would be fireworks in it.'

'You don't know a thing about it—I mean about me.'

'No?' His monosyllable was polite but skeptical.

'You've seen me about six times.'

'Eight,' he corrected unwarily.

So he had counted, she thought, delighted, but concealed her pleasure.

'You're the kind of man who understands women,' she mocked. 'You've read me through and through.'

'It would do you good to change places with Janet for a year. The trouble with you is that you have always eaten out of a silver spoon.' He smiled with amiable malice and explained her to herself. 'You are spoiled, of course. I expect you weren't paddled enough when you were a kid. Naturally you've become self-centered. One of these days that is going to be tough on some poor man who marries you. It's too bad, for I think there is good stuff in you at bottom.'

Excitement sparked her eyes. 'It's nice of you to think that. I suppose you couldn't be mistaken.'

'About the good in you? I'm sure of it.'

'The vilest sinner has some redeeming traits, they say. When did you start disliking me—the first time we met? Or has the feeling been growing on you?'

He showed surprise. 'I didn't say I didn't like you. Fact is, I find you interesting.'

'A new kind of specimen to study. After you and Janet are married, if she decides to risk you—'

'I told you to stop that nonsense,' he interrupted. 'I won't have it.'

It was strange, he thought, how when they met he and this girl nearly always fought. They seemed naturally to be flung into antagonism. Yet there was an attraction that drew them together. In spite of her cool impertinence he could feel her come to life when they looked at each other. Perhaps there was a deeper repellant force that dominated them, an instinctive wisdom that warned them the codes by which they lived were at complete variance.

She said, chin lifted, 'I usually do and say what I think, Mr. MacGowan.'

'I know you do,' he answered, 'but it's not too late yet to do something about that.'

'You ought to have been a missionary,' she told him. 'But you must remember we can't all be gamblers and killers. We'll have to stay the poor things we are.'

They had reached the end of the lane. Eleanor looked in the mail box and found it empty.

'Nothing for us,' she said.

'It's the wrong day. Old Bob comes Tuesdays and Fridays.'

'Yes, I knew that,' she said sweetly. 'I thought it would be nice to have a walk with you and find out your intentions about Janet.' She took off her hat and swung it by the ribbons, imps of mischief in her dancing eyes. 'I've sorta adopted the family, you know.'

She was an enticing figure of soft loveliness, the flowing lines stressed by a summer breeze that wrapped the dress closer about her limbs. The loose tendrils of her hair, caught by the sun rays, were fine-spun gold. Neal's blood quickened. Their eyes met and held fast. He moved closer.

'You little devil,' he cried, and took her in his arms.

This was what she had unconsciously wanted, but she made a perfunctory resistance. 'You don't approve of me, you know,' she murmured, the color hot in her cheeks.

He kissed her quite thoroughly. It takes two to

make kissing worth while. Eleanor did not have her ripe red lips for nothing.

'Well,' she said, after he freed her. 'I'd heard you had violent impulses. I'll have to catch my breath before I say, "How dare you, Mr. MacGowan!" You're so—so eager.' A ripple of laughter swept her face. 'You never mentioned cattle or grass or winter feed.'

She was moving back up the lane again and he fell into step beside her. 'If I've scotched your silly talk about Janet and me, that's something,' he told her.

'I've been kissed before,' she tossed at him lightly. 'But Janet hasn't. She wouldn't understand it doesn't mean anything. You'd better watch your step with her. She isn't a—what is it you called me, a little devil?'

But though Eleanor chaffed him gaily she felt excitement racing through her. When they reached the house she was glad to escape while he went into the big room to say good-bye to Janet.

Janet found it difficult to tell Neal what she wanted to say. She felt a river of gratitude flowing out to him. He had risked his life to arrest the man who had murdered her father and tried to kill her. It was more than gratitude, she knew. When he smiled it warmed her. His sun-tanned reckless face, his lithe graceful body, the free way he walked—she remembered them at night when her room was dark and she could let herself go. But she schooled herself to stamp down the emotion. Even if he had wanted her, it would have been impossible for her small steps to keep pace with his wild uneven ones. She could not travel with him the trails such a man was bound to follow. And between them was the dreadful thing he had done in Rustlers' Gap. The fact that he had done it for her made the barrier between them more insurmountable. No doubt Blackburn had forfeited the right to live. Neal was an officer of the law. He had been forced to kill to save himself. She did not feel that it was wrong to shoot down the villain. But to take a human life was so awful—so final. If anybody but Neal had done it she would not worry.

MacGowan drew up a chair and sat beside her. His cheerful friendly smile was reassuring. 'You're worrying because I had to kill this man,' he told her. 'Don't you, Janet. I didn't kill him. The law did. You are trying to blame yoreself. No need of that. He was just a wolf that had to be rubbed out for the good of the rest of us. If he had lived you would not have been safe. Neither would Doctor Seneca. He would have gone on murdering to the end of his life. He's better dead.'

'I know,' she agreed in a small voice. 'I know, but—'

'But you'd rather somebody else had killed

him,' he finished for her. 'So would I. Still, it was something I had to do, and I'm not going to let it spoil my life.'

'I'm awfully grateful,' she said, choking a little. 'I'm so glad you weren't hurt.'

'Me too,' he agreed, grinning at her. 'And one thing is sure. Several people will sleep easier now the fellow is off the map.'

That was true, Janet knew. She did not understand the reference to Doctor Seneca, though she had heard that he had been taking care of a wounded man in Rustlers' Gap.

CHAPTER XIV

A man hunt

Neal pulled up to rest his winded horse and looked down into the golden valley far below him. The river wound through it, a thread of silver. Well back from it were the red buttes, below them a stretch of pine forest marching down to the cow-backed foothills. On both sides of the river he could see the checkerboard squares of grain and alfalfa belonging to the Blue Bell Ranch. The buildings were dwarfed to toy size. A moving wagon might have been a crawling ant, for the bluff on which he stood was two thousand feet above the valley floor.

There had been sunshine, but clouds had gathered and now a fine drizzle began to fall. Neal put on his slicker as the rain increased. The foothills grew vague and misty. He could hardly make out the buildings of the Blue Bell. Soon the whole valley would be blotted out.

He put Keno to the trail running along the ridge and descended to the gulch below. Through the sound of the rain there came to him a faint murmur of voices approaching. Out of the mist appeared three riders. They pulled up abruptly. Two of them carried rifles across their saddles.

The third, Robert Muir of the Blue Bell, removed his fingers from the butt of a revolver when he recognized Neal. There was a short pregnant silence.

'Off yore usual beat, aren't you, gentlemen?' MacGowan said dryly.

One of them answered harshly. 'It's a free country.' He was a big hard-faced man with slaty eyes and a mouth like a steel trap. Jack Cross of the Bar A B. Neal knew him well. He was a leading member of the Association and had for the owner of the K-B an intense dislike.

One of Neal's eyebrows lifted quizzically. 'Quite right, Mr. Cross. I agree with the Constitution. All of us entitled to life, liberty, and the pursuit of happiness. Or is that in the Declaration of Independence?'

The third of the trio was a heavyset squat man in chaps. Neal knew him, Tug Hack, a rider for the Circle Double T. He was chewing tobacco steadily, the eyes in his impassive face now set on MacGowan and now sweeping the misty background from which he had emerged. Apparently he wanted to be quite sure that Neal was alone. His rifle ready for action, he was as wary as a cat at a rat hole.

Neither Cross nor Hack smiled at MacGowan's pleasantry. They watched with the concentrated attention a prize fighter gives his opponent during the first few seconds of a bout.

'You alone?' Cross asked, his voice grating.

'I was, until I met such pleasant company,' Neal returned, dragging the words ironically.

Muir spoke for the first time. 'MacGowan is all right,' he said, to soften the dourness of his companions. The Scotchman had the high color and the clean scrubbed look peculiar to many of his race. He was an athletic, broad-shouldered young fellow. In the Flood River country he was well liked for his friendly cheerfulness. His open countenance was a guarantee of integrity.

'Is he?' Cross replied. The words were a sneer rather than a question. They carried more than a doubt.

Neal's manner was as jaunty as ever, but back of his cool indifference was a keen attention. The grimness of these men held a menace. There could be only one reason for this. They were hunting cattle thieves, very likely were part of a larger posse split up to cover different trails into the mountains. Probably within the past twenty-four hours rustlers had raided the range and cut out a bunch of stock. The outlaws must have run it fine, since the pursuers were hoping to head them off before they reached the hidden cache in the hills where the stuff was to be held, rebranded, and later driven to a buyer outside of the territory.

What concerned Neal was that the attitude of two of these men suggested that he was a suspect. They thought that the stolen cattle and the men

129

driving the bunch might be somewhere back in the mist within a mile or two, that he was scouting to make sure the way was clear. Of course this was ridiculous, but with the feeling as tense as it was now, nothing was too fanciful for partisans to believe.

'It's not a week since MacGowan went into the Gap to arrest Blackburn and killed him?' Muir reminded his allies.

Cross laughed harshly. 'You swallow everything you hear, don't you, Bob?' he said derisively.

Muir's blue eyes were puzzled. 'There were witnesses, Jack,' he insisted. 'Allan Dunn and Tim Owen.'

'One of the rustlers and a guy whose pay check is signed by MacGowan,' Tug Hack jeered.

'You mean that Neal didn't kill Blackburn?' Muir asked.

'Sure he killed him.' The words of Cross dripped malice. 'But why?'

'Because Blackburn murdered Lane and was resisting arrest,' Muir answered.

'Says who? That sounds to me. Why would an outsider take on a job like that—go into the Gap to arrest this bad man, knowing he likely wouldn't ever come out alive?'

'But he did.'

'He went in all right and he rubbed out Blackburn. Maybe he was welcome to ride in any time he liked.' The hard slaty eyes of Cross were fixed on the K-B man. 'Maybe he and Blackburn quarreled. Crooks do.'

Neal spoke, softly, his voice like steel. 'You used a word, Cross. I don't like it.'

'Then you can lump it,' the Bar A B man said bluntly.

'No.' Neal's words came low but clear. 'You can't call me a crook and get away with it. I've taken a good deal from you and yore friends, but I can't take that.'

Muir moved his horse forward, to stand between them. 'He's right, Jack. You have no right to say that without proof, and you have no proof.'

'Proof!' Cross spat the word out bitterly. 'Why be so damned legal? When we get the deadwood on these birds we can't convict them, not with nester and rustler juries. Take MacGowan here. He cuts loose from the Association, which is trying to stop thieving. The outlaws make a convenience of his ranch, riding over it whenever they please. His friends are the riffraff of this country.'

'He wears a badge of a United States marshal,' Muir said.

'What for?' demanded Cross. 'To protect the scalawags he runs with. Cullen is an officer too. He sits on his fat behind and never lifts a hand against the crooked friends who elected him.'

'Look at the facts straight, Jack,' urged Muir.

'You have no right to name Cullen and MacGowan in the same breath. Let's be fair. MacGowan discovered that Blackburn had killed Lane and wounded his daughter. Knowing that Cullen wouldn't move, he had himself appointed marshal to drag the scoundrel to justice. Reynolds and I are convinced of that. When Blackburn resisted arrest he killed him.'

Neal said nothing. The Blue Bell man had put the case fairly. It was up to Cross now. The Bar A B owner was mulishly obstinate. He had a virulent dislike of MacGowan. But he was not a fool. That he had gone too far he knew. In this frontier country you could not call a game man a crook without a fight. If he did not modify what he had said guns would smoke. He was moved now not by fear but by the knowledge that to go farther would be a mistake.

Cross sat his saddle heavily, the rancor in his hard face slowly ironing itself out. 'All right, Bob,' he said at last. 'I'll take it back. Like you say, I've got no proof.' His gaze fastened bleakly to the face of the man he hated, the man he thought a traitor to his class. Passion leaped out of him hotly. 'But, by God, I know what I think.'

'Think what you like,' Neal replied quietly. 'That's nothing to me, so long as you don't say it.'

The Scot thought the talk had been personal long enough. Trouble might still flare up between

132

them if he was not careful. 'Meet any fellows driving cattle this morning, MacGowan?' he asked.

'No. I'm quite sure there is no drive back of me between here and the K-B.'

'We'll look for ourselves, I reckon,' Hack announced.

'Why not?' Neal murmured. 'Then you'll be sure.'

He guided his horse past Cross and into the mist beyond. Would they find and capture the rustlers for whom they were looking, he wondered? If so, the men would get short shrift. They might be killed in a running fight, or hanged to the nearest cottonwood. His mind ran over the men he knew who could have been in this raid. This was not the job of nesters. The homesteaders might run their brand on a stray calf belonging to a big outfit or they might kill a beef for meat, but they would not tackle a raid like this. A night roundup and drive would require half a dozen men. There must be a hidden cache in which to keep the stock and a point of delivery for a subsequent sale arranged beforehand. An organization was necessary. Neal's guess was that Cad Clemson was back of it. He had the men, the cache, and the outside connections to dispose of the stolen stuff.

CHAPTER XV

In a tight

When Neal reached Sundog, he found the little town buzzing like a beehive. News of the raid had been brought in by a cowboy, and the story of it was in everybody's mouth. Men were huddled in small groups. They talked guardedly, in undertones, and expressed opinions only to those they felt could be trusted. Fifty head had been taken, it was said, belonging to the Bar A B and the Circle Double T. There might be other brands too in the gather, but this was not known yet. Sol Bassett, a rider for Cross, had come on the rustlers at work and had been severely wounded.

No raid of such proportion had occurred before in the Flood River country. It was a barefaced challenge to the cattlemen from the rustlers. That the big ranches would lie down and take this without fighting back nobody believed. To put a running iron on a calf or to blot a brand on a heifer was one thing. A wholesale drive like this was quite another.

Neal stopped Doctor Seneca's buggy on the way to his office. He noticed that the flanks of the horse were stained with dried sweat.

'Been out to the Bar A B, doc?' he inquired.

'That's just where I've been,' Seneca answered. 'This is a bad business, Neal.'

'Yes. I hear one of the ranch boys was wounded.'

'Sol Bassett. He'll be lucky if he makes it. Sol had been galling[1] and was on his way back to the ranch when he ran into the thieves. Before he could get away one of them shot him. Whoever did it certainly stirred up a hornets' nest. I'll bet the outfits around here have five or six posses out after the thieves.'

'Did Sol recognize any of the men?'

'No. He wasn't close enough. But I don't see how the outlaws can get away unless they push the cattle hard. Some of the Bar A B boys were in the saddle inside of three hours.'

'I met Cross and two other men away up on Piney Ridge,' Neal told the doctor. 'The old man was sure living up to his name. He almost picked a row with me.'

'What for?'

'He got it into his noodle that I was one of the thieves.'

Seneca stared at him. 'He wasn't fool enough to say so?'

'Not exactly. He *did* imply that I was in with the Rustlers' Gap outlaws.'

'Holy smoke! That was fighting talk.'

[1]A cowboy went 'gallin'' when he called on a girl in his best clothes.

135

'I thought so,' Neal agreed. 'I mentioned that I didn't like it. He took it back, halfway.'

The doctor frowned down on MacGowan. 'This raid will make trouble, Neal, sure as you are a foot high. The district has been ripe for it quite a spell. The pot will boil over now.' He added irritably, 'I thought Cad Clemson had better sense than to pull a thing like this.'

'He has got away with so much I reckon he thinks there is no limit.' A smile danced in Neal's brown eyes. 'I expect I had better be drifting out of town before Cross gets back and tells me some more of my delinquencies, derelictions, and depravities.'

The doctor watched him ride away, a lithe trim figure in his whipcord suit, the broad hat tilted a little rakishly. He thought he had seldom seen a more likable man or one more likely to find favor in a woman's eyes. Seneca sighed. Even as a young man he had possessed none of this cattleman's gay charm, and now middle age was creeping up on him. But he found a good deal of pleasure in observing the younger generation from the side lines. Unless he was mistaken he knew two girls who were intrigued by the personality of this reckless light-stepping individualist. He meant to watch with interest the course of events. Just now the odds were in favor of the Titian-headed entry, but he thought the dark-eyed brunette had a chance too. She might be a surer long-time bet.

At this moment Neal was headed for the home of one of them, but he was not thinking of the lady at his journey's end. His mind was full of this new development in the feud between the rustlers and the cattlemen. It meant that passions, already inflamed, would find expression in violent action. The hotheads in the Gap must have put a good deal of pressure on Clemson before he consented to such a raid. For though Cad was greedy, he was also cautious. He must know that it would be better not to stir up the latent power back of the big ranches. There were places in the Gap which a dozen men could hold against five times as many attackers, but if the law ever set itself seriously to clean out the bandit's retreat, enough troops could be sent in to do so. That was the trouble about being the leader of a band of outlaws held together loosely. Cad had a good deal of the sly shrewd wisdom necessary for self-preservation, but he could not always restrain the dangerous impulses of those with whom he was associated.

Neal rode along a wooded prong and his gaze swept the sun-warmed valley below. Far up it his trained eye picked up a puff of dust. The hoofs of five horses had stirred it. He counted the animals as they came up out of a draw. Another posse looking for last night's rustlers, he guessed. Probably Cullen was with one of the pursuing parties. He had to make a bluff, but the sheriff would be unhappy if he found the men for whom he was searching.

Neal did not descend into the valley. He followed the shoulder of a hill that led him to a draw. Skirting a grove of quaking asp, he crossed the sage flats below and came to a small creek where he could see trout resting on the bottom in the clear water. It brought him to a fenced field of hay. In it were two stacks Stuart Lane had put up a few months earlier.

He rode around the field to the house. Mary ran to meet him, and he lifted her to the saddle in front of him. She took the reins.

'We got home yesterday,' Mary explained. 'Mr. Reynolds brought us back. I like it better at the Triangle R. Harry and I are just startin' for the Finn Woods. We're gonna have supper there.'

A six-months-old puppy came wriggling out of the house to join Mary. She clasped her hands joyfully. 'Looky, looky, Neal. Isn't he the most sweetest dog you ever did see? His name's Eleanor, on account of that she gave him to me.' The little girl slid to the ground and picked up the misnamed dog, encircling its belly with her arms and holding it close to her own. She brought it to MacGowan for admiration. He gravely agreed that the Flood River country had not produced a finer mongrel.

Harry came from the stable with a harnessed horse. 'Mary calls him a girl's name,' he said with the patronizing wisdom of his extra years.

'Course he's her dog, but I call him Lin for short. He likes that better.'

'He doesn't either,' Mary protested. 'He likes his own honest-to-gosh name.'

'Honest-to-goodness sounds better than honest-to-gosh, Mary,' her sister suggested.

'Well, anyway, his name's Eleanor,' the child insisted stoutly.

Janet stood in the doorway giving last instructions to Harry as he hitched the horse to the buggy. They weren't to stay long after supper. He could take his father's watch, to make sure he started in time to be home by nine o'clock.

After the children had gone Neal sat on the porch and watched her knitting needles flash. She was making a pair of stockings for Harry. He had never seen her look so well. Her cheeks were fuller and the color in them warmer.

'Are you quite all right?' he asked.

'Yes.' She smiled. 'Everybody was too good to me. The Reynolds spoiled me, and of course I can't thank you enough for looking after things here. You didn't have to build me a henhouse. But we needed it. I'm to have the school. When I get some money I'll pay you for it.'

'You're still a tenderfoot,' he scoffed. 'Can't I be neighborly without you talking about pay? But I'm glad you're to get the school. I reckon I'm too old to be one of yore pupils. I'll have to stay uneducated.'

'You spent a year at college,' she said, 'and that is one more than I have had.' She asked curiously, 'Why did you stop?'

'My money gave out, and I didn't like it much anyhow.' He swept out an arm to include Wyoming and adjacent states. 'I like this better than being cramped up in four walls and reading what Plato thought about life. Here is life in the raw—plains, mountains, blue skies. A man has to stand on his own feet. He has to do his own thinking. If he is incompetent he had better go back and live in a town. Reynolds went to college. I expect it was good for him. But what he learned there hasn't helped make him the first-class cattleman he is.'

'Maybe not, but it has made him a bigger man. I like him. At first I didn't, till I began to know him. He isn't arrogant or proud. It's his shyness that makes him stiff. He might be a little prejudiced about the homesteaders.'

'A little,' Neal agreed.

'You don't like him,' she charged.

'Wouldn't it be better to put it that he doesn't like me?'

'He didn't say a word against you all the time I was there.'

Neal grinned. 'So you think he feels right friendly toward me.'

'No, I don't. He feels that it is a question in Wyoming now whether the honest men or the

140

thieves run it, and I suppose he thinks you haven't come out clean for the right side.'

'He would think that. With him there is black and white, and no shades in between. A nester kills one of my calves to feed his family. What he has done is not right, but he isn't a criminal because of it. A cowboy has a little place of his own and a brand. He is just getting started, and he can't live off his earnings from what he has. But no ranch will hire him for fear he will put his own brand on the company stuff. So he starts getting too free with a running iron. He is wrong, of course, but the way to make him better isn't to hang him to a cottonwood. Cattlemen aren't such sticklers for the law themselves. Reynolds has not fenced government land, but plenty of his neighbors have. Because they do it openly does not justify them. That land belongs to any homesteader who wants to take it up.'

'Yes,' Janet sighed. 'I used to think it was easy to know right from wrong, but—'

'But most of us are human,' he concluded for her lightly.

His eyes fastened on a movement in the sage across the creek. A horse emerged from the brush. One man was riding it, another walking by its side. They crossed the creek and came up to the house. Neal watched them alertly. The horse was spent, the men harassed and weary. The one in the saddle leaned heavily on the pommel. His gaze swept the sage back of them hurriedly, as if to make sure they were not being followed. He was a mere lad, with smooth cheeks from which the blood had been drained. Neal recognized him—Russ Miller, who had been his guide to Blackburn's hole-up in the Gap. The boy's companion was Dave Dagwell, another of Clemson's henchmen. Both were dusty, sweat-stained, and disheveled.

Dagwell held his right hand concealed under the left side of the coat. MacGowan knew what the man's fingers clutched. No words were necessary to let them know that they were two of the raiders cut off from their fellows by the pursuit before reaching the Gap.

'We're in a tight, MacGowan,' Dagwell snarled. 'This boy has been hurt. We've got to get outa here—quick. I want two horses.'

The words and manner of the man frightened Janet. There was something dreadful about this. She did not yet know what it was, but no doubt it had to do with the feud that rent the country and held it full of fears and hatred.

'I won't try to keep you from taking my horse, Dagwell,' Neal said quietly. 'But Miss Lane has only one horse here. He is old and heavy-footed. Afraid he won't be of much use to you.'

The hands of Miller clung so tightly to the saddlehorn that his knuckles whitened. 'We've gotta—get—outa here.'

Neal caught his body as he began to slide from his seat.

'He got shot in the leg,' Dagwell explained. 'I reckon his boot is full of blood. He can't travel farther.' The troubled eyes in the leathery face probed into those of the cattleman. 'Will you hide him, MacGowan? He's only a kid.'

'Where?' Neal asked. 'If they come here they'll search the place.'

'They'll be here—soon,' the rustler replied. 'Cain't you put him in the root house?'

'We'll do our best!' Janet cried. 'Maybe they won't search the ranch.'

Neal had been thinking fast. Neither the house nor the root dugout would be safe for the fugitive. One of the haystacks would be better.

'Here, Dagwell. Help me lift him to the horse. We'll get him to that haystack and hide him on it.' Neal gave a crisp order. 'You take him there while I get bandages for the wound.'

They put the lax figure of Russell on Keno, and Dagwell guided the cowpony through the hayfield. A minute later MacGowan reached the stack carrying a pail half full of water and some clean dishtowels. While he washed and bound the wound he told Dagwell to climb to the top of the stack by standing on the saddle and to take the lariat with him.

The boy came back to consciousness as Neal was tightening the loop of the rope around his waist.

'Don't hang me,' he begged, misunderstanding Neal's intent.

'He's trying to save you, buzzard head,' Dagwell explained, and hauled him up the side of the stack.

'Bury yoreself in the hay and stay there till I come for you,' MacGowan called up to Russell.

Dagwell slid down and swung to the saddle. 'If I get outa this jam I'll not forget this,' he promised, his voice rough and hard.

'Take the pinto with you so that it won't be here if a posse comes,' the cattleman said. 'You can't make a getaway by the valley. As I came along the ridge I saw a bunch of fellows headed this way. Any chance for you to double back up Squaw Creek?'

'No.' The giant in butternut jeans sat motionless for a moment, the bulldog jaw in the leathery face jutting out as he considered his situation. 'Not a dead man's chance that way. They were right behind me, fannin' out as they came.' His eyes narrowed in concentration as he looked across the sage flats to the Antelope Hills. If he could reach them he might work back through some of the gulches to safety.

He rode back to the house, picked up the rein of the pinto, and splashed through the creek. Two minutes later he had disappeared behind a dip in the flats.

Neal joined Janet again, the pup capering beside

him as he went. Eleanor had taken a very active interest in the proceedings and had done a good deal of barking at the strangers.

'Is the boy all right?' Janet asked. 'You don't think his wound is dangerous, do you?'

'Not too bad.' He looked at the stained rags. 'You'd better burn these in the stove.'

She put kindling beneath the cloth and got rid of the evidence. 'They are fugitives from the sheriff?' she asked.

'Not from the sheriff, from the cattlemen,' he corrected.

'What have they done?'

He told her of the raid and of the man they had left wounded.

'If they are caught—'

'It won't go well with them,' Neal replied.

She did not ask him to elaborate. Already she knew her West well enough to guess at the rough lawless punishment that would be inflicted on them if captured.

'I hope they don't find them,' she said in a low voice.

It was what Neal hoped himself, but he gave her his friendly derisive grin. 'Now look here, girl, you're not going over to the side of the rustlers, are you? Austin Reynolds wouldn't approve of that. They are miscreants, you know, and in this fight between honest men and thieves you have to come clean for the right.'

Janet knew he was teasing her to take her mind from thinking of the possibly impending tragedy. She sighed.

'Back home you don't have to worry about what is right and what is wrong. You can tell. But out here they get so mixed.'

'They are probably mixed back there too, but in Ohio you don't accept personal responsibility for the punishment of crime. You turn it over to the police and wash yore hands of it. Sometimes we can't do that out here. It's laid right down in our laps to handle.'

'I suppose that's true,' the girl agreed. 'But I don't like it. I wish it wasn't that way. You don't think that poor boy they shot deserves to—to have his life taken, do you?'

'Put yoreself in the place of the cattlemen. They can't send him to prison. A rustlers' jury won't convict him, or even a jury that has some decent homesteaders on it. The ranchmen are up against a bad situation. They must either turn him loose to steal more of their stock—or they must rub him out.'

'Isn't there any other way to punish him?'

Neal had to admit that he didn't know of any.

CHAPTER XVI

Mary's pup barks

Five men rode up to the fence at the Lane place. One dismounted to open the poor man's gate. Neal recognized the leader as Sheriff Cullen. He was past forty, face plump and soft and pink, bones well cushioned with fat. After he had laboriously lowered himself from the horse, he pulled down the trouser legs that had climbed to the top of the boots. It stuck out all over that he was no rider. Tomorrow he was going to be a sore stiff man.

He bowed to Janet, who was waiting on the porch, fear fluttering through her. Neal was standing beside her.

'Howdy, Miss Lane! Howdy, MacGowan! I'm lookin' for some fellows who raided the Bar A B range and druv off a bunch of cows. I don't reckon you've got 'em hid in yore vest pocket, MacGowan, have you?' His voice was heavily jocose, full of the false heartiness of the small-town professional politician.

Neal laughed at the pleasantry. He was willing just now to be amused at even a feeble joke. 'I saw you in the valley as I came along the ridge. Know yet who the fellows are you're hunting?'

'No more than a rabbit. I reckon they made a

clean getaway. You're lookin' peart as a new painted wagon, Miss Lane. Glad you recovered so nice from yore accident.'

'Thank you, Mr. Cullen. Won't you sit down in the shade?' Janet indicated a rocking chair on the porch. 'I expect you are thirsty. I'll get a bucket and a dipper, if one of your young men will go to the creek and bring back some cool water.'

The sheriff lowered himself carefully into the chair, choosing a position not too painful. 'Much obliged, Miss Lane. I'm sure spittin' cotton. Bill, you are young and spry. I reckon you wouldn't mind bringing Miss Lane a bucket of water.' He relaxed and mopped his fat perspiring face with a bandanna.

Bill Brock picked up the bucket and walked down to the creek. He was a thickset bowlegged man with a harsh sullen face, a stock detective in the employ of the Association. Most men avoided being too familiar with him, for he was suspected of being the man who had shot from ambush the rustlers Thorne and Norwood. On both occasions he had been seen close to the spot where the crimes were committed.

While they drank Neal made talk cheerfully. 'It's certainly hot for this time of year. We could do with a good soaking rain.'

'You've said it,' the sheriff agreed. He added irritably: 'No sense in me combing the sage hills for these birds now. They've done gone into their hole and pulled it after them.'

'Sounds reasonable,' Neal assented.

The misnamed Eleanor was doing a good deal of yelping, most of the time at a young fellow in the posse who kept teasing him. Occasionally he varied his performance by racing over to the haystack and barking there.

'He was chasing a rabbit awhile ago,' Neal observed. 'It ran over that way. He thinks it went into the haystack.'

'A dog has a mighty fine life,' the sheriff ruminated aloud, shifting in his chair to ease the saddle sores. 'Most all the time he lies in the shade and sleeps. If he gets rarin' to go all he has to do is run around and bark and act important. When he is hungry he is fed. Just enough fleas on him to keep him from gettin' lonesome. No troubles on his mind. Sometimes I figure I'd as lief be a dog with a good master as be king of Prooshia.'

The sound of a rifle shot whipped across the sage flats. An instant later, like a fainter echo of it, came a second explosion. That would be a revolver, Neal guessed, and the answer to it a rifle speaking again.

The nerves inside Janet's stomach knotted. Her eyes, big with dread, fastened on Neal.

'What's that?' Cullen asked, sitting up in the rocker.

The young man who had brought the water from the creek, Bill Brock, answered grimly, 'It ain't thunder.'

They listened for more shots, but none came.

'Don't you reckon we better drift over and see what's doing?' one of the posse asked.

Cullen was comfortable where he was, for the first time in hours. 'Might of been a hunter,' he suggested.

'Shootin' first with a Winchester an' then with a pistol,' Brock replied with obvious sarcasm.

'Whatever it was, it has died down,' the sheriff answered. 'No use going over there now. Still and all, if some of you boys want to run over—'

Brock interrupted bluntly. 'We're huntin' a bunch of rustlers who shot down poor Sol Bassett. You won't find them by sittin' here fannin' yoreself with yore hat. I don't care whether you go, but I aim to find out what the trouble is over there.' He turned to the others. 'How about you boys?'

The others agreed the shooting ought to be investigated.

Cullen eased himself out of the chair reluctantly. All his movements were made with exasperating deliberation. He thanked their hostess elaborately and ambled down to his horse. The others had fastened the girths of their mounts and were in the saddle before he had started to get ready. He took his stirrups up a notch.

'Maybe we'll get going again some time today,' Brock said curtly.

The sheriff made fast the belly band and hoisted himself to the seat, his motions as graceful as those of a hippopotamus. He lifted his hat to the girl. She was not looking at him.

'Someone else coming,' Janet said to Neal in a low voice, her eyes fixed on some riders topping a rise the other side of the creek.

'Four of them,' the sheriff said. 'By golly, one of 'em is a prisoner. His hands are tied behind him.'

Janet went white as a sheet. The prisoner was Dave Dagwell. Tug Hack was leading his horse.

Cross of the Bar A B dismounted in front of the sheriff and jeered at that officer. 'You'll be glad I've got one of the scoundrels, Cullen,' he said, the sting of a whip in his voice.

The sheriff did not look glad. Arrest of the guilty men meant trouble for him. The cattlemen and their enemies would be tugging at him from different directions. No matter what he did he would be blamed.

'Sure you've got the right man, Mr. Cross?' Cullen ventured.

'Dead sure,' the ranchman answered brusquely. 'He and another guy were bringing up the drag when we jumped them. I shot the horse this fellow was on, and he lit out back of the other thief. Both of them astraddle the same bronc, a pinto. I know who owns it too. He got away—for the present.'

'Who is he?' Cullen asked.

'One of yore friends,' Cross answered harshly. 'I'll get him, like I did this scalawag.'

Dagwell looked at him hardily. 'You got me because I didn't have a rifle to stand you off, you and Tug having one each. That's a hell of a thing to brag about.'

'Drag him from that horse,' ordered Cross.

Hack pulled him down into the dust, and when he tried awkwardly to rise, hampered by his bound wrists, hit him in the face with his closed fist.

Neal came down from the porch. 'That will be all of that,' he snapped.

'Is that so?' Hack inquired ironically. 'Orders from Mr. MacGowan, whose horse the damned rustler was riding when we took him.'

The words rang a bell for silence. All eyes turned on Neal. How had Dagwell come by the animal, they asked without words.

MacGowan laughed. 'Much obliged, Tug, for bringing back Keno.'

'Come clean,' demanded Cross harshly. 'I want to know how he got yore horse.'

'He borrowed it,' Neal said. 'Claimed he was in a hurry and needed it. So I let him have it.'

The slaty eyes of Cross smoldered. 'By God, if you—'

Dagwell cut in scornfully. 'Try not to be too big a fool, Cross. I held him up and took it, of course.'

'Where?'

'Here,' Janet spoke up. 'A little while ago.'

'Was the other fellow with him?'

'What other fellow, Mr. Cross?' Janet asked.

'We split up before we got here,' Dagwell said.

'You and Russ?' Cross insinuated.

The big prisoner in the butternut trousers and the blue shirt checked with white was giving out no information. 'I didn't mention any names.'

'We know who was with you,' Hack retorted.

'Then why ask me?'

'You might as well come through, Dave,' Brock spoke up. 'We've a mighty good idea who rode with you on that raid. Allan Dunn for one, and that fellow Purdy.'

'So you say. I'm not talking.' Dagwell's salient jaw jutted out.

The sheriff made a proposal. 'What say you boys go on with the hunt while I take Dave back to jail with me? Ned Smith can go with me to make sure our prisoner doesn't get away.'

The slaty eyes of Cross met those of the officer. 'He's not your prisoner, Cullen, *and he's not going to jail.*'

A cold wind blew through Janet. The words, so cruel in their meaning, the look that went with them, told her that the big rustler was doomed. He must have known it all the time, but he stood there with no evidence of fear in his cool demeanor. Instinctively she knew that he would die without weakening. He would not betray his fellow raiders nor would he ask mercy for himself. A wave of sickness swept the girl. He might be a bold and hardy miscreant, but deep in him somewhere was a self-respect that held him to his code, that burned like a white light and would not be put out as long as they let him live.

Cross turned to the two on the porch, his steel-trap lips so tight that the man's mouth looked like a slit in his face. His close-lidded eyes took in first Janet and then the K-B Ranch-owner.

'I'm not satisfied,' he told them harshly. 'Yore story is that Miller wasn't with Dagwell when he came here. Sounds fishy to me. They wanted fresh horses—had to rustle them somewhere. This was the nearest place to get them. We weren't far back of them. Why would they separate?'

Neal said, a touch of frosty insolence in his quiet voice: 'I couldn't tell you anything you don't know, Mr. Cross, since you're always right. I could guess that they talked their plight over and decided that there was a better chance for one of them to escape if they split up. Then if you followed one the other would make a getaway. How could they tell they weren't riding into a trap in coming here?'

'I'll talk to the girl,' Cross told him angrily. 'How did Dagwell come, Miss Lane—afoot or on horseback?'

Fear and excitement choked the throat of Janet. She must not make a mistake. The life of the wounded boy might depend on what she told this man.

'Afoot,' she answered.

'Did he mention his pal?'

'No.'

'Just covered MacGowan with a gun, took his horse, and rode away?'

'Yes.'

Hack pointed triumphantly to the lowest step. 'Look!' he cried.

There were three drops of blood on it.

'By cripes, we wounded one of the thieves,' Hack went on, his voice lifted with excitement. 'I thought I did. And it wasn't Dagwell. They're lying. Miller was here.'

'I had the nosebleed this morning,' Janet explained. Her own words came back to her with a strange quaver in them. She wondered if she was going to faint.

Cross paid no attention. He pushed past her into the house, looked the two rooms over, and came out again a few seconds later.

'Search the stable and the root house,' he ordered.

Mary's pup was at the haystack again, barking furiously.

'I reckon that dog has holed another rabbit,' Smith said.

Jack Cross stopped in his stride and looked toward the stack.

CHAPTER XVII

Neal makes an arrest

Janet thought her heart would stop beating during the long moment while Cross was looking silently at the haystack.

A hard bitter smile creased his thin lips. 'Maybe it's a skunk he has jumped up,' the man said, and walked into the field with rifle ready.

'Look out,' Brock warned. 'If he's there he may pump lead into you.'

Cross neither stopped nor hurried. 'If he's there we'll collect him. Come on, boys.'

The sheriff lost for once his deliberation. He moved fast, to stop the shooting if possible. 'Throw down yore pistol, Russ,' he ordered. 'The boys have got you. We're eight to one.'

His opinion was that Miller was not on the haystack, but it was better to be on the safe side.

No answer came from above.

'Drag up that wagon, boys, and one of you skin up there,' Cross snapped sharply.

Neal moved to the front. 'Don't push on the reins,' he drawled. 'Miller is up there all right, Cross, but he is my prisoner.'

Cross glared at him, anger in his cold eyes. 'So that's it. I get the idea now. You worked it to be made a marshal to protect yore friends, the thieves and criminals.' His big body swung round to the other men. 'By heaven, he won't get away with it. Pull up the wagon boys. We'll hang Miller with his partner Dagwell.'

'No.' Neal did not raise his voice nor make any motion toward the forty-five at his hip. His manner was as quiet and as sure as if he had been discussing a cattle cut. 'Just now I'm the United States Government, boys. I've arrested Miller for helping to hold up the Sheridan stage. No mob can take him from me without a fight.'

A moment of blank silence followed this challenge. Two of the sheriff's posse were ranch foremen, Brock was a gunman who had been employed by the Association as a cattle detective, and Smith was a drifter at present living at Sundog. Undecided, they waited for a lead.

Cullen said, his voice smooth and hearty: 'Of course if the government wants Miller that's different. I reckon Uncle Sam comes first.'

Derisively Brock's jeering laugh rang out. 'A slick trick, MacGowan, if it works.'

'It won't work.' The face of Cross was flushed to an angry purple. 'I'm damned if I let him double-cross me. Even a fool could see he's playing with the Rustlers' Gap crowd. If he wants a showdown right now he'll get it.'

The Scotchman Muir had said nothing as yet. Trained to law-abiding habits, he disliked very

157

much the business upon which he was today engaged. He had ridden with Cross because he thought it his duty, but he did not intend to see a wounded boy hanged if there was any reasonable excuse to prevent it.

'Not so fast, Mr. Cross,' he interposed. 'If this Miller is MacGowan's prisoner we can't interfere. He took him first, and we must recognize the government claim.'

Tug Hack had brought the prisoner into the field. The heavyset Circle Double T rider wanted to be in on any excitement that might arise.

He flung a jeer at Muir. 'Trouble with you is that you're soft. You'd like to back outa this whole thing. It's too thorough for you.'

Muir flushed. 'If I'm soft because I don't like to see a man hanged without having a chance to fight for his life, you're right,' he retorted hotly.

'You don't have to see it,' Brock said. 'You can ride hell-for-leather back to the Blue Bell right damn now. We're going to rub Dagwell out. That's sure. Miller too, if I have my way.'

Dagwell spoke up. 'You've got me. Isn't that enough for one day? Russ is only a kid. He's had his lesson. You can afford to let him go.'

'We're not going to let him go,' one of the ranch foremen differed. 'We're here to clean up this business. There's only one way to do that.'

'I'm standing with you, MacGowan,' Muir announced quietly.

'Me too.' Smith grinned apologetically at Cross. 'I don't aim to have the U.S. Government ridin' my neck.'

'Now, boys, we don't want any trouble,' the sheriff began, and was cut off by Brock.

'Trouble is one thing you sure duck, Cullen,' he agreed. 'What if Miller is a kid? Nits grow up to be lice. He knew what he was headin' for when he started brandin' other men's stock.'

'And when he helped shoot down Sol Bassett,' Hack added.

Again Dagwell said a word for his companion. 'He had nothing to do with that, boys. Another man did that.'

'What man?'

'No information on that point,' the blue-shirted rustler countered.

'Well, where do we go from here?' Brock wanted to know. 'Do we bump them both off or only one?'

The desertion of Muir had shaken Cross. He knew he could not get young Miller without a fight. That meant men would be killed and others wounded. In the ranks of the cattlemen there would be division. It would be better to let the marshal have his way with the wounded man.

'Have it like you want it.' Cross threw up a hand angrily. 'Call yoreself a cattleman and throw yore neighbors down at every chance.' He swore bitterly.

'Get yore friend down from that stack,' Hack growled at Neal. 'I'm gonna ask him some questions or know why.'

The wounded young man was brought down, the eyes in his colorless face filled with fear. Manifestly he was fighting to control his terror. As Neal took the gun from the youngster's belt, the rustler's hands shook.

'Who killed Bassett?' was the first question flung at him.

'He doesn't know,' Dagwell interrupted. 'Russ was bringing up the drag and Sol was at the point when he was shot.'

'Let him do his own talkin',' Hack warned. 'He's got a tongue, ain't he?'

Miller moistened his dry lips. 'It was like Dave says. I couldn't see from where I was at.'

'Don't try to run a sandy on us!' Brock cried, and caught him by the coat collar, dragging his face close.

'Hands off my prisoner,' Neal ordered, bringing his fist down hard on the wrist of the cattle detective. 'Ask whatever questions you like but don't touch him.'

Brock fell back, nursing his wrist. He cursed angrily.

For an instant he crouched, hand hovering toward the weapon on his hip, but the steady eyes of Neal covered him so relentlessly that the fingers fell away from the butt of the forty-five.

Perhaps he thought of Jess Blackburn, who had let a similar idea attract him and had been snuffed out.

Cross flung questions at Miller harshly, but with Dagwell present to stiffen his will the wounded man refused to tell who had been his companions on the raid.

'Who was yore leader—Dunn, or that fellow Purdy?'

'I ran the gather,' Dagwell said evenly. It was plain that he already counted himself a dead man and was trying to protect his associates.

'Under orders from Cad Clemson,' Hack chipped in acidly.

'Clemson never saw the day he could give me orders.'

'If you arrested Miller, Neal, how come it you didn't take his gun from him?' the foreman of the Circle Double T asked sharply.

'Miss Lane and I were busy patching him up,' MacGowan explained. 'Since I knew he wouldn't use it, I didn't bother taking the gun.'

'But you bothered putting him up on this stack where you figured we wouldn't find him,' Cross charged.

The marshal's smile was blandly insulting. 'I thought I would take away the temptation for you to start something you couldn't finish, Cross.'

The owner of the Bar A B ripped out a furious oath. 'For a plugged nickel I would carry through!' he cried. 'I think you're up to yore neck in this, MacGowan. You and the girl have lied ever since we came here. If I had my choice I'd rather hang you than Dagwell.'

'I'm with you there,' Brock agreed. 'But what's the use of talking? Let's cut the cackle. We've got a job to do.'

'Right,' said Hack.

The men trooped back to the house in two groups. Those in the rear were MacGowan, Muir, the sheriff, and the wounded man. They moved slowly on account of Miller. When they reached the house Dagwell had been hoisted to the back of a horse and the others also were mounted.

The doomed rustler looked across at those not going on this last ride with him. His leathery face was completely without expression.

'So long, Russ—Neal,' he said quietly.

Janet had come out and was standing in the doorway. Her lips were colorless. A man was being taken to his death. From her throat a strangled sob broke. She turned and ran into the house, her face covered by her hands.

Neal left his prisoner in charge of the sheriff and followed Janet. He found her lying face down on her bed crying into the pillow.

His fingers rested gently on her shoulder. Presently the sobs died down. A stifled voice came out of the pillow.

'It's so . . . horrible, Neal. Can't you save him?'

'No. I saved Miller. They let me get away with it because he is a kid and wounded, and because Muir backed my play. But Dagwell is a confirmed thief. If they let him go, he would be at it again in a week. Before he went on this raid he knew the stakes if he lost. He made his choice. It has to be this way.'

'Isn't there ever going to be peace in this country? Must men keep on killing one another and claiming it is necessary?'

'We'll have peace, sooner than you think, perhaps, and this will seem to you just a bad dream you have had.'

Her fingers groped back, to find the comfort of his strong warm hand.

CHAPTER XVIII

Two discuss matrimony

Ostensibly Robert Muir had driven over to the Triangle R to get Austin Reynolds's opinion of a bunch of whiteface yearlings the Lazy D were offering for sale. A more important reason was that he wanted to see Eleanor. This was a desire that grew increasingly urgent.

Eleanor was writing a letter, but she put down the pen at sight of him. 'Hello, Bob,' she sang out. 'I hear you were out after the raiders.'

'Yes,' he told her, and hoped she would drop the subject.

The girl had no intention of doing that. She had just heard from the cook, who had caught only a rumor of the facts, that two of the rustlers had been captured.

'Get any of them?' she asked.

'Two were taken prisoner.'

'Are they in jail at Sundog?'

'No.'

'Where are they?' At Muir's hesitation she flung at him a swift demand. 'What's this mystery you are trying to keep from me?'

Muir looked to Reynolds for help. 'You ask too many questions, Eleanor,' her brother said.

'I'm going to keep asking till I find out.'

Reynolds gave a lift to his shoulders. 'Might as well tell her, Bob. She'll pester you till you do.'

'MacGowan took one of the rustlers to Sheridan for safe keeping,' the Scot explained.

'Was it Neal MacGowan caught him?'

'Yes.'

'You're not a communicative witness, Bob,' Eleanor told him dryly. 'What did he do with the other prisoner?'

Austin carried on. 'The less said about this the better, Eleanor, but I suppose you have to know. The man was hanged.'

His sister stared at him. 'Not by Neal!' she cried.

'No, by the men who captured him. I'll not tell you their names.'

She rose from the desk where she had been writing and came across the room to Muir. 'All right. You needn't tell me names. But I want the whole story—all of it.'

Muir told her how he and the men with him had cut off two of the raiders from the rest and driven them down to the Lane place, of the capture of Dagwell and of what had occurred at the homestead.

'So your friends think Neal must be a rustler himself because he wouldn't let them kill a wounded boy,' she cried resentfully.

Muir flushed, but it was Reynolds who answered.

'Why not try to be fair?' he reproved his sister. 'None of these men are Bob's friends. If he had not supported MacGowan, young Miller would probably have been hanged too.'

Eleanor offered Muir her hand and a warm apologetic smile. 'Sorry. You didn't tell me you stood with Neal, but of course you wouldn't. I should have known it, as I ought to know you wouldn't let them kill a wounded boy. You come as near being right as anybody on either side. If everybody was like you there wouldn't be all this hatred on the Flood.'

The young man was embarrassed but pleased. 'I didn't do anything but say what I thought.'

As Eleanor looked at this good-looking young Scot, friendly, wholesome, and strong, a man to be entirely trusted, she knew that some day he would ask her to be his wife. It would be foolish not to accept him, she thought. There were few as fine as he in this raw frontier land. It was fun to be with him. He liked the things she did, and he was a man of honor whose integrity she would never have to doubt. Was it important that she did not find him very exciting? She felt a touch of scornful impatience at her own temperament. No friend had ever been dearer to her. If she took the plunge, she would very likely fall head over heels in love with him. He would make a wife happy.

The thought of him remained with her after he had left. Her mind shuttled back and forth between him and another man, one wild and reckless and audacious, by the judgment of her associates half scamp, half fool. Neal MacGowan was an intruder in the picture she had drawn for her own future. He had pushed into it against her sense of fitness and perhaps against his own. She was not going to marry him, of course. Probably he did not want that any more than she did.

None the less when she caught sight of him later in the day at Sundog, he set a pulse beating in her throat.

She was in a store buying groceries for the ranch. Three men stopped to talk on the sidewalk and their voices drifted to her. She glanced out, to see Cross of the Bar A B and Manson of the Circle Double T. The other man she did not know.

'I've heard he took Miller to Sheridan and put him in the jail there,' Cross was saying sourly. 'That's only a stall. Next we'll hear will be that the fellow has escaped.'

'If you ask me, he's hand in glove with Cad Clemson,' Manson replied bitterly. He was a small man, wrinkled as a dried apple, with black beady eyes that did not miss much.

'He's got the nerve of a rhino,' the third member of the group said. 'Met him a half hour ago, and he asked me whether I had any stuff stolen in the big raid. He looked as sober as a judge, but I knew he was laughing at me. I told him where he could go.'

'You can tell him again,' Manson piped in his squeaky voice. 'Here he comes now.'

Eleanor moved toward the front of the store. 'I'll take ten pounds of Arbuckle's coffee and a barrel of flour. I think that will be all.' Her mind was no longer on her purchases but on the eavesdropping she meant to do.

Neal came forward, with the rippling motion that was light as a cat's tread.

'What for did you take Miller to Sheridan?' snapped Manson.

Mirth twinkled in MacGowan's brown eyes. 'Nice of you, Mr. Manson, to take me back into fellowship,' he said. 'Last time we met you were breaking my heart by not speaking to me. I took him to Sheridan because our jail here is so ramshackle. He might push a hole through a wall and walk out. You wouldn't want that.'

'Or we might push a hole through it and walk in,' Cross corrected, a snarl in his manner. 'You know what I think?'

'I can guess. We agreed you were to think it and not say it, Mr. Cross, at least where I can hear it.'

'I'll say it if I please,' the Bar A B man retorted angrily.

Neal lifted a deprecatory hand. 'Don't stomp on my corns, please,' he drawled. 'I'm peaceful as Parson Wadley, and I don't want to get mad and lose my religion.' His grin was gay and guileless.

'You're the durndest idjit I ever did see,'

Manson told him acidly. 'Don't fool yourself, MacGowan. You're playin' with fire. If you weren't plumb addled you would know you can't run with the hares and hunt with the hounds.'

'He's not runnin' with the hounds,' the third man pointed out. 'He's with the thieves lock, stock, and barrel.'

'Meaning exactly what, Jackman?' Neal inquired very gently and clearly. 'In sentiment— or in action?'

'If you let Miller bust out of the jail at Sheridan we won't need any more evidence,' Cross cried, and hammered a fist into the palm of the other hand. 'We'll know for sure.' He added, bristling, 'Far as I'm concerned, I know already.'

Eleanor thought this had gone far enough. From further talk an explosion might develop. She sauntered out of the store, nodded a greeting to Cross and Manson, and showed surprise at the presence of MacGowan.

'Why, Neal!' she cried. 'Aren't you in the penitentiary yet?'

His eyes brightened. 'Not yet. When I go, will you visit me there?'

'Let's talk that over.' She tucked an arm under his and walked him out of the danger zone.

Neal laughed. 'Thanks awfully for saving me from these desperate characters,' he said, loud enough for the words to drift back to the group they were leaving.

Her long slender legs moved in step with his. 'I see you work hard at making yourself popular,' she said. 'I have to admit you are impartial. First it is one side and then the other that you annoy.'

'It's a gift,' he mentioned airily. To be walking down the street beside her, the girl's hand resting against his beating heart, filled him with exhilaration.

A good many eyes watched them, wondering what this meant. To the plain people of Sundog and vicinity she was an unpredictable girl. They were not sure about her morals, and they knew nothing as to her mental reactions. She did as she pleased. But she belonged with the Cattlemen's Association crowd, with the big outfits, and it was surprising to see her arm in arm with MacGowan in broad daylight. Modest girls of the Flood Valley did not do that sort of thing, anyhow. If they liked a man they took care to show indifference to him in public. This young woman was an outsider, one they did not understand, and therefore subject to criticism more than their own.

She tilted her chin sideways at him, mocking lights in her eyes. 'You're going to lose your reputation—or I am—or both of us,' she prophesied.

'Mine has already gone. The Sundog Madam Grundy has thumbed down on me.'

'Why?'

'I'm considered a little wild by careful mothers.'

The girl considered him thoughtfully. 'And yet, if I were a mother, I think I would trust you with my daughter farther than most men.'

'I ought not to have let you kidnap me,' he told her, not very repentantly. 'It won't do you any good with the tabbies.'

'A lot I care about that.' Her mind was on something more important. She frowned at him with an elder sisterly look that made him chuckle. 'I thought you knew this country. It's as Mr. Manson told you. If you play with fire, as you are doing, you'll be destroyed. Men are violent here. Neal, it takes the pressure of just one finger to kill you. Do be careful.'

'What have I done that I could help doing?' he asked. 'Every step I have taken has been forced on me.'

'Were you forced to stand there deviling those men a few minutes ago?'

'If you are going to play yore own hand you have to do it boldly. If yore opponents think you are scared—'

'Do you have to play a lone hand? Maybe the cattlemen aren't angels, but Bob Muir and my brother Austin are good men. So are most of the others. Why can't you throw in with them?'

'That's water under the mill. I didn't see it as they did, and we came to a parting of the ways. Don't worry about me. I'm going to live a great many years.'

They had reached the river bridge. He gave her a hand down the slope to the bank of the stream below. They strolled along it to the bend which cut them off from the sight of the town.

They walked in silence for a little while. She broke it by telling him reluctantly what was in her mind. 'I think you and I had better say good-bye. You're not good for me. I find you too . . . exciting.'

'What do you want—slippers by the fire?'

'I want a lot of things you can't give me.'

'And some I can.'

'The fact is . . . I think I'm going to be asked to marry a man, and if he does I'll say yes.'

'Robert Muir?'

'A gentleman isn't supposed to put to a lady an intimate personal question like that,' she said with mock demureness. 'He waits until she wants to tell him.'

'But I'm no gentleman, just a man who wants to know.' His mind ranged over the field. 'You have had a lot of fine guests at the Triangle R. There have been several college friends of yore brother who come out to shoot and fish. It might be any one of them. If it's anybody local, it must be Muir. He'll do to ride the river with, even if he's the son of a lord. My guess is still Muir. Aren't you afraid he is too good for you?'

'Because he is the son of Lord Mauchline?'

'Good gracious, no! In spite of that. You're a

bit of a rip, and he's just a little on the formal side.'

'I need somebody like that.' Mirth bubbled in her face. 'But since he hasn't asked me yet we needn't go into details.'

'He will. I've seen it breaking out all over him—like the measles. Don't make a mistake.'

'That's why I'll accept him—if he gives me a chance. To keep from making a mistake.'

'He'll go home in a few years,' Neal mused aloud. 'They all do. Somebody will leave him a fortune, or his father will die and he will be Lord Mauchline. The wife of an Englishman of family has to toe the mark. You'll have to be a great lady, sedate and proper, till you want to shriek with boredom. No, you won't like it at all. I've decided against it.'

'How nice of you to take so much interest!'

'I have a kind heart.' He took her hands in his. 'You are entitled to a little play, since you are not wearing the yoke yet.'

As he drew her closer he saw golden flecks of excitement dancing in her eyes. For a moment she held back, lips parted, mobile face alight with the emotions warring in her. Then she gave herself to his kiss.

He said, when he found time for words, 'A nice cattleman's wife *you'll* make.'

'Fortunately it is Robert I have to please,' she retorted. 'He may have a different opinion. And, as you pointed out, he won't be a cattleman all his life.'

'I'm not talking about Muir. It won't do to have him waste his career on you. I'm going to marry you myself to save him.'

Eleanor drew back, surprised, her heart pounding. He sounded in earnest. 'So generous of you, if you mean it, which you don't,' she mocked.

'Never meant anything more in my life,' he insisted. 'I can see now that we were made for each other.'

She fought down the tide of joy that raced through her veins. It would not do to be let down later when she found he was larking.

'I could not accept so great a sacrifice,' she said, and tried to keep her tone light. 'You don't owe Robert Muir that much.'

'No, I owe it to myself,' he cried, and took her in his arms again.

'Not so fast, please,' she objected, with a husky little laugh. 'You must be crazy—if this isn't a part of the game. We don't think alike about things. My friends aren't your friends.'

'I'm asking if you love me. Your friends don't matter. I'm not talking about marrying them . . . or your opinions.'

With his kisses on her lips the objections faded away. She felt as though her essential spirit was melting into his. He was the man she loved, the one she wanted for time and eternity. Nothing else was of importance.

Minutes later she said, with smothered laughter, 'We'll probably fight half the time.'

'But the other half . . .' he reminded her gaily.

'Life would be much more peaceful with Robert Muir.'

'Who wants peace?' he asked happily. 'We'll have lots of that after we grow old.'

'Old!' she echoed with the superb scorn of youth. 'Not you and I, Neal. Not ever.'

He looked at the girl, her beauty tempered as finely as a Damascus blade, the warm blood glowing in her face. For a moment what she had said seemed to him truth, that they could make time stand still for them. Then it came to him with tragic poignancy that even her youth would not endure forever. Already she was dancing on the quicksands of the future. They could be sure of only now.

CHAPTER XIX

All chips in the game

Austin Reynolds did not take kindly to the idea of his sister's marrying Neal MacGowan. He opposed it vehemently and with acrimony, explaining to Eleanor that no matter how much opinions might differ concerning him, on one point they would agree, that he was no kind of material out of which to make a good steady husband.

'I don't think I want a good steady husband,' the girl replied. 'I have had a few chances to get one like that, and they made marriage seem like a dull business to me. If I take Neal I won't be bored. I know that, anyhow.'

'You talk as if marriage was like—like going on a picnic!' he exclaimed impatiently. 'It's a serious business, and of course it is often dull. What you must have above all is a man who is reliable and—'

'Stodgy,' she cut in. 'No, thank you. Life with Neal will be exciting, at least.'

'You don't know what you are letting yourself in for. He has you under a kind of enchantment.'

'I hope I stay under it.' She shook her lovely head. 'No use talking, Austin. My mind is made up. He's due here in five minutes. You had better be getting ready to tell him how pleased you are.'

Reynolds did not say that. He told MacGowan bluntly that he disapproved of the engagement. It was, he thought, unsuitable in every way. Eleanor was the victim of a delusion, and if he would give her time she would get over it.

'That's reasonable,' Neal agreed. 'She can have all the time she likes, and any day until we're married she can change her mind. That's only fair. I'm certainly a risk.' He looked at his girl and smiled. 'I don't reckon any responsible person would recommend me. My own opinion is that this would be either the worst marriage in the world for her—or the best. Eleanor and I are gambling all our chips that it will be the best.'

Austin explained patiently. 'Eleanor has been brought up differently from most girls here. I'm afraid you don't realize how expensive she is. Her traditions are those of the East. She has traveled—gone to college—had a great deal of money spent on her. Do you think she would be satisfied with what you could offer her on the K-B Ranch?'

'I don't know,' Neal answered frankly. 'That's a risk.'

'I'm willing to take it if Neal is,' Eleanor said.

'You think so now, but you will feel differently later,' her brother insisted.

Eleanor rose from the lounge. 'All marriage is a

risk, but not so great a one when those who go into it love each other. . . . If we're going to ride we'd better start, Neal.'

Reynolds shrugged his shoulders. 'I've said my say. I don't like this. There's nothing more I can do. Eleanor has to make her own choice.'

The girl walked across to Neal and slipped a hand into his. 'I know all your arguments, Austin, and agree with some of them,' she said, smiling at him. 'Neal is reckless, and he can be violent, I hear. His standards aren't yours—or mine. I don't think I'm going to approve of all he does. But that doesn't mean he will be wrong. He thinks freer than we do. His mind isn't so clamped and prejudiced. Anyhow, he is the man I want to marry. Maybe we won't always be happy. But I would rather be with him than anybody else even if I am unhappy sometimes.'

Looking at them, Reynolds thought he had never seen a finer-looking pair, the lean sun-tanned man with the sardonic devil-may-care gaiety, and the vivid girl, a gallant and defiant courage in the bright and sparkling face. He did not like MacGowan, nor did he trust him fully. But there was an *élan* about this pair of lovers that he envied, a vital glow he would never feel. Some poet had sung about the world well lost for love. There was no wisdom in it of course. A man should keep his balance. Love should fit into his life but not dominate it. Still—

As Neal and Eleanor rode along a hill shoulder, knee to knee, the warm sunshine painting the trail, an escaping tendril of the girl's hair flying in the wind, she pulled up from a canter to take up again the talk where it had been dropped.

'Austin thinks I'm crazy,' she laughed. 'Maybe I am. I didn't mean to fall in love with you. All I wanted was to flirt with you and get a thrill out of it. It was when I began not to feel so sure that I told you we had better not see each other any more. But when you told me you were going to marry me I knew I was lost.'

'Found, not lost,' he substituted.

She had brought luncheon in his saddlebags and they picnicked in a little park all golden with the autumn foliage. The memory of that lovely lazy day, a peaceful interlude between others filled with excitement and danger, remained for long with both of them.

After they had eaten he rolled a cigarette and gave it to her. Doubtfully she looked at it.

'Maybe I ought to give up smoking now I am engaged to you?' She lay on an elbow, her lissom outstretched body basking in the sun. 'I don't want people to think you are marrying a loose woman.'

He grinned at her. 'I don't see why. I'm not marrying you to reform you. We'll be ourselves. Some night I'll probably sit down in the Round Up and play poker 'round the clock.'

'I'd want you to,' she told him. 'But just the same I think I'll drop smoking, except maybe once in a great while when we are alone and you want me to keep your pipe company.'

That pleased Neal. He held the view, common for outdoor Westerners, that a good woman was something precious, to be treated with great respect, even to be reverenced a little if her character justified it. He thought Eleanor had the loveliest mouth under heaven, with even teeth that shone like pearls when she laughed, and he did not want it spoiled by a cigarette dragging from it.

'All right,' he agreed. 'I'll do the smoking for the family.'

'Just the same,' she predicted, 'it won't be very long till half the nice women we know will be smoking cigarettes.'

At Sundog, later in the day, Brick Carson met Neal on the street. Brick made talk for a minute, in the way one does when debating in his mind whether to broach a doubtful topic.

'Pretty busy these days, Mr. Marshal?' he presently asked guardedly.

'I can answer that better if you'll be a little clearer, Brick,' Neal replied. 'Are you inquiring whether the marshal is busy—or the boss of the K-B—or just Neal MacGowan?'

Brick rubbed the palm of a hand across a bristling chin and amended the question, watching to see how the other would take it. 'I was thinking of the marshal,' he admitted.

'Not since I took young Miller to jail. I hope I'm through.'

'I hope so.'

Neal stared at him a moment. 'What's on yore mind, Brick? Let's have it.'

'Word just got here that the kid broke jail. They claim he was helped from outside.'

'Who helped him?' Neal demanded sharply.

'I wouldn't know that.' Carson's voice was dry and noncommital.

'Details?'

'The story is that when the jailer went to feed him he shoved a pistol under his nose. A horse was waiting tied outside for Miller. He jumped it and went outa town like the heel flies were after him.'

'Where was he headin' for?'

'He didn't send me word.'

MacGowan laughed, without mirth. 'I'm certainly left holding the sack.'

'You're not to blame,' Carson said.

'Tell that to Cross and Manson and Jackman and the other members of the Association. See how far you'll get.'

Neal remembered the bitter warning of Cross, that if he let Miller escape from jail they would know he was in with the rustlers all the way. It would be of no use for him to protest that he had not contrived or at least been cognizant to the jail break. The cattlemen would not believe him. Already most of them completely distrusted him and believed he had established some sort of relation with the gang in Rustlers' Gap. He could hear in imagination the harsh strident voice of Cross demanding why he had taken the rustler to the Sheridan prison except to arrange a getaway for him.

CHAPTER XX

Questions asked and answered

Allan Dunn came out of the store in front of which Carson and MacGowan were standing. At sight of the marshal his sardonic eye lit.

'I hear one of yore prisoners has done escaped,' he said.

'Not one of mine,' Neal corrected. 'He quit being mine when the sheriff of Sheridan County signed for him.'

'Not anybody's now.' There was a jubilant note in Dunn's voice. 'I reckon Cross and some of his friends will froth at the mouth.'

'Know any particulars of the jail break, Allan?' asked Neal.

'Seems he stuck up the jailer with a gun somebody slipped him from the outside, and there just happened to be a saddled horse waiting in the cottonwoods fifty yards away. Now, I wonder who could have given him that pistol.'

There was such a smooth triumphant purr to Dunn's wonder that MacGowan's gaze held fast to the lank puncher's brown face. He would have liked to know whether Dunn was in Sheridan at the time of the escape, but that was not a question he could ask here.

'Miller's friend went quite a way to help him,' Neal said evenly.

'How do you know the fellow doesn't live right there in Sheridan?' Dunn demanded.

'I wasn't talking about how many miles he went. What I meant was that he must have been a good friend.'

'You're right he was.' The rustler corrected that. 'At least he sure acted like one.'

Brick Carson looked up the street. 'Be seeing you again, boys. I got to get back to business.' He turned and walked rapidly away.

Four men were coming down the sidewalk, all abreast. Cross and Manson were two of them. Nearest the wall was Brock, and on the outside a fattish man in blue Levis with curly hair and a rolling gait. This was Christy, manager of the Blue Bell.

'Brick ran out on us,' the mordant puncher commented. 'Well, I don't blame him. When you are in business a fellow like I am is kinda poison to trade. It will be all right with me if you beat it too, MacGowan. They won't like the company you keep, not right after the Sheridan episode.'

Neal said quietly: 'I'm not keeping company with you, Dunn, but it is all the same to me what they think. I'm not making apologies or explanations.'

Without any preliminaries Cross flung a question at the man from Rustlers' Gap. 'Where were you this morning at eight o'clock, Dunn?'

'At eight o'clock? Why, I was eating breakfast at a camp on Skunk Creek. Where were you?'

'Never mind where I was,' Cross retorted arrogantly. 'I'm asking the questions. But I can give answers too. You were seen at Sheridan half an hour before that time.'

'Not unless I can be in two places at once,' Dunn jeered. 'Were you at Sheridan too? If not, how come you to know so much about where I was?'

'We've just been talking to Sheriff Alcott over long distance. He tells me you were recognized by a man who knows you when you were eating breakfast at the Bon Ton Restaurant.'

'Some other man or some other day,' Dunn drawled.

'Where were you at that time, MacGowan?' asked Manson.

'I'll not answer that, Manson, until you have shown a right to ask it,' Neal replied.

'I expect Dunn has been reporting to you how he fixed it up for yore friend Miller to escape,' Cross fleered at him.

'You're giving me too much credit, Mr. Cross.' Dunn showed his teeth in a defiant grin. 'I'd sure like to say I'd pulled off that getaway, but I can't honestly do it. It was certainly a nice slick job.'

Austin Reynolds walked out of Gibson's New York Emporium and turned down the street toward the Journey's End Corral. Cross called to him. Without answering in words the Triangle R man crossed the dusty street. That trouble was in the air he could guess.

'Mebbe you haven't heard the news, Reynolds,' Cross said, a strident anger riding in the words. 'That thief Miller has escaped from jail. Dunn here just happened to be in Sheridan at the time. Somebody gave Miller a pistol for to hold up the jailer. Somebody had a horse waiting for him outside. Miller lit out. So did Dunn. He must of done some traveling, since he was in Sheridan at eight this morning and now he's here having a nice cheery talk with friend Marshal MacGowan. Don't ask me what they're saying. Like enough Dunn didn't have to tell his friend the news. He may have been right with him all the time.'

'Not possible,' Reynolds demurred. 'MacGowan was at my ranch at eleven o'clock this morning.'

Christy laughed ironically. 'Mr. MacGowan isn't such a jug-headed chump as that. He wouldn't pull his own chestnuts outa the fire while he has a handy man like Dunn to do it.'

'Why would I care whether Miller got out of the jail or not?' Neal asked. He spoke quietly, but his eyes were as dangerous as half-scabbarded steel.

The curly-headed man in the Levis did not lift his eyes of gunmetal blue from the owner of the K-B outfit. Reynolds noticed that the men with

Cross had fanned out to a half-circle. Neal did not move, but a tense wariness advertised that he was ready.

'Maybe you didn't want Miller to talk. Maybe he could tell too much.'

'Tell what?' MacGowan's voice was as cold as wind blowing over a glacier.

'How would I know?' Christy jeered. 'He might tell who robbed the Sheridan stage and killed Cole Tracy.'

'Or the inside story of how come you to rub out Blackburn,' snapped Manson, the black beady eyes in his tanned wrinkled face fixed on MacGowan.

Brock made a contribution. 'Or spill the beans on who was back of the big raid.'

'Wait a minute.' The strong figure of Reynolds moved forward. 'Don't get on the prod too fast. MacGowan had nothing to do with the stage holdup. He killed one of the men in it.'

'I wonder why,' Brock murmured, just loud enough to be heard.

The lanky rustler had something to say about that. 'I can tell you why. Lane was his friend. He had reason to think Blackburn killed him. So he came up into the Gap to arrest Jess, who resisted and was killed. I was there and saw it.'

'That's right, Mr. Dunn.' Derision rode in Christy's voice. 'So you were. And now you are with him again.'

'Tim Owen was also present,' Reynolds reminded the Blue Bell manager.

'One of MacGowan's hired hands,' Brock suggested.

'Whose hired hand are you?' Dunn demanded, turning on Brock. 'Before you do any talking tell us how much the Association paid you for murdering Thorne and Norwood from the brush.'

Reynolds caught Brock's wrist as the man's revolver flashed out and pushed his arm down. A bullet plowed into the road and flung up a spurt of dust. Dunn crouched, snarling, gun out and close to his hip.

'Don't shoot, Allan!' MacGowan cried.

Dunn backed away, slowly, stiff-legged, his feet wide apart. He moved across the sidewalk and passed into the store.

'Why did you do that?' Brock demanded of Reynolds. 'He might of killed me while you were holding my hand.'

'Fork yore saddle and get outa town, Brock,' ordered Reynolds.

The stock detective glared at him. 'You heard what that damned thief called me. Why should I get outa town?'

'Because I say so.' The stony eyes of Reynolds drilled into the man stormily. 'You take orders. I give them. If and when we want trouble started, we'll give the word. Get going.'

Brock hung in the wind a moment, his face dark

with anger, the sense of outraged pride strong in him. He wanted to tell the owner of the Triangle R that he would go or stay as he pleased. But in the looks of these men who employed him to do their dirty work he found no encouragement. They paid him and despised him. He thrust the revolver back in its scabbard, turned on his heel, and clumped back in the direction from which he and his companions had come.

'Exit Mr. Brock,' drawled Neal, 'who objects to being reminded of Thorne and Norwood.' He added, in a murmur just audible, 'I wonder why.'

'They got what they asked for,' Cross retorted brutally. 'As Dagwell did. You'll live longer if you keep that fixed in yore mind, MacGowan.'

'Sounds a little like a threat,' Neal said.

'Call it a warning. The time has come when you can't any longer protect thieves from their deserts. It's a showdown.'

'With Mr. Cross being the lord of the high justice?' Neal's smile was a scornful challenge. 'I think not.'

He let his eyes drift coolly from one to another, brushed past Manson, and walked up the street without once looking back.

CHAPTER XXI

A 'difficulty' adjusted

Neal walked lightly along Trail's End Street, head up, the broad hat tilted jauntily, the you-be-damned expression still in his eyes. He dropped into Gunter's hardware store to buy a spade, and some cartridges for his shotgun. From there he gravitated to the postoffice to send off a money order. While he was writing the application a hand fell on his shoulder and a voice cried gaily, 'Run down at last, you old son-of-a-gun!'

The owner of the hand and voice was Pete Driskill, a cowboy he had not seen in five years. They had been sidekicks once, but Pete had the *Wanderlust*. His driftings had taken him into Arizona and Mexico, and later into the Oregon and Idaho cow countries. At last he was back again, pockets empty, jobless, but as carefree as ever.

'You've got a place waiting for you at the K-B right now,' Neal told him.

To which offer Pete replied promptly. 'You've hired a hand.'

Neal looked at his watch. 'We'd better be hitting the trail if we expect to get to the ranch for supper,' he suggested.

Outside the store they met Doctor Seneca. He glanced at Driskill and made a motion of his head to draw MacGowan away.

'Say anything you like before Pete. You know Driskill, don't you, doctor?'

'I mended a busted leg for him once, but I didn't recognize him at first.' The two men shook hands. Seneca went back at once to the subject on his mind. 'Heard about the trouble between Allan Dunn and that fellow Brock?' he asked.

'Yes. I was present. Brock has left town, hasn't he?'

'No. He's here drinking. He sent word to Dunn that he would shoot on sight unless he took back what he said.'

'Where is he?'

'In the Yellowstone. Dunn was down at the Babcock Corral a little while ago.'

'I've got to stop this if I can.' Neal thought fast. Cross probably would not lift a finger. Reynolds was the best man to handle Brock. He could put the pressure on and force him to give up his intention, since the fellow was an employee of the Association.

Seneca offered to carry a message to Reynolds.

'Tell him I'll try to call off Dunn if he will work on Brock,' Neal said. 'We haven't much time left. They will both be on the street before dark.'

Driskill walked down toward the corral with MacGowan. They met Dunn coming up town. He

191

and Driskill shook hands with cheerful friendly profanity. They had worked for the same spread once. But Neal noticed that his eyes strayed past Pete and searched the street warily.

'Meet you at the Round Up for a drink in half an hour or so,' Dunn promised. 'I've got to see a man first.'

'We know who that man is, Allan,' Neal said. 'Do you have to see him? Can't this be arranged? I'll be glad to try to fix it up.'

Dunn shook his head. 'Nothing I can do about it. It's his choice, not mine. He sent word for me to be ready.'

'Will you wait in the Round Up a few minutes while I talk with him? Maybe he'll take back his message.'

The rustler considered. 'Yeah, I'll wait. But understand, you're not seeing him for me. Half the folks in town know he's served notice. I've got to go through.'

Neal left the two men in the Round Up and hurried to the Yellowstone. On the way he met Seneca with the news that Reynolds had departed for the ranch.

'That's bad,' Neal said. 'I don't believe I can do much with Brock. He never liked me.'

He found Brock at the bar with two or three cronies.

'May I have a word with you?' MacGowan asked.

'Sure. Right here. Spit it out.'

'I mean alone.'

Brock's face was flushed with drink but he was not intoxicated. 'No. I don't want to have a thing to do with you. If you've got anything to say, unbutton yore lip right where you're at. Or get the hell out of here if you'd rather.'

Neal knew he had to speak here or not at all. It was already plain to him that what he was going to say would do no good. But he had to try.

'About you and Dunn. I've just been with him. I think he would call this quits if you'd meet him halfway.'

'He sent you here to crawl for him, did he?'

The mouth of the man was a thin close slit. A red-hot devil of rage looked out of his eyes.

'No, Brock. I'm on my own. If you and he meet on the street tonight one or both of you will be buried tomorrow. Why? Because he used a few blunt hard words when he was being hounded. It doesn't make sense, man. Let me tell him that you'll withdraw what you have said if he will do the same.'

In moments of decisions when passions are involved there is sometimes present a fool who can with a word undo the influence of the wise. There was one in the room now.

He said: 'Better take back what you said, Brock. Dunn is a tough customer. He might get you.'

Neal saw instantly that whatever chance he

193

might have had of moving Brock was gone. The cattle detective ripped out an oath. 'He never saw the hour he could get me. Tell him, MacGowan, that at six o'clock I'll walk down Trail's End to meet him.'

'I'll not carry that message, Brock. Do you want a killing? You're forcing this fight.'

'You bet I am. If he's scared he'd better fork a bronc and ride outa town hell-for-leather. He's got just fifteen minutes.'

Neal walked back to the Round Up. Dunn and Driskill were sitting at a small table. The rustler was not drinking. Time enough for that if he came through all right. He looked up at Neal, a grim sardonic smile on his face.

'You didn't get anywhere,' he said.

MacGowan shook his head. 'No. He told me he would be coming down the street looking for you inside of fifteen minutes. There is still time to leave town, Allan.'

'Tell *him* that.' The eyes of the man from the Gap were bleak. Out of them the life seemed to drain, leaving them opaque and stony.

'We'll see fair play,' Driskill promised.

'All I ask.' Dunn rose and tested his revolver. He made sure the draw was easy.

Neal spoke to all in the room. 'I tried to talk Brock out of this, boys. Allan offered to meet him halfway, but he wouldn't have it. Remember that, whatever happens.'

They walked out of the place to the sidewalk. Dunn crossed the street to the doorway of a vacant store. 'I'll wait for him here,' he said.

'Luck,' Driskill wished him, and took a position beside a hitching-block forty yards farther down the street.

Neal moved up to the postoffice entrance. One or two men passed along the walk on their way home to supper. A horseman cantered down the road. After that traffic died away. Already the rumor that there would be shooting had swept the street.

The clump of boots sounded on the sidewalk. A man came out of the growing dusk, two others trailing him fifteen yards in the rear.

Brock was the man in the lead. 'Where is he at?' the cattle detective demanded hoarsely.

'He's down the street,' Neal answered quietly. 'Still time to turn back, Brock.'

'Quit skulking and show yoreself!' Brock cried, and jerked out his gun.

Neal stopped the men in the rear supporting Brock. 'Far enough, gentlemen. We're seeing fair play. You're not in this.'

'That's all right.' They crowded into the entry beside MacGowan, to be out of the way of bullets.

The sound of a forty-five went crashing up the street. A second and a third shot picked up the echo of it. Neal saw Brock's body plunge into the dust, the weapon still in his hand, a trickle of smoke rising from the barrel.

Dunn moved forward, very slowly, his gaze clamped to the huddled figure on the ground. Already men were coming out of stores and saloons.

'He asked for this,' the rustler said. 'I couldn't help it. But he had it coming. Brock sold his saddle[1] when he killed Norwood and Thorne for pay.'

'That's right!' a voice shouted.

Finn Wood was one of those present. He was a heavyset graybearded old-timer who held the respect of all.

'Did you see this killing?' Neal asked him.

'Yes. Brock passed me farther up the street. I didn't know what was up, but I heard one of the men with him say, "You'll get him sure." His gun was out before the first shot sounded, but I don't know which of them started the shooting.'

'He did, as it happened,' Dunn said. 'But that doesn't matter. He was out to get me—had sent word for me to be ready.'

Neal corroborated that. 'You had better give yourself up to the sheriff,' he advised. 'Plenty of witnesses will prove you couldn't avoid this.'

A minute later Sheriff Cullen arrived on the scene. He listened to the evidence and took Dunn to the prosecuting attorney, who released the rustler on bail offered by Neal and the owner of the Round Up.

[1]In cowboy parlance a man who 'sold his saddle' had lost all self-respect.

CHAPTER XXII

Trouble ahead

Neal had ridden into Sundog in a gay and happy mood, an accepted lover returning from a meeting with his sweetheart. He left it feeling depressed and unhappy. For he knew that the breach between him and his fellow cattlemen was wider than ever. On the courthouse steps he had met Cross, who had charged him bluntly with trapping Brock to his death.

That his enemies would not listen to reason Neal knew. A perverse fatality was dogging his steps. Whatever he did turned out wrong and could be twisted to support the prejudices of those who despised and hated him. Within the hour he had added another black mark to the score against him. He had no obligation to go bond for Dunn. But the man had been forced to kill in self-defense. Somebody had to stand by him. If he had not tried to prevent the shooting he would not be involved in the blame for it. As usual, he had ram-stammed into other men's troubles.

As he took the short-cut hill trail for the ranch he smiled sardonically. He was thinking how every move he made mired him more. Even the trip taken to the scene of the stage holdup had been given a false construction. It was claimed that he had gone there to blot out any sign he might have left at the time of the robbery. He had killed Blackburn on account of a row about the division of the spoils. He had obtained an appointment as deputy United States marshal to protect his rustler friends. To keep Russ Miller from betraying him he had saved the boy's life and later arranged a jail break for him.

From the ridge above he looked down into the valley and saw the windmills of the Bar A B flashing the rays of the sun as the blades whirled. The wry grin came to his lips again. Jack Cross considered him a scoundrel and a renegade. In earlier days Cross had mavericked so freely that he had narrowly escaped punishment as a thief. Of late years he had fenced government land arrogantly, had burned out and driven away homesteaders. Now he sat in the seat of the righteous and judged offenders who were far less guilty than he had been.

Neal could not feel that he had been wrong-headed and obstinate because he had stood up for the rights of the little fellows. A man had to do right as he saw it. He had to walk his own way of life. It was true that his manner offended others. He had met harsh words and threats with a cool scornful insolence. Well, what did they expect of him—that he would turn the other cheek meekly?

His relation with Eleanor complicated the difficulty. Some of these men's wives were her friends. They visited back and forth. The managers and owners of the big outfits were in constant association with her brother. If she married Neal she would be cut off from any social outlet—and she was a girl who loved the pleasant amenities of being hostess and guest. It was a lot to ask of her that she forego this easy give and take. Perhaps it was asking too much.

Pete Driskill left him alone with his thoughts while they were taking the steep hill trails. But as soon as they could ride two abreast he began to ask questions about the changes that had come to the Flood Valley since he had left. In those days the cattleman had been top dog with none to dispute his sway, rustling had been sporadic, and homesteaders had not yet begun to come into the district.

'Ten years from now there won't be any very big ranches left,' Neal explained to him. 'The large outfits depend on free grass, and that's going. The wise stockman now must breed up his cattle, buy and fence land, and raise hay. I think the smartest cowman I know is Austin Reynolds. Men like Cross can't see the handwriting on the wall. They will stick to the old way till they go broke.'

Next day Neal rode across to Squaw Creek to see Janet. Presently she sent the children out to dig some potatoes for dinner, and as soon as they had gone congratulated Neal on his engagement.

'Eleanor is the finest girl I know,' she said. 'If you are not happy it won't be her fault.'

'No, it will be mine,' he assented. 'I'm a little worried about it, Janet. If she marries me she'll have to give up so much.'

'Does that matter, since she loves you?'

'I don't know. I'm going to do well. That's not the trouble. It's my reputation and my standing. They get worse all the time.'

'I heard about yesterday. Some people blame you. Tell me about it.'

He related to her what had occurred at Sundog.

'I don't see how you could be blamed for that, except maybe for going on Allan Dunn's bond. He's one of the Gap gang. Did you have to do that?'

'I felt I must. If he stayed in jail there I think he might have been lynched, and he really wasn't to blame . . . How did you hear about it?'

'From Finn Wood. He thought you did right. And this morning Eleanor and Austin were here. He brought me my contract for the school. Austin did not give an opinion, but I don't think he agrees with Mr. Cross and some of the others about how guilty you are, though he doesn't at all approve of you.'

'I haven't seen Eleanor since. How does she feel?'

'I don't know. But I would see her soon if I were you, to tell her how it all happened.'

'She is going to have a tough time, with all her friends against me.'

'That won't bother her, if she is sure you are right.'

He gave her his gay friendly smile. 'But I'm probably not right a good deal of the time. In her place what would you think?'

A wave of warmer color beat into her cheeks. She hoped he did not know how wildly her heart was beating. 'But I'm not in her place. Why should I judge you?'

'Like Austin Reynolds you disapprove of me,' he told her, mischief sparkling in his eyes, 'but unlike him you find some good in me and pray that there may be more.'

She looked at him with startled eyes. 'How do you know I . . . pray for you?'

'Because I am yore brother, even though I am a sinner, and you would like to have me join the ninety and nine who are safely in the fold.'

'You laugh at me for that?' she asked, and there were tears in her eyes.

'No, by heaven.' He caught her small hands in his. 'I am very grateful that I have you for a friend.'

A wave of emotion crashed through her. She felt the strong beat of her heart, as one does that of a frightened bird imprisoned in the hand. Scornful of the desire in her to be near and close to him, she drew away stiffly. He was engaged to her friend, yet she was wildly longing that he would break through her defenses and take her in his arms. What kind of wanton was she?

Janet reverted to a subject less personal. 'This hasn't ended yet. Austin is afraid the trouble has just started. He didn't tell me so, but I think the cattlemen are drawing together to do something.'

'To do what?' Neal asked.

'I don't know. He was keeping something back, I felt.'

'Some sort of retaliation, maybe. I hope not. There is evidence to show that Brock was a paid killer, and anyhow he brought this on himself.'

But Neal knew the fight had gone too far for the merits of the trouble between Dunn and Brock to be weighed justly. Even though the cattlemen despised and disliked the stock detective, he was on their side in the struggle. That would be enough for them. He rode home disturbed in mind.

That night two haystacks in one of his fields were set on fire and destroyed. An anonymous letter received next day advised him to leave the country if he wanted to stay alive.

CHAPTER XXIII

Sincerely yours

Eleanor read over the letter she had just written to a school friend who lived at Cheyenne, the daughter of the cattleman governor of Wyoming. In it she had declined an invitation to spend a gala week with her former room-mate, during part of which time the President of the United States was to be a guest of her father.

The program you have outlined [so she had written] sounds thrilling. You know how I love dances and dinners and young officers in uniform. At least I did in the prehistoric period before I came to the ranch to live.

Couldn't you get the President to postpone his Western trip for a few days? Tell him that I am taming a Wild Man of the Desert and I can't possibly get away just now. I think I had better plump out my news to you at this point. I am engaged to him. (To the W. M. of the D., not to the President.) And it is the most exciting adventure of my life. He isn't very tame yet. A few days ago he killed a desperate outlaw, and only yesterday he acted as a kind of second for another outlaw who shot a man in a duel. Yes, I can hear you say I am crazy. Perhaps I am, my dear. At any rate I am very much in love with him.

I expect him here this afternoon to explain his outrageous conduct. Since I am greatly vexed at him, I intend to be quite severe. But he has the most charming smile, and when he turns it on I melt.

There was a good deal more of it, and Eleanor debated the question of deleting the whole of the part relating to the love affair but in the end decided to send it.

She sealed and stamped the letter, put on her hat, and started down the lane to leave the epistle in the mail box.

A man rode up to the porch, took off his hat, and handed her a letter. She tore open the envelope and read a paragraph.

'There may be an answer,' she told the messenger, and walked into the house.

The letter was from Neal. He wrote that he had expected to get over in person but he had an appointment to meet a man on a cattle deal. But he would be over without fail on Saturday. It would take too long to write her of the unfortunate events of yesterday, and he was not sure he could make things clear except by word of mouth. So he would save his story until he saw her. Meantime he was, he concluded, very much her lover. There was a postscript which added that he thought of her a hundred times a day.

Eleanor was quite annoyed. He was too busy to come and explain his part in the killing of the man Brock, was he? She could sit and worry, and when work was less pressing he would graciously ride over and make explanation of why he had backed this murderous thief and had gone bond for him. His note was like a slap in the face. Could he not see that if they were to be close and dear to each other he ought to lose no time in making clear to her the cause of what had occurred at Sundog? Instead, he acted as if it were a mere casual incident.

The reply she sent to Neal was crisp and curt. Fortunately he would not have to waste his valuable time coming to see her Saturday, since before then she was leaving on a visit and expected to be gone some time. She was, Eleanor mentioned, sincerely his.

It was close to supper time when Neal read the girl's answer. He did not wait to eat but ordered Keno saddled at once. Tired though he was with a hard day's work, he could not delay before setting himself right. His clothes he did not change, though he rammed into the saddlebags clean underwear, shirt, and socks. Inside of ten minutes he was climbing to the mesa where he could strike the short cut leading to the Triangle R. The trail followed a prong and dropped down to a winding creek which descended into a park partly wooded and partly open meadow. In the gathering darkness he could see cattle standing on their heads.[1]

He grinned wryly, remembering that Janet had warned him to get to Eleanor and tell his story at once. That was what he had intended to do, but Kinsley had sent word he was on his way with the whiteface heifers Neal had ordered. After the man had driven three hundred miles he could not decently walk out on him.

The ranchman talked to his horse, as men sometimes do who live much alone. 'I reckon what I don't know about women would fill a book, Keno. My plumb demented notion was that she would understand.'

He drew up where the creek flowed deep and swift along a bank at a bend. Grounding his reins so that the horse could graze freely, he took from the saddlebags the clean clothes and stripped to the skin. From the bank he dived into the deep water, still ice cold from the small lake at the foot of the glacier that fed it. The shock was bracing. When he climbed out a few minutes later, his fatigue was gone. He felt clean and fit, though his stomach was flat as an empty leather mail sack.

Since he had forgotten to bring a towel, he dried as best he could with the bandanna that had

---

[1] A term for cattle while grazing.

been around his throat. The discarded underwear he put into the saddlebags.

It was well past nine when Neal reached the
Triangle R. Eleanor was curled up on a lounge
trying to read a story in the *Century* by Mary
Hallock Foote about a shy Quaker girl on a train
who was falling in love with a wild young fellow
in care of a sheriff taking him back to Boise on a
murder charge. She was not making much head-
way with it because her mind kept flitting to a
wild young man of her own in circumstances not
very dissimilar. That is, he had been her own until
she had relinquished him a few hours earlier.

A crisp step sounded on the porch. She looked
up, to see Neal standing in the doorway. He was
in chaps and dusty boots. The dust of travel had
sifted into every crease of his coat. Yet she had
never seen him more debonair and graceful. The
short curly hair above the lean tanned face, the
fine slope of the neck muscles into the strong
shoulders, sent a little shiver of delight through
her. She might have forgiven him on the spot if it
had not been for his first words and the way he
said them, with a flashing smile that showed a set
of perfect ivory teeth in the brown countenance.
Both the words and the confident manner took
too much for granted.

'I've come to see the girl who is sincerely
mine,' he told her.

Decidedly it was the wrong approach. She asked

for penitence and not assurance. Since he could forgive himself so easily, he could do without forgiveness from her.

'Probably you would have understood it better if I had written yours very truly,' she replied coldly.

He came forward to the lounge, grinned down at her, and offered both his hands. 'Come, honey, there's a better way to settle this than with words.'

Eleanor did not see his hands. 'I don't think so.'

'You wouldn't condemn me without listening to my side, would you?' he asked gently.

'Is it my fault you have been too busy to tell me your side?'

'I was coming, and I got a letter from a man who has been on the trail three weeks driving a bunch of heifers to me. He said he would get in this afternoon. I couldn't run out on him, could I?'

'So you ran out on me.'

He began to resent her stiff aloofness. 'Don't put it that way. I thought you were grown up and would understand.'

Eleanor rose from the couch, to get the advantage of her slim straight height. She was angry, and back of her anger was an awareness that she was not behaving well. Like a small girl, she knew she was being naughty and could not seem to help it.

'I'm spoiled, of course. You gave me a nice little lecture about it once, you remember. I wasn't whipped enough when I was a child. So I'm self-centered, and it's going to be tough on anybody that marries me. It can't be helped now, but I didn't have the excellent upbringing that has made you such a model.'

He laughed. He could not help it. For a moment she thought of laughing with him but decided instead to stay angry. Rather than getting amusement out of her displeasure he ought to be groveling.

'That's telling me off,' he chuckled. 'Let's agree I should have come earlier but didn't. I'm sorry. Now that's out of the way we can take up what took place at Sundog.'

'You mean about you and that cattle thief Dunn quarreling with some cowmen, then supporting him in a gunfight, and after he had killed a man helping him get free.'

'Yes,' he answered. 'That's what I mean. It isn't exactly the way I was going to put it, but I daresay I'm prejudiced in my own favor.'

He said it carelessly, almost scornfully, and her shoulders set themselves defensively against the tug inside that drew her to him.

Her words took on the timbre of sharpness. 'When I came to this country I liked its big clean spaces, its wide freedom. I thought the golden valleys sitting in sunlight and the breath of the wind in the pines lovely. They brushed out of one's mind the silly little gossip of the cities. It seemed to me a fine brave land.'

'All those things are still here,' he mentioned dryly.

'But all spoiled by the people who live here. In the Flood valley there isn't any trust or friendliness. In Sundog men walk the streets watching one another like wolves. In the ranch country there are fear and treachery. You can see it written in men's faces when you talk with them. You have a feeling of something concealed and hateful. So we have murders from ambush and killings on the street.'

The color tide ran into the fine planes of her cheeks and fired the beauty of her face. Neal wanted to take her warm supple body in his arms and make an end of this misunderstanding. But he knew it was more than a quarrel. There was a fundamental question that had to be settled or it would rise up between them again and again.

'That is something you and I can't change. Only time can settle it by softening the present hatreds and bitter animosities.'

'The quarrels are between honest men and thieves, between law and crime.'

'Is Jack Cross an honest man, a defender of law?' he asked. 'In the old days he was almost run out of the country as a rustler. Now he fences government land which homesteaders have a right to take up. I think he hires killers to destroy the men who oppose him.' He spoke without hope, for he knew that at present he could not change her view.

Eleanor deserted her argument abruptly, harking back to her personal grievance.

'Do you have to get mixed up in it every time there is trouble in the Flood River country?' she asked. 'Couldn't you just once sit on the side lines?'

'I do seem to be a kind of stormy petrel,' he admitted. 'Where I am trouble is.' There was a glean of sardonic mirth in his brown eyes. 'And I thought I was right gentle this time. I didn't bark or bite either one. Oil on the troubled waters was what I tried to be. I reckon I'm not cut out for a good Samaritan.'

'You sided with Dunn in the gunfight, didn't you?'

'I wished him well. Brock was crowding him into the difficulty. And when it came I stood by to see fair play.'

'Afterward you helped get him free, I hear. You and a saloonkeeper.'

'That's correct. We were afraid his enemies would tear down the jail—it's only a shack—and rub him out.'

'You can explain everything, can't you?'

His eyes rested on her a long time. 'No, I don't

think I can—to you. I've said all I'm going to say. It will be good-bye for the present between us.'

She was startled at his words, so quietly spoken but with no lack of decision. It was one thing for her to dismiss him, in the expectation that after a few days he would come back chastened, but it was quite another to have him make the choice instead of her.

'What do you mean—for the present?' she asked.

'Till you have thought this over. Perhaps yore brother is right—that my ways aren't your ways.'

'Perhaps he is,' she flung back, intent on saving face. 'If so, we'd better find it out now.'

They parted on that note. As soon as he had gone Eleanor went to her room. She did not want to meet her brother now, not till the turmoil in her heart was stilled. This was not what she had wanted or expected. He had made a declaration of independence. If she married him—and she was not sure that he still wanted her—it must be on his terms. He would lead his own life, and she would have to fit into it.

After the first burst of anger was over she knew that she had a greater respect for him than ever before. She had tried to dominate him, to tell him how to rule his life, and without quarreling, without even raising his voice, he had made it quite clear to her that she could not do it. He was intensely masculine. She loved the leashed strength of him, cased in the lean tough supple body that so charmed her.

But she was proud and headstrong. Fiercely she told herself that she was not going to make the first move for a reconciliation. It had to come from him or not at all.

CHAPTER XXIV

Advice offered

To Neal came rumors of unusual activity on the part of the cattlemen. These reached him first as casual and unimportant bits of news. Tim Owen, back from Sundog, where he had gone to buy a bridle, mentioned that Cross had hired as a rider a notorious gunman named Chris Morgan, a fellow who two years earlier had been a refugee in the Gap. A chance remark of Gunter told Neal that he had within a week sold three Winchester rifles, one to Christy and two to Manson. While hunting strays Pete Driskill from a wooded prong looked down to see a wagonload of supplies left at a Bar A B line camp far up in the hills. Three men carried the goods into the cabin. Two of them remained there after the empty wagon had departed.

These incidents taken together, in conjunction with Austin Reynolds's hint to Janet Lane about trouble imminent, pointed to some kind of organized offense. If the attack was to be against the rustlers and outlaws in the Gap, it was no affair of MacGowan's. He was not carrying a banner for either side. But it was disturbing to feel that the feud was about to break into open warfare. Men who would far rather not lend a hand to one faction or the other would be driven to take sides.

Even though Neal kept out, as he meant to do, he knew he would not be considered a neutral by Cross and his allies. His opinion was that the haystacks at his ranch had been set on fire by some of the Bar A B men as a punishment for having gone on Dunn's bond. When he hunted cows on the range he had a sense of pressing danger. In spite of himself he was likely to become a victim.

Neal rode down to Janet Lane's place to tell her that some spools of barb wire she had ordered would be brought out to her from Sundog by one of his men before the end of the week. As he rode up to the house he saw a horse tied to one of the porch posts. It carried the ⚠ brand.

Mary ran up to him. 'Mr. Reynolds is here,' she called out. 'To see Janet about the school. It will be funny to call her teacher.'

At the sound of their voices Janet came to the door. She showed embarrassment, blushing a little. 'Come in, Neal,' she invited. 'Mr. Reynolds is here. We are talking over what books we ought to order for the school.'

Reynolds joined them. He bowed stiffly to the other man.

Neal's eyes twinkled. 'It's important to get good textbooks for the children. I hope you'll stick to the McGuffey Readers, ma'am. Studying them made me what I am.'

'Then we'll certainly have to keep them,' Janet said, laughing. 'And you don't have to call me "Ma'am!" I'm not a teacher yet.'

'If you need the big boys jounced around you can call on Mr. Reynolds, since he is a director.'

'I'll take care of the big boys myself or quit the job,' Janet told him.

'I'll bet you will. Smile at 'em and look like you are depending on them to help out, and they will line yore desk up with red apples every day.'

Janet explained a little more fully the presence of the school director. 'Mr. Reynolds expects to be away for a week or more and thought he had better come while he had a chance. I suppose you know that Eleanor is visiting the Governor's daughter at Cheyenne. She will have a lovely time. The President will be there two days and she will meet him.'

'Nice for the President,' Neal commented.

'Nice for both of them,' Janet agreed.

'Will you be meeting the Great White Father too?' Neal asked Reynolds.

'No. I have other business.'

MacGowan wondered if he could guess the other business. He hoped not.

He mentioned to Janet that the spools of wire would be delivered at her place within a few days.

'Are you sure it will be convenient for you to bring them?' she asked. 'I don't want your man making a special trip to get goods for me.'

'He won't do that. When he is in town he'll stop at Gunter's and toss the wire in the wagon. No trouble at all.' Neal turned to the Triangle R owner and asked if he could see him a moment alone.

The men walked to the stable.

'Since I'm not a fool, Reynolds, I know there is trouble afoot,' Neal said bluntly. 'I'm not asking you what it is. I don't want to know. But I'll say this: If you and yore friends have any idea of trying to comb Rustlers' Gap for outlaws you want to hang, I would advise you to give it up.'

Reynolds took a few seconds before he answered. 'It might come to sending a posse into the Gap some day. We're not going to let those scoundrels rob us forever.' He added, with a touch of ironic scorn, 'If that day ever comes I'll consider your advice—and probably reject it.'

'I am not talking about some day but now—this week or next.' Neal's gaze rested steadily on the other. 'Likely you won't give any weight to what I say. But you had better. I don't know any terrain in the country rougher or more tangled than the Gap. The hills are all huddled together. One gorge runs into another. It is full of traps where a posse can be ambushed and wiped out to a man. There are fifty places where a few sharpshooters can stand off scores of gunmen.'

'You seem to know it very well,' Reynolds replied dryly.

'I've been in it three times. The last time I barely

got out with my life. If you go into the Gap you haven't a chance.'

'Are you speaking for yourself?' The Triangle R man asked coldly.

Neal looked at him, anger darkening his eyes. 'Just what do you mean by that?' he demanded.

Reynolds had the courage to back his insolence. 'I was thinking you might be a messenger for somebody else, perhaps for Cad Clemson.'

Bluntly MacGowan snapped, 'Try not to be a fool, Reynolds.' He added, restraining his temper, 'I'm speaking for the men of yore party who will be massacred if you try this.'

'They will be obliged for your interest in them.'

'All right. I've said my say. Take the poor fools in and have them rubbed out.'

Neal strode to his horse, mounted, waved a hand at Janet, and rode away. The girl was disturbed. Something had occurred that annoyed him, a difference of opinion between him and Reynolds. She watched the latter walk slowly to the house.

Reynolds was pondering the advice that had been given him. No doubt it was good. Probably he had been unfair to MacGowan. That was the trouble in not liking a man. It made you distrust his motives. But all along it had been his opinion that the campaign insisted upon by Cross and his group was a foolish one. It was, he felt and had said, both too lawless and too dangerous. He had been outvoted and had surrendered to the will of the majority. He could not back out now.

Janet said, 'Neal acted a little peculiar.' That was as near as she could come to asking for information. Reynolds offered no explanation. He also seemed to be put out by what had taken place.

'Then everything is settled about the books,' he said, coming back to the official reason for his visit.

'Yes,' she agreed.

Austin did not want to go but he could find no valid excuse for staying. 'I'll bring that magazine I spoke of,' he promised, and gave her his hand.

He held her small one in his longer than he ever had before, his gaze searching her eyes. It was in his mind to speak out now, but something in her look daunted him. What he wanted to say to her he decided to leave unsaid. Abruptly he turned away and swung to the saddle.

A flush had crept into Janet's cheeks. A pulse of excitement beat through her blood. She knew what he had come so near to telling her, and she was glad that he had restrained himself. For she did not love him. She had not yet banished from her thoughts the memory of another man. But she liked Austin Reynolds very much. He had saved her life, had been very kind to her and very considerate. She was grateful to him. He was often in her mind. It had occurred to her more than once that some day she might think of him not only as a friend.

CHAPTER XXV

Cross plays his own hand

Darkness still hung over the valley when the small cavalcade drew out from the Bar A B. Cross came out of the house after it had started, pulled himself heavily to the saddle, and moved at a swift road gait past the wagon to the van of the party. Stars were still out and the ranch buildings shrouded in a blur of gloom.

'Where does Reynolds join us?' Manson asked, ranging alongside Cross.

'At the line camp. Two–three others will meet us there. Delavan for one—and Oldfield.'

They traveled through the sage, mile after mile. Out of the blackness the distant hills marched vaguely. Gradually night began to lift. Gray day sifted over the desert. The pungent scent of the sage filled the nostrils. A startled bunch of antelope crashed into the brush and disappeared.

The terrain grew more broken as they moved into the foot-slopes. This was a brush country. Along Willow Creek the young shoots whipped at their legs. As the wagon tore through the aspen growth the slender saplings beat a rat-tat-tat on the bed and axles.

Before they reached the Bar A B line camp the

sun was coming over the eastern hills and sending long shafts of light across the gray-green sage desert. The expected reinforcements were waiting at the cabin, and with them three pack-horses already loaded. Additional supplies were transferred from the shack to the wagon.

Oldfield had a word to say before they started. 'This is serious business, boys. We may get in a tight. Anyhow, we ought to choose a leader, and after we have him obey orders. If we make mistakes we're headed for trouble.'

'That's right,' agreed Delavan. He was a big blond giant with close-set eyes and a taciturn manner. 'Reynolds is my man for boss of the outfit.'

The dark blood beat up into the beefy face of Cross. His steel-trap lips tightened. He considered this his expedition. It had been organized at his insistence after acrimonious discussion against the advice of Reynolds. Now the Triangle R man was being proposed as leader.

'I don't get this,' he snapped. 'We know what we've come for—to get a bunch of thieves and outlaws. Let's go get 'em. We don't need any boss.'

'I don't agree with you.' Oldfield spoke quietly. He was an old Indian fighter, a gray-haired man well past fifty who had an excellent reputation as a good citizen. 'We are not a crazy mob of killers but a posse of decent men who have an unpleasant job to do. There are four names on our list. All four are killers and desperadoes. We want them and no more. If we don't have a leader, somebody is liable to go hog-wild and start killing.'

'It would be all right with me if we did bump off half a dozen others too,' Cross snarled. 'There are twenty known rustlers holed up in the Gap.'

'We've been over all that, Jack,' Reynolds said firmly. 'If we get the four decided on the others will be scared off. They will let our stock alone. Either we stick to our agreement or you can count me out.'

'Here too,' Oldfield assented.

'I didn't say I wasn't sticking to it,' Cross replied sullenly. 'But we're grown-up responsible men. We don't need any boss.'

'Every roundup has one,' Oldfield insisted. 'Let's go at this right.'

There was a chorus of approval. The fact was that most of those present distrusted Cross and the hotheads who supported him. They wanted a leader who would not lose his head.

Reynolds was elected.

The party struck across country, aiming for a rocky truncated cone which stood out above the surrounding landscape. They reached it late in the afternoon. At the base of the great slab was a pile of large boulders that had crashed down through the centuries. Among these they made a temporary camp. The wagon was unloaded and supplies cached in a cave. One man was to be left there as a guard. The plan was that if the food taken in by the pack animals gave out, the posse would get fresh pro-visions from the cache.

Reynolds advised the men to snatch a few hours sleep since they would be in the saddle most of the night. No fire was lit until after dark for fear the smoke might betray their presence to some chance rider.

They ate supper under the stars, after which the regulators took up their journey to the Gap and the driver of the wagon returned to the Bar A B. With Reynolds in the van rode the guide, Chris Morgan, the gunman recently taken into the employ of Cross. While a fugitive from justice a year earlier he had spent a month in the Gap. He knew its more traveled trails, though he admitted that there were a hundred gulches, pockets, and ravines he had never seen.

It was the full of the moon, and after they had passed through the defile which led into Rustlers' Gap they could see vaguely below them the huddle of hills fading into the gulf of blackness beyond. Along a rock scarp they descended, following a narrow trail that ran close to the edge of what seemed to be a bottomless pit. Rubble started by the feet of the horses slid over the precipice and fell so far that no sound of its striking reached those above.

'They call this Breakneck Trail,' Morgan said to

Reynolds after the cowpony of the rancher had slipped on the gravel and been reined up just in time. 'It's bad enough in the daytime. At night it's plain suicide.'

Carefully they worked down the ledge and came at last to a shoulder which broadened and offered a safer path. It led to a stretch of timber and that in turn to a walled cañon through which a stream ran noisily, plunging over rocks and falls. They descended to the bottom, so far below the top of the walls that only a narrow line of the sky could be seen. The mounts of the raiders found a footing in a black darkness that pressed in on them like something tangible.

They emerged into a valley of meadowland flanked by heavy growths of pine marching up the hillsides. Here Reynolds called a halt. His watch showed that it was four o'clock. In another hour the darkness would lift.

'Morgan says that there is a camp about four miles ahead where Cad Clemson spends a good deal of time,' he explained. 'He may or may not be there now. If we keep going it will be daybreak before we get there. That might not be so good if he has four or five men with him. My idea is that we had better camp today in the timber and close in on Cad tonight.'

'If he is there,' Christy amended.

'If he isn't we'll have to look farther. We'll move well back in the timber and get through with breakfast so the fire will be out before it is light. All day we'll stay holed up. Any objections?'

'I'm for going in and cleaning up Cad's nest right now,' Cross objected. 'We came to get these scalawags. I say, go get them.'

'He always has two or three fellows with him,' Morgan said. 'Sometimes more. If you bull right in they'll sure pick off four or five of us. The thing to do is surprise them.'

'Sure,' Oldfield agreed. 'We've got to slip up on them, mop up quick as we can, and get out.'

Cross gave way sulkily. It was clear that he intended to be a malcontent and find fault with whatever was done.

They found a pocket back of the timber on their right where the horses could find grass and the party would be out of sight of a traveler riding through the valley. While it was still dark they drank their hot coffee and ate flapjacks and steak around the campfire. Before the first streaks of blue showed in the sky the fire was put out.

Reynolds divided the day into two-hour stretches for the guard, with explicit instructions that they were to stay back of some flat rock outcroppings at the lip of the pocket and not show themselves at all. Those not on picket duty could sleep, except for a wrangler who was to keep the horses from straying out of the pocket.

The day was warm and sunny. Tired with the long night trek, most of the men slept the hours away. Reynolds was busy until nearly noon, then retired to the shade of a pine tree for rest. He was awakened by Delavan about four o'clock.

'Cross and Hack are gone,' the big blond giant said.

'Gone!' Reynolds rolled over on an elbow and brought himself back from the heaviness of sleep. 'What do you mean, gone? They must be near.'

'No, sir. They've lit out. They're nowheres around.'

Reynolds rose and looked at the other. 'I don't get it. Where could they have gone?'

'Search me.' Delavan added, 'They could of lit out for home.'

'Did they take their horses?'

'No. Probably they figured they would have been seen if they tried it.'

'They haven't started to walk home. That's a cinch.' Reynolds moved another step forward on the problem. 'And they are not running out on us. They're fighting fools, both of them. More likely they are trying to pull something on their own. Cross didn't like it when he wasn't chosen to run this roundup.'

'That's so.' Delavan considered. 'I reckon he is pulling a fast one to show how much better he could of done.'

'I expect they will be back in a little while. They can't have gone far.' But Reynolds was disturbed. He knew the rash ungovernable temper of

226

Cross. He might bring disaster on the whole outfit.

He joined the rest of the party. They were discussing the absence of their companions.

'We ought never to have started on a Friday, and thirteen of us,' a sandy freckled cowboy moaned. 'I dunno how I come not to notice what day it was.'

'We ought never to have started with Cross,' Oldfield differed bluntly. 'He's got too much hell in the neck.'

'They must of slipped away down that draw,' another guessed. 'But what for?'

Reynolds answered bitterly. 'To prove how smart they are and to show me up. You chose the wrong majordomo, boys.'

They heard the faint far sound of a shot, and before the silence had fairly closed on it another. Three or four more followed.

'That shooting is between here and Cad's hideout,' Morgan said.

Oldfield hazarded a guess. 'Their idea was to get Cad, then come back and brag to us about it. Looks to me like they have slipped up.'

Another shot came to them, like the pop of a distant firecracker.

'They are probably in a jam,' Reynolds commented sharply. 'We'll have to go rescue them.'

'And after that what?' Delavan inquired angrily. 'The durn fools have cut the ground from under our feet. Word will spread we are here. We'll have to fight our way out.'

'Yes,' Reynolds assented. 'They'll come swarming at us like a bunch of hornets. But the damage is already done. The point is, do we try to save Cross and Hack? I say yes.'

'Then let's slap our saddles on and get going,' Oldfield snapped. 'We haven't any time to waste.'

Within five minutes they were riding through the timber into the valley. They had not waited to load the supplies or bring the pack animals. The only spares they took were the saddled mounts of the absent men.

As they galloped up to the lip of the mountain park Manson found himself knee to knee with Reynolds. 'We ought to let 'em fry in their own juice,' he complained sourly. 'They've blown the lid off this whole business. We'll probably lose several men trying to get them out of the tight they are in.'

Reynolds nodded grimly. 'Yes. But we can't leave them to die without lifting a hand.'

'I know. But they got no right to put us up against such a proposition. Cross always was a bullheaded fool.'

The sound of more shooting came to them. Reynolds put his horse to a canter. From the summit he looked down a long steep slope dotted with scrub pines. A puff of smoke rose from behind one of these. A man with a rifle lay crouched there. Reynolds recognized Cross. He saw no sign of Hack.

Recklessly Reynolds dashed down the hill, Chris Morgan at his heels. He pulled up beside Cross.

'Where's Hack?' he cried.

'They got him, plumb through the heart,' Cross answered.

'Get on behind me.'

From a draw below them a shot whistled along the shoulder of the hill. Morgan's hand caught at the horn of his saddle. His heavy body swayed and pitched to the ground. Cross seized the rein of the horse and Reynolds dismounted. The gunman had been shot through the forehead just above the eyes.

'Dead,' Reynolds said, and vaulted to the saddle.

On Morgan's horse Cross followed him up the hill. Bullets whipped past them as they rode. The fire of the invaders crackled an answer from the ridge above.

CHAPTER XXVI

Run to earth

As Reynolds looked back from the cut leading into the park, he saw men below swinging into the saddle. No doubt messengers were already on the way to summon reinforcements. A swift retreat from the Gap was the only course left him and his riders.

Oldfield, Delavan, and Christy gathered round him. Without slackening their pace they talked over the situation. Their hope had been to surprise Cad Clemson, rub him out, and in the darkness push on to get the other men on their black list. There was no chance of that now. They would be lucky to escape with their lives. It was decided to abandon the pack animals and the supplies. Food could be picked up at the cache after they were safely out of the Gap.

Reynolds held the party together at a road gait. There was a tendency among some of the riders to hurry. He could see them looking back to see if the pursuit was in sight, and he could read the thoughts urgent in their minds. Two of them had been killed. Were the rest to be picked off one by one?

That sort of fear led to panic. They had a long

way to travel, and they had to keep their heads. At the summit of a long hill Reynolds called for a short halt to breathe the horses. Far down in the valley below they saw two horsemen following them.

Austin shifted to ease himself in the saddle. He spoke with quiet confidence. 'We're all right, boys. There isn't going to be any attack, not right away. Clemson can't get his men gathered before morning, and by that time we ought to be getting out of the Gap. Those fellows below are just keeping an eye on us to see where we go. The one important thing is for us to stick together.'

'Nothing to worry about,' Oldfield added in support of Reynolds. 'Too many of us. They would lose a dozen men trying to clean us up. Cad isn't fool enough for that.'

Christy and Delavan led the advance. The rear was brought up by Oldfield and Reynolds. With them rode Cross. Neither of the other cattlemen reproached him, unless it was an imputation of blame to ignore his presence. He slumped dejectedly in the saddle, all the arrogant obstinacy for the moment stricken out of him.

Dusk came over the land and then darkness. Later the sky was lit by stars and a moon at times obscured by scudding clouds. With Morgan gone they were forced to stop more than once to decide on the way to go. The district was a tangle of hills and gulches tossed up by explosive

231

energy a million years earlier. In the subdued light one slope looked exactly like its neighbor.

At last Delavan pulled up. 'I don't know whether we are right or not,' he said.

'I'm wondering about that,' Christy replied. 'The direction seems okay. But that doesn't mean a thing if we get balled up in some of these cañons that twist around every which way.'

Others took a hand in the discussion. Only one of them had ever been in the Gap before, and it turned out that he had no sense of direction. It was decided to follow the gulch at the mouth of which they had halted. After they had reached the upper end of it, coming out on a long prong which overlooked an undulating floor that concealed a dozen defiles and gorges, Reynolds felt a cold sinking at his stomach. To find the path they wanted in all this welter of land waves would be almost impossible. His eyes met those of Oldfield. Each read in the gaze of the other the admission that they were lost.

Later this became a certainty. After another hour of travel Delavan again called for a huddle.

'No use loadin' ourselves, boys,' he told the others. 'I throw in my hand. It's a busted flush. I don't know where we are.'

'I haven't known for quite some time,' Christy admitted.

'We went wrong back at that draw where we jumped up the deer,' a cowpuncher said.

'There or somewhere else,' another cut in. 'Seems to me we been bearin' too far south.'

'We'd better throw off and camp till morning,' Reynolds proposed. 'No use wandering around in the dark. We'd only get more confused.'

'By morning they'll have the gateway blocked up so we can't get through,' Cross objected.

Christy looked at him. A shutter dropped over the eyes of the manager of the Blue Bell, a film that left them opaque and blank. 'It's some late for you to think of that now,' he drawled bitterly.

They built a fire and slept around it. Reynolds divided the night watches. To Cross he assigned no duty. Austin himself got only a few snatches of sleep toward morning. He guessed they were in for very serious trouble. Already the men were hungry, and they had no food with them. If they did not find the exit to the Gap soon, they would be forced to try to fight their way out. The prospect was a dreary one.

With the first light of day they were in the saddle. It was clear that they had to work eastward. But the range in which they were trapped, or at least that particular spur of it, ran more north and south. They had to find clefts in the mountains through which they could pass.

A narrow gulch ran down into the cañon they were following. It was steep, and the bed of it was filled with rubble and loose stone. Reynolds guessed that there were times in the year when a torrent of water ripped through there at tremendous speed. They put their horses at the incline. It grew stiffer, with large boulders here and there filling the tilted floor. In the end it brought them to an impasse, a rock wall their mounts could not possibly climb.

Disheartened, they turned back and retraced their way, to follow the major cañon on its devious path. Noon found them still wandering through deep gullies and over the shoulders of great hills. A grassy pocket at the foot of some high cliffs offered grazing for the animals. Unexpectedly a deer broke for cover from out of a clump of aspens. One of the cowboys shot it.

Delavan looked at Reynolds and shrugged his shoulders. The sound of that shot might bring their enemies on them, but after all they had to eat to live. Whatever they did now was more likely to be wrong than right. The buck was cooked, and the hungry men ate enormously. They took with them the meat that was not eaten, tying it to the saddles of two of the men.

But they did not take it far. As they started out of the cove a volley of guns crashed at them. A horse went down, hit in the neck. Christy let out a yelp of pain.

'Get back into the pocket,' Reynolds ordered harshly. 'Find cover among the rocks.'

The Blue Bell manager slid to the ground and collapsed. Cross and Reynolds dragged him back into the aspens and through the grove to the shelter of the rocks beyond.

They were trapped, a sandstone wall behind them and entrenched riflemen in front.

CHAPTER XXVII

Janet asks for help

The Lane family were all busy. Janet was kneading a batch of light bread. On the porch Harry operated a dash-churn, his arms moving up and down regularly. Mary was teaching Eleanor to lie-down-and-play-dead.

Of the three only Harry was discontented with his occupation. The two chores he detested most were turning a grindstone and churning, and of the two this was the worse. In the first place it was woman's work, and he was reaching an age when he wanted to be and act like a man. Moreover, for him the butter would never come. He reckoned he had been lifting the dasher up and down for an hour. Churning was the doggondest, most provoking thing in the world.

A man rode into the yard on a sorrel horse that showed signs of having been hard-ridden. Dried sweat flecked its withers. When the rider pulled up, the animal's head drooped dejectedly.

Janet came to the door, the sleeves of her dress rolled up, a dash of flour on one of the forearms. She knew the visitor. He had been here once before, and she had helped to save his life.

'Hell loose in the Gap,' he blurted out. 'A bunch

of cowmen came in to make trouble, and Cad has got them rounded up where they can't get out.'

'Rounded up!' Janet's eyes grew big. A cold tight hand gripped at her stomach muscles. 'You mean he's . . . going to—'

'He aims to clean up on them,' Russ Miller told her bluntly. 'They got no chance to get away.'

Harry stared at him open-mouthed. 'What cattlemen?' he asked.

'I dunno all of 'em. Reynolds is one—and Cross. Two of the bunch have got themselves killed already.'

The color washed out of Janet's face. 'What two?' she faltered.

'Fellow called Hack and Chris Morgan. I'm headin' for Neal MacGowan's place. I don't reckon there's a thing he can do about it, but—'

Janet interrupted. 'Saddle old Buck—quick!' she told her brother. 'I'll go with you.'

'With me?' Harry asked.

'No—no! With Mr. Miller. Hurry, please.'

The girl and the outlaw were on their way inside of a few minutes. She was greatly disturbed. Her friend was in appalling danger. Already it might have destroyed him. Over the steep trails between the homestead and the K-B Ranch they could not make fast time, and every second seemed to her important. Neal was her only hope. He must do something about this. She did not know what. But somehow he must find a way to save Austin Reynolds. It came to her with complete surprise that if anything happened to Austin her world would go to pieces.

MacGowan was in the corral branding calves when he caught sight of the two riders coming down the hill. He recognized Janet first, and a moment later Russ Miller. This was a queer combination, he thought. Something out of the ordinary must have sent them here together. He walked out of the corral and watched them approach. His trained eyes picked up the brand on the sorrel horse of the man, and his mind flashed to an advertisement he had seen that morning in the *Flood River Bulletin.*

One sorrel horse stolen from the Babcock Corral. Branded Bar B A on left shoulder and I O on the jaw. Fourteen hands high. Three white feet. Shod in front. Reward will be paid for recovery and for conviction of thief.

Neal's jaw set. He did not wait to find out why they had come.

'In spite of hell and high water you're bound to stay a thief, Miller, aren't you?' he said angrily.

'Listen, Neal,' the young man pleaded. 'I didn't steal this horse. Maybe somebody else did. There's trouble up in the Gap. I grabbed the first mount I could slap a saddle on. A bunch of cowmen butted in there, and Cad has got them cornered.'

'Austin is one of them,' Janet contributed miserably. 'Two of the men have already been killed. We must do something to save Austin— and the others.'

'What can we do?' Neal demanded, his voice strident, the muscles of his strong jaw knotted. 'I warned him not to go—told him how it would be. And he as good as insulted me for telling him. How can I save the fool from the consequences of his folly?'

'I don't know.' Janet lifted her hands in a little gesture of despair. 'But we can't leave him there to . . . to die.' Her sentence broke. A sob choked up into her throat.

Neal knew he meant to save the beleaguered men if he could, but he bitterly resented the need of trying. Most of them were his enemies. Two or three at least were almost ready to give the word to have him assassinated. Why did he have to interfere when this was none of his business? Rage welled up in him—at their stupidity, at his own temperament, at the tragic intolerance which had built up the murderous feud.

He strode back to the corral. In two curt sentences he put the facts before his men.

'I'm going up into the Gap to see what I can do to stop this damn foolishness,' he continued. 'If you've got any sense you'll stay here on the job. If you're as big a lunkhead as I am, you'll ride up there with me and maybe get yore heads shot off.'

Pete Driskill freed the rope he had just tossed around the neck of a blatting calf. 'Invitation to go and get massacred,' he drawled with a laugh. 'Let's go, boys.'

Tim Owen scratched his red head and grinned. 'I done been there once and didn't like the company I met. I'd be plumb crazy to go again, but I reckon I'll mosey along.'

The other man in the corral asked for more information from Miller, and after getting it decided that he would stay where he was.

'Cross treated me mighty bad one time,' he explained. 'I guess I won't butt in.'

'You're certainly smart,' Driskill agreed ironically, 'for Cad Clemson's gunman would be liable to treat you a whole lot meaner if you went.'

'There's no obligation for Yorky to go if he doesn't want to,' Neal said. 'We'd better get off right away, boys.'

As they saddled he gave instructions to Yorky to ride to Sundog and urge Sheriff Cullen to start a posse from there at once. To Janet he said: 'We ought to get the word to the Triangle R too. Can you send Harry over with a message?'

'I'll go myself,' the girl promised. 'And then I'll see Mr. Muir at the Blue Bell.'

'Doctor Seneca has been in the Gap two or three times,' MacGowan told Yorky. 'I think Cullen could get him to guide a posse in. Russ will return to the gateway to bring them to the right place.'

'Sure,' assented Miller with a wry grin. 'I've done managed to get both sides in this feud sore at me already. The cattlemen want to hang me and now Cad's crowd will pump lead at me when they get a chance, so I might as well go the whole hog.'

Neal did not take the time to explain that he too had for some time been considered an enemy by both sides. He tightened the cinch on his horse and poured out suggestions to Yorky and Janet.

'Spread the word quick as you can. Rouse the town and the ranches. If any of the Gap men are at Sundog, be sure they know how much trouble is brewing. There's a chance they might hustle back home with the news and scare Cad off.'

Yorky's face was flushed. 'Let Miss Lane do that. I've decided to go in with you boys.'

MacGowan understood his embarrassed shame. 'That's fine, Yorky, but you can do more good outside. After you have got things moving you can come in with a posse if you like.'

While the men looked to their weapons and ammunition, Janet supervised the Mexican cook as he packed in saddlebags all the prepared food in the house. Into one gunny sack he flung coffee-pot and frying-pan and Dutch oven, into another flour, navy beans, a slab of pork, and a package of Arbuckle's roasted and ground. She hovered about Neal as he disposed of the supplies on the mounts. There was no time to bother with a packhorse.

This lean tough man had never seemed to her more remote than now. The harsh grimness of the face, the tigerish litheness of the body all set to pounce, the hint of primeval savagery boiling up into the jade-hard eyes! These were no part of the blithe friendly neighbor who had become so much a spur to her happiness. The thought stabbed her that the message she had brought might be sending him to his death.

She murmured, knowing the uselessness of it, 'You'll be awfully careful, won't you?'

In his laughter there was mockery rather than mirth. 'Oh, yes, we'll be careful.'

Swift compunction seized her. She could not be responsible for his death, even to save Austin. 'Don't go because I asked you, Neal. Maybe you can't do anything. Maybe—'

Her face was so gray and drawn that he cut off the bitter words crackling on his lips. It was not her fault that an inner urge in him drove him angrily to this adventure.

'It will work out all right, Janet,' he told her gently. 'I'll bring him back to you alive.'

'And yourself,' she added, pleading in her voice.

'I've never thrown down on myself yet,' he answered shortly, and swung to the saddle.

Watching them ride away, hope almost died in her heart.

'He sure flings his shadow a long way,' Yorky said, his admiring eyes followed the man who signed his pay checks. 'What has he got that will make men jump at the chance to ride with him into such a hell broth as this? Neither Pete nor Tim has any call to go risking his life on such a crazy business nor Neal himself, for that matter. What have these cattlemen ever done but act like he has the smallpox? Not a week ago they burned up his hay and sent him an anonymous letter to get out or be killed. Now he's starting out to try to save their lives. No sense to it. And anyhow all he can do is get himself and his boys bumped off.'

'Do you think so?' Janet asked anxiously.

'There are probably fifty outlaws and rustlers on the peck to settle the hash of the fool cowmen who went into the Gap. They will get them sure. And when our boys butt in they'll get wiped out too.' Yorky was doing his grumbling out loud, trying to satisfy his conscience that he had been right in declining to go. 'And me, I'll feel like a coyote because I didn't slap a saddle on a bronc right off and go whooping into the outlaws' net with Neal. I'll be doggoned if it ain't enough to drive a fellow to drink.'

Janet felt her stomach muscles sink at Yorky's prediction. If anything harmful befell these three men it would be her fault. Maybe the cowboy was right, that there was no sense in Neal's taking a hand. For that matter, there was no sense to any of this caldron of hate that was boiling over to ruin the lives of women and children as well as men. She had thought Austin Reynolds so conservative and law-abiding, yet he had been swept away by it too. He had not wanted to go. She knew that. But he had been dragged into this madness by a mistaken sense of loyalty to his group. She thought of Tennyson's lines:

His honor rooted in dishonor stood,
And faith unfaithful kept him falsely true.

Eleanor flashed to her mind. She ought to let her know what was taking place, since of course she would want to come home as quickly as she could.

'Will you send a telegram for me when you get to Sundog?' she asked Yorky.

'Sure, ma'am,' he promised.

Janet went into the house, found paper and pencil, and wrote a message to be wired to Eleanor.

CHAPTER XXVIII

A willful woman has her way

Eleanor read the telegram as she was starting to dress to go to the afternoon reception for the President. The message read:

AUSTIN TRAPPED IN RUSTLERS' GAP WITH OTHER CATTLEMEN. TWO OF PARTY ALREADY KILLED. NEAL STARTING IN TO TRY HELP THEM.

JANET

To her friend, who was doing up her hair before the mirror, Eleanor said abruptly, 'I've got to go home, Ann.'

Her hostess turned. 'Is it bad news, Nell?'

'Yes.' Eleanor handed the yellow slip to the other girl.

Ann read the message. Her eyes grew wide. 'But, my gracious, this is dreadful!' she exclaimed. 'How in the world did Austin ever get into such a mess? He's so . . . so conservative.'

'I don't know. The feeling is very bitter. Neal is going into it too, Janet says.'

'Who is Janet?'

'A girl on a homestead near us. Austin is in love with her.'

'It's so mixed up.' Ann frowned at the paper in her hand. 'You told me Neal and Austin aren't friendly—and that the other cattlemen hated your wild man.'

'They do. But that's just like Neal. He's . . . quixotic. Fights for the underdog. I've got to catch the first train.' She began flinging her things from a drawer to the bed.

'But there's the reception,' Ann protested.

'Sorry, dear, but I've got to go. I'd never forgive myself if—if anything happened and I didn't try to get there.'

Half an hour later Eleanor was waving good-bye to her friend from the window of a coach. She had never been on a train that seemed to travel so slowly, though the conductor assured her they were making very good time.

At the junction she caught the Sundog stage five minutes before it started. The only other passengers were two brown-faced lads in dusty chaps, run-down-at-the-heel boots, and old weatherstained big drooping hats. They were on their jovial way to spend four months' pay as swiftly as they could at Sundog.

Eleanor asked them if they had heard anything about the trouble at Rustlers' Gap. It appeared that they had heard a good deal. A rumor had come down the line that a bunch of cowmen had been wiped out.

'Is it true?' she asked. 'Do they know?'

Her ashen face and bleak eyes startled them. She was asking not from curiosity but because of an urgent vital interest.

'We don't know a thing for sure, ma'am,' one of them answered gently. 'You know how stories get started. Maybe there is mighty little to this.'

'Do the stories give names about . . . about who has been killed? I'm Eleanor Reynolds. My brother is with the cattlemen.'

For a split second the cowpuncher hesitated. He had heard the name of Austin Reynolds given among the dead, but he lied without shame. 'No names have come through, ma'am.'

They had the exaggerated respect all of their fraternity held for good women. This lovely girl's fear-stricken eyes appealed to the chivalry in them. It was their opinion that she would hear tragic news as soon as they arrived at Sundog, and they did their best now to look after her comfort with gentle and unobtrusive consideration.

Eleanor found Sundog buzzing with excitement. At the hitch-racks in front of saloons and stores many horses were tied. She passed a little huddle of men on the sidewalk, and as they recognized her their talk died until she was out of hearing.

From Gunter's hardware store a man walked. He was carrying a rifle. Eleanor called to him, 'Bob—Bob!'

Robert Muir turned and came swiftly toward

her, warm sympathy in his eyes. 'Eleanor!' he cried.

'Tell me,' she begged. 'What about Austin?'

He noticed how anxiety and fear had thinned her rich voice down. But he did not try to hide the truth. She had to know it sooner or later. 'Austin is in Rustlers' Gap with a bunch of cattlemen. I am afraid the outlaws have them trapped.'

'He's . . . all right?'

'As far as I know. Neal MacGowan went in to help them soon as he heard of the trouble. I have been in the hills looking after a gather of strays and didn't hear about this till an hour ago. I'm taking up some of the Blue Bell and Triangle R boys now. Try not to worry, Eleanor. Austin is probably all right.'

'What about Neal? Has anything been heard from him yet?'

'Not yet.'

'How many men did he take with him?'

'Two of his punchers.'

She let that rest in her mind a moment. 'Bob, I want to go into the Gap with you. I know what you are going to tell me—that it is no place for a woman. But I don't agree. I'm going. My brother may be . . . wounded. Perhaps he needs me.'

Eleanor was not thinking only of her brother. Vividly to her mind there rose the graceful light-stepping figure of Neal MacGowan, reckless laughter in his dark eyes, the beat of excitement pulsing through his blood, and in swift succession another picture, one of his supple body lying lifeless on the ground.

Muir shook his head. 'You can't go, Eleanor. I know how you feel. As soon as I can get word to you about Austin I'll do it.'

'I'm not asking whether I can go,' she said. 'I'm telling you that I'm going.'

He told her, quite firmly, that he would not take her. It was no place for a lady.

'I'm not a lady,' she urged. 'I'm a woman, worried sick. If you don't take me I am going anyhow. There will be wounded men. I can nurse.'

'There will be plenty of men to look after them. Of course Doctor Seneca is going. You won't be needed. Be reasonable.'

'I am reasonable. Nobody would hurt me. You know that.'

'Sorry, Eleanor. I can't take you. No use talking.'

'Very well. I'll meet you in the Gap.' She turned away, eyes bright with resentment and the firm intention not to be denied.

He had given her a thought. She walked to the office of Doctor Seneca. She found him gathering dressings and putting them in his bag.

'I'm going with you,' she told him.

He had just returned from taking care of a broken leg on a ranch twenty miles away. Most of last night's sleep he had lost, and he was not in the best of humors.

'Not if I know it,' he returned bluntly. 'The Gap is—'

'—no place for a lady,' she cut in sharply. 'Did you ever hear of Florence Nightingale?'

'The situation is different.'

'Why is it? Nobody would hurt me. My brother is there in danger—and the man I am going to marry.'

'Young Muir?'

'Neal MacGowan. Don't you see, doctor, that if a few women were in the Gap all this fighting would have to stop? My going with you might make a difference.'

He stared at her, struck by the suggestion. Among these wild bandits, as among all outdoor Westerners, there was a very great regard for good women. It was a long shot, of course, and the chances were that it would not score a hit, but her presence might just possibly save her brother. It came to him that he had no right to refuse her.

'Can you take it?' he demanded. 'The long ride—rough country—poor food, if any—maybe wounded and dying men.'

She nodded. 'I'll be all right. I'm strong, and I won't quit on you, or faint.'

'All right. Get a good easy horse and a boy's saddle. Get out of those duds and put on a pair of Levis. And be back here in fifteen minutes if you expect to go with me. I'm starting right away.'

She ran out of the office and up the street. It took her less than five minutes to buy Levis, a flannel shirt, a belt, a boy's pair of boots, and sombrero, and not more than two more to slip them on in the office of the merchant. At the livery stable she found a horse and saddle. As she rode down the street to the office of the doctor she saw men watching her in surprise. They had seen her a short time before in a trim fashionable dress, one that could not have been bought in any Sundog store. Now she was in a man's outfit ready for the brush. They were thinking, she guessed, that there was no telling what this crazy girl would do.

Eleanor tied the horse and put her head in the door. She called to the doctor, 'Miss Nightingale reporting for service, General.'

Gruffly he barked, 'I expect I'm a fool for letting you go.'

'That's what they thought about taking Florence the other time,' she retorted.

Though she counted herself a good rider, Eleanor was saddle-weary long before they reached the gateway to the Gap. Mile after mile, hour after hour, the horses plodded over the rough trail. But the girl did not let her companion know how heavy were her shoulders. When he inquired once whether she was tired she flung back the chipper response, 'We've hardly started yet.'

Night fell long before they came to the pass. They rode through it and looked down on the dark churned land below. Seneca swung stiffly down from the saddle. He tied the horses to bushes.

'Where away now?' she asked as she followed him to the ground.

'Nowhere yet,' he groaned, and sank into a bed of moss beside a boulder. 'We wait till a guide comes to get us.' He looked at her with rueful admiration. 'You must be made of iron.'

She did not mention how stiff and sore and exhausted the ride had made her. This did not matter. Her anxious thoughts were full of the peril so close to the two men she loved. Her imagination churned up pictures of their plight, all of them with the sound of roaring guns in the background.

'You'd better try to sleep,' Seneca advised. 'It may be hours before we have a chance to start.'

'I couldn't sleep,' she told him. 'I'm so dreadfully worried.'

'Anyhow lie down and rest.'

To please him she lay down in the moss, face to the stars so many million miles away. Her eyes began to droop. Inside of five minutes she was sound asleep.

Doctor Seneca tucked a blanket around her. Looking down at her gracious body and charming face, he had a moment of poignant regret for his own lost youth. She would suffer and know grief, but she would live abundantly.

CHAPTER XXIX

Reynolds reports

The cove in which the Reynolds party was trapped narrowed at the mouth. Austin saw at once that any attacking party coming through the jaws of the pocket would be exposed to a flanking fire from the aspen grove and the boulders at the foot of the cliff. He and his party were caught. There was no way out except by the one through which they had entered. But though escape had been cut off, their position was such that it would be very difficult to dislodge them without heavy loss.

He stationed two men in the aspens with orders not to fire unless absolutely necessary, and if forced to do so to shift position afterward as soon as possible. Others he placed where they could command a view of the entrance. Austin did not believe the outlaws would try a frontal attack, but he intended to be prepared for the possibility.

The weakness of the defenders was that they had very little food and could expect no help from outside. All Clemson had to do was to sit tight and starve them out. Since he was both shrewd and cautious, that was what he would probably do. There would be no profit in getting half a dozen of his own men killed.

Between the rock wall and a huge slab of granite at the foot of the precipice ran a narrow gallery. Here Reynolds attended to the wound of Christy. The manager of the Blue Bell had been shot in the side. Fortunately the wound was not a deep one. Austin washed it with water from a canteen and bound it up with a piece of a shirt. He knew that Christy was going to have an unpleasant time, but that could not be helped. Before the rest of them got out of this difficulty—if they ever did—the injury to Christy might seem to them all a very minor casualty.

Reynolds could not see any way of escape for his men. In a semicircle around the cove mouth a dozen sharpshooters would lie back of cover and wait for them. If in the darkness of night two or three of his party managed to slip past the cordon, they would be little better off. All they could do would be to wander about the Gap for days and in the end very likely be picked off like hunted coyotes.

'We might be worse off,' he said cheerfully to those within hearing.

'Will you tell me how?' growled Cross. 'We're trapped rats, with no water and very little grub.'

'For the present we're safe. They can snipe at us, but they daren't attack in force.'

'They don't have to come in after us,' a cowboy answered. 'All they got to do is stick around and wait till we starve.'

'Unless we rush them in the night,' Delavan suggested.

Reynolds shook his head. 'Not unless we have to do that. Those of us that got through would be separated. They would have a tough time getting out of the Gap.'

'I doubt if any would get out,' Oldfield said. 'They would skulk around in the hills till the rustlers bumped into them.'

'So we starve,' Manson contributed acidly. 'Well, they say that's an easy way to die—after the first week or so.'

'We're not talking about dying,' Reynolds snapped gruffly. 'One way or another we'll get out of here.'

'Fine,' jeered Cross. 'Tell us how.'

'I don't know how yet.' Reynolds looked at him with cold scorn. 'But ten able-bodied men armed with rifles aren't going to lie down and quit like sick cats, are they?'

'No. I vote with Delavan. Let's bust through them.'

'We may have to do so in the end, but not yet,' Oldfield disagreed. 'News of this is going to spread. Our friends outside will get busy. Time will work for us.'

'What makes you think news of it will get out?' Manson wanted to know. 'Cad is no fool. He'll play his hand close till he's raked in the chips.'

'He can't control all of the wild desperate

fellows in the Gap. Some one of them is going to want to celebrate having got us holed up here. He will race off to Sundog to brag about it and to drink. Inside of twenty-four hours everybody in the town will know about us. Our friends won't sit still and take it without making a move.'

Oldfield talked confidently. He wished he felt as sure of his prediction as his words sounded, but in any case it did no harm to bluff. He suspected some of the men were feeling very downhearted, and it was up to him to help Reynolds build up their confidence.

'Yore idea is that the Association will send a regiment with a brass band up here,' jeered Manson. 'Nothing to it. We're stuck, unless we can fight our way out.'

To huddle behind rocks and broil in the hot sun was not Reynolds's conception of a pleasant afternoon, especially with occasional bullets pinging past him and spattering fragments of rock from the face of the wall. He could think of a good many places where he would rather be. But until night they had to stick it where they were without moving about too much.

There was not cover enough to keep all the animals out of sight. A slug struck a horse and sent it screaming through the aspens. Half an hour later the roan Christy had been riding was killed. One of the men stationed in the young grove slipped back to report a flesh wound in the calf of his leg. The prospect before the defenders was grim enough to discourage the hardiest.

It took the sun an interminable time to travel down the long inverted sky bowl and disappear behind the range in a blaze of splendid color. The glow died out of the hill crotches and darkness crept over the land.

In the gallery back of the upended granite slab a fire was built of brushwood to cook the rest of the deer. They had no water except that left in the canteens. Reynolds rationed both this and the food.

While they ate, a council of war was held. It was important, Reynolds said, to find out the disposition of the enemy. There was a chance that most of the outlaws had left, content with the damage they had already done. Most of them were thieves but not murderers. They would not want to exterminate this whole party, though pressure from Clemson and others might drive them toward that. Austin proposed that one of them slip out of the pocket and discover what he could.

'Fine,' Cross agreed ironically. 'Who's yore choice to go? After he reaches the mouth he wouldn't get any farther than you could throw a bull by the tail. He'd be picked off sure. When we go out we've got all to pile out together.'

Several volunteered to make the scout. Reynolds rejected all offers. He was going himself, he insisted, adding casually that Cross was greatly overestimating the danger.

He carried a revolver in his belt but no rifle. Within a half-hour or perhaps a little longer he would be back, he promised. If he did not return, no search was to be made for him.

Reynolds vanished among the aspens. He worked from the grove into the boulder quarry that had crashed down from the rock wall above at the mouth of the pocket. Taking what cover he could, he crept out from the rocks and turned sharply to the right along the hill shoulder. His advance was very slow, since he scanned every clump of sage before starting for each new base. That a cordon of sentries had been placed to guard the exit he had no doubt. It would not do to be seen by any one of them.

He had been in Cuba with Roosevelt's Rough Riders and had learned how to worm his way through brush with a minimum of sound. The snapping of a twig might betray him. By this time the stars were coming out. A sentry might catch sight of him, an unrecognized moving body, and therefore a suspicious object to be stopped with a bullet.

From where he lay he could see the two campfires of the outlaws. That probably meant a considerable force. Most of the men would be resting at one or the other of these. The remainder were no doubt scattered along the hill to prevent a surprise attack or to check an attempt on the part of the defenders to escape during the night.

Reynolds followed a small draw, creeping forward on his hands and knees. To him there came the sound of a voice, from the lip of the little basin to his left. One sentry was hailing another. The men converged toward him. They stopped not ten feet below the clump of brush behind which he crouched. Fortunately the moon was momentarily back of a cloud.

The men took up a subject that had already apparently been under debate. The hidden listener recognized the first speaker's voice. The man was Allan Dunn.

'I'm not gonna stand for it, Buck—wiping out this whole bunch. Cad isn't czar of the Gap. He can't tell me what to do and what not to do. We've done got Hack and Brock and Morgan, all of them bad men who are better dead, all enemies of ours from where they laid the chunk.'

'That's so,' agreed the other man. 'Seems kinda rough to me to wipe 'em all out. But some of those left are just as bad as the ones we got. Take Cross, now. And Reynolds. He put me in the pen when he was sheriff.'

'Suits me. You can have Cross. That's fair. He hanged Dagwell. We'll see how he likes it himself. And I won't make any fight for Reynolds either. He rode us damned hard when he was on top. But no more. I've talked with some of the other boys. They feel that way too.'

'How do you figure on gettin' the ones you want and not the rest?' Buck asked.

'Starve 'em out. They'll ask for terms. We've got them where the wool is short.'

'Maybe so. Time our relief showed up. My belly is flat as a pair of chaps hangin' on the wall. I'm ready for grub.'

The pickets drifted apart, each turning back along the way he had come. Reynolds had picked up more information than he had expected to get. He retraced his steps, still traveling with the greatest care. When he reached the boulder quarry the tension relaxed. He passed from it to the aspens and rejoined his companions.

Cross was the first man who saw him. 'Thought you might have made up yore mind to keep on going,' the owner of the Bar A B said with sour impudence.

There never had been any love lost between the two men. Reynolds looked steadily at him and passed without answering. Those not on guard duty gathered to hear the report of his scout.

He told them how he had worked down the draw and encountered the rustler sentries, the men so near to him that with a fishing rod he could have touched them.

'Learn anything worth while from them?' Oldfield asked.

'One of them was Allan Dunn. He called the

other Buck. I don't know him. Cad Clemson wants us all wiped out. Dunn says he won't stand for that. Evidently some of the others are with him. When it comes to a showdown I don't think they will let Cad have his way.'

'Good!' Manson cried. 'All we got to do is fix up some agreement with them.'

'I think that could be arranged,' Reynolds agreed quietly. 'But there is a catch to it. Dunn and this fellow Buck both said that two of us would have to be rubbed out.'

'Which two?' Cross demanded.

Reynolds let his gaze rest on the Bar A B man. 'You for one, because of what you did to Dave Dagwell.'

Cross ripped out an angry oath. 'I knew that's what you were going to say—and I don't believe a word of it. You're trying to frame me. Ever since you came to this country you've been against me. I'm just a plain dust-eating cowman, not good enough for a high and mighty gentleman like you. But by cripes, you can't sell me out. I'll pump lead into yore belly first.'

Delavan's close-set eyes fastened on Cross. 'Reynolds hasn't offered to sell you out yet far as I've heard. But I'll say this, since you're asking for it. We don't owe you a damn bit of loyalty. You got us in this jam. Nothing would suit you but we had to come up and clean out some of these birds that roost here. And after that you had to get smart and let the scoundrels know we were here. You threw us all down. Why shouldn't we give you up to them?'

'Not so fast, boys,' Oldfield interrupted. 'We're all in this together. It doesn't matter who was to blame. We're not going to turn anybody over to these bandits. And now, first off, let Austin finish his story.'

'Just so it's understood I don't believe a word of it,' Cross flung out harshly.

'Who is the other fellow they claimed they would have to bump off?' Manson asked.

On Reynolds's face there was a thin grim smile. 'I'm the other one.'

There was a moment of blank silence. The cowboy who had been shot in the leg broke it with a totally inadequate comment.

'Well, I'll be jiggered!' he said.

'I reckon you believe him now, Jack,' Manson snapped, his black beady eyes on Cross, a gleam of malice in them.

'What's the difference? Maybe he wants to be sold down the river, but I don't. And I'm not going to be either.'

'Neither of you are,' Oldfield told him bluntly. 'We'll play this hand out together, like we started to do. We're not going to turn yellow just because we bumped into a little hard luck. To hell with that kind of an offer, if they ever make it.'

Delavan justified himself. 'I didn't mean I

wanted to turn Cross over to these fellows, but I'm tired of hearing him shoot off his mouth after the play he made.'

'Point of fact,' Oldfield explained, 'it's good news that Austin brought back.' He elaborated the statement. 'There's a split among the outlaws. Cad isn't going to have this all his own way. Dunn is a tough game rooster, bullheaded as a government mule. He'll take a lot of these scamps with him. Only a pretty thorough devil wants to wipe out a whole bunch of men even if he doesn't like them. Most of the Rustlers' Gap fellows are just wild cowboys gone bad. The only killing they could stomach would be that done in a fight. They would draw the line at a massacre.'

Two or three of the others nodded agreement with this. They judged the rustlers by themselves. A killing in cold blood shook the nerve of those doing it almost as much as it did that of the victim.

Reynolds knew that Oldfield had put his finger on a truth. If these outlaws made a clean sweep of them, it would have to be in the heat of battle. For the men who lived in Rustlers' Gap—or most of them, at least—were not essentially different from the cattlemen who were such sticklers for the established order. A good many of the ranchmen too had lived elemental lives, had walked along the narrow line which separates the honest man from the rogue. They had known raw and violent moments, yet they lived by a code that was funda-mentally decent; and this same code, even though warped to strange and evil shapes, dominated the lives of many of those who followed fugitive trails outside the law.

In spite of which, he knew that Cross and he would be considered in a class by themselves. Their lives would be held forfeit.

CHAPTER XXX

At Lonesome Valley Ranch

As they headed into the higher hills Neal talked over with his companions the problem that confronted them. To rush in and attempt a rescue would be fatal. They would either be taken prisoners or exterminated. The occasion was one that called for finesse combined with audacity. No success was possible unless they could pull off a *coup* that would give them something with which to trade. If they could capture Cad Clemson, a deal might be worked out. This was a forlorn hope, but they had to back a long shot or nothing.

The chance of surprising Clemson had been lessened by the failure of the cattlemen's raid. It must have given him a scare to know that he might have been rounded up by them except for the folly of some of the invaders' allowing themselves to be seen.

Miller could give them no assurance as to where Clemson might be found. He might be with the besieging party, in which case there would be practically no chance of seizing him. But as Neal judged his character he was more likely to be in the background, close enough for consultation but not actually in the camp of the attackers. Cad always tried to play as safe as he could in his nefarious undertakings. He would reason shrewdly that it would be wise to let others do the violence his shrugs and hints stimulated.

Young Miller's guess was that the old fox might still be at the Lonesome Valley Ranch. It was his favorite stopping place, the point where most of the stolen stock was driven for concealment and rebranding before pushing it on to a market in Montana or Idaho.

'We'll be lucky if we find him there,' Neal said.

'Maybe we'll be luckier if we don't,' Driskill chuckled.

That might be true, Neal thought, and knew it was in the minds of the others too. A burst of gunfire might mow them down. For a moment his heart failed him. He ought not to ask these men to follow him into such a wild adventure, even though they were willing to go wherever he might lead.

In single file they rode into the Gap through the boulder-strewn pass, after listening for long minutes at the mouth for any sound that might tell them the defile was guarded. They passed deep into it, fear catching at their throats. Not until they were moving out of its shadowy depths did any of them utter a word.

Tim mopped his moist forehead with a handkerchief and laughed with relief. That hundred yards, with the chance of death at every step, had shaken him.

'Remember the last time we went through, Neal?' he asked in a low voice just a little jumpy.

Neal smiled. A pulse of excitement was beating in his throat. 'With bullets whistling at us,' he mentioned.

Breakneck Trail lay before them, along a precipice which fell away to a black gulf of space that showed no bottom. They could have had no better guide than young Miller. He led them down the ledge, warning them now and again of tricky bits where the path of rubble sloped outward or narrow turns came out of the darkness unexpectedly. At the foot of the steep declivity he swung sharply to the left and took them along a hill shoulder from which they dropped to a box cañon with walls sheer and close.

Miller had lived two years in the Gap and he knew its fastnesses as a cattleman does his range. He led them into gorges through which streams tore down furiously, and he took them up stiff ascents into wooded parks dropping to narrow trails winding along draws issuing into other gulches. The horsemen depended on their guide absolutely. Without him they would have been completely lost. But he never hesitated. When he stopped it was to breathe the mounts.

By the light of the moon Neal read the face of his watch. The time was half-past two.

'Not far now,' Miller assured him. The young man's voice was dry, his throat parched. He knew what a dangerous game he was playing. If he was captured by the outlaws, he was doomed. There was a slender chance the others might be allowed to escape, but there would be no mercy for a traitor. He did not know why he had dared ride out to warn the friends of the cattlemen, unless it was because Cad Clemson's slimy cruelty had sickened him. Another reason had moved him— his deep gratitude to Neal MacGowan for saving his life. He had promised Neal to turn his back on lawlessness. It was a pledge he had meant to keep. But when Allan Dunn arranged the jail break, with the pursuit hard on his heels, he knew of no place of safety for him except Rustlers' Gap. It had been his intention to slip away from there as soon as he dared. The trapping of the cowmen brought his determination to the point of action. It was too late for him to turn back now.

Deep within him he was glad of it. He might be going to his death. But he was riding beside honest men. He had turned his back forever on the crooked trails that had led him into evil ways.

From the rock ridge that formed the near lip of the park they looked down into Lonesome Valley. Even in the moonlight no details were clear, but even in the blur of darkness they could make out that the floor was rough and uneven. This was no gentle meadow, but a park of ragged scarps, scarred gorges, and pine forests marching up the hills to the enclosing boundaries.

Miller led them along the ridge to a wooded point from which they dropped down to the ranch. The silvery light showed the place asleep, apparently peaceful as old age. There were the usual log house and cluttered out buildings. What differentiated it from the usual hill nester's home were the large corrals. There were three of them instead of one.

'I wonder how many K-B cattle and horses have been driven into those corrals,' Neal said.

'Not so many,' Miller replied. 'There was a sort of understanding among us to leave yore stuff alone because you stood up to the big outfits for the small man. Once in a while the boys picked up a K-B animal, but it was kinda by chance mostly.'

An unseen dog began to howl mournfully.

'Just exercising his lungs,' Driskill said. 'He can't know we're here.'

'His bark would be more vicious if he did,' Owen agreed. 'But he'll know soon as we get closer.'

'Unless Russ rides up alone and takes the curse off,' Driskill suggested.

Miller sat his saddle in a heavy silence. He knew the others were waiting for his answer. 'I don't reckon I can do that,' he replied at last. 'I'm through with Cad. I brought you here. The rest is up to you. I can't betray him cold, and

that's what I'd be doing if I held him unsus-
pecting in talk while you fellows rushed him.'

'We don't intend to kill Cad or anybody else,'
Neal mentioned quietly. 'If there's any shooting
done, his side will start it.'

'About a dozen men's lives hanging on this,'
Driskill murmured.

'Including one mighty important to me,'
chipped in Tim.

'I've been a pretty wild coot,' the rustler
admitted unhappily, 'but I haven't ever sold my
saddle yet.'

'Would you be selling yore saddle, Russ?'
asked Neal. 'Look at it this way. Cad is a bad
man and a killer. Right now he is contriving the
death of a lot of decent citizens. All four of us
are risking our lives to stop it if we can. To kill
Cad would ruin our plan. All we want to do is to
take him prisoner. Your job is the most dangerous
because he is liable to be suspicious of you for
not having been around all day. If this attempt
goes wrong, you're done for.'

'All right. I'll try it. How am I to explain
showing up at this time of night?'

'Better tell him Reynolds's party have hoisted
a white flag and want to surrender. Say Dunn
thinks Cad had better come to the camp right
away.'

They agreed on details of the plan and Miller
rode forward.

CHAPTER XXXI

The battle in the stable

As Russ Miller approached the house the hound broke into angry and noisy protest, but while he dismounted the dog leaped up joyfully in affectionate greeting. Before the door was opened a voice demanded roughly, 'Who's there?'

After Miller had given his name a man stepped out, revolver in hand. He was a short bowlegged, barrel-chested fellow with flinty eyes, and one of his unshaven cheeks showed a long scar where a bullet had ripped along it.

'The old man has been lookin' for you all day,' he grunted, the rasp of a file in his speech. 'He'll give you billy-be-damn, you chump.'

'Great Jehoshaphat, Tuck, I got to do as I'm told,' complained Miller. 'The old man has got no call to jump me. I'll tell him so. Is he up?'

The young man passed into the house. Tuck followed him, after he had bolted the door. Cad Clemson came out of a bedroom carrying a small coal-oil lamp in the left hand and a Colt's six-shooter in the right.

'What in Tophet kept you away?' he snapped, putting the lamp on a table. 'And why do you have to come waking us up in the middle of the night?'

Miller flared up resentfully. 'Why, I been up there with the boys pluggin' the cork into that pocket where we got the Reynolds crowd trapped. Ain't that where every guy that can shoot a gun ought to be?'

'I didn't see you there while I was with them.'

'Well, I was there, till Dunn sent me on a scout to see there wasn't any more of those birds coming along.'

'Dunn didn't say anything to me about that,' Clemson retorted suspiciously.

'There's quite a lot he don't tell you,' Miller sneered. 'Onct in a while he likes to be wagon boss himself, I've noticed.'

'So that's it, is it?' There was anger in the lame man's sly evil face. 'If he wants a showdown he'll find out who runs the Gap.'

'I dunno as he does. Point is, Allan is quite a he-man. As to why I come waking you up, it's because Reynolds sent a fellow out offering to surrender if he and his men would be allowed to march away safe.'

The eyes in the ratlike face of Clemson quickened with life. 'Did Dunn fall for that?' he demanded.

'The boys are having a pow-wow. I didn't wait to find out what they decided, but slipped away and rode here hell-for-leather to let you know. And all I get for it is to be bawled out.'

A fourth man walked into the room—the

outlaw Purdy who had been pistolwhipped by MacGowan on the day of Blackburn's death.

'What's all the shootin' about?' he wanted to know.

'Reynolds wants to make a deal to leave the Gap with his men, and Dunn would be just fool enough to let him,' Clemson yelped. 'You stay here, Tuck. The rest of us will saddle up and see about that.'

'Why not wait till morning?' Purdy protested.

'Because it may be too late, then. We've got these lunkheads where we want 'em, and I don't mean to let them get away. Russ, you slap saddles on Two Bits and Blackie while Purdy and I get dressed.'

There had been moments during the past three minutes when the pit of Miller's stomach had gone icy cold. Now he breathed again as Clemson limped from the room with Purdy at his heels.

'Better come help me saddle,' he said to Tuck.

'Might as well,' the bandylegged man said. 'I won't get any more sleep tonight anyhow. The old man doesn't trust Dunn much, does he?'

'Allan has got a lot of bull in his neck. He likes his own way. Cad wants to run the whole show.'

The two walked to the barn, caught the horses, and led them to the stable. As they saddled, a man appeared at the head of the stairs leading to the loft.

'Anything doing, boys?' he asked sleepily.

'The old man has heard Reynolds wants to throw in his hand and he aims to sit at the table when the pot is raked in,' Tuck explained. 'So he's lighting out for the camp now.'

The querulous voice of Clemson announced that he and Purdy were approaching. Cad limped out of the darkness, a step or two behind the other man.

'Those horses ready?' he asked unpleasantly.

'All ready,' Miller answered.

At the sound of a crisp command the outlaws froze in their tracks. It came out of the black night unexpectedly.

'Throw up yore hands,' Neal ordered harshly. 'We have you covered.'

He moved forward from the shadowy darkness of a stall. Owen and Driskill showed themselves at the same time. All three carried revolvers ready for action.

Purdy ripped out an oath. 'It's that damned meddler again,' he cried.

'Get yore hands up,' Neal repeated, and watched the man closely. Purdy had made him trouble once before. He did not want him to start anything again.

Clemson slanted a sly anxious glance round him. Miller had betrayed him. He was sure of that. No use trying to put up a fight, not with the guns of three men trained on them. His loose lips trembled. Fear choked up in his throat. Did they mean to kill him? If so, why had they not blasted away without warning?

'Let's not go off half-cocked, boys,' he pleaded. 'Neal means to be reasonable, I reckon. He's got nothing against us. We'll talk this over.'

He raised his arms. Those of Purdy and Tuck went up reluctantly, but the narrowed hate-filled eyes in the vice-ridden face of Purdy held fast to MacGowan.

'Disarm them, Tim,' Neal commanded. 'And you fellow on the stairs come down reaching for the ceiling.'

'Now, looky here,' Clemson protested, his voice unctuous with false heartiness. 'We always been friends, you and we'uns. Together we've stood against the big outfits when they were crowding the poor folks. There's no call for a play like this. Let's all sit down over a drink and fix things up. It'll be the way you want.'

'We're not going to hurt any of you,' Neal explained. 'You're as safe as a lot of old ladies in a church—if you don't start trouble. You on the stairs, come down and join the party. I reckon we'll collect the artillery to prevent any mis-understanding later. Begin with Purdy, Tim.'

Owen moved forward to gather the guns. The man on the stairs came down another step and stopped. From his revolver flame darted. The knees of Tim buckled and he staggered against a grain bin. Together the forty-fives of Driskill and MacGowan blazed. Head first, the outlaw above plunged down. His huddled body lay lax at the foot of the ladder.

In the narrow lane below the guns roared. Men closed with each other, too near for pumping lead. Fists drove out into furious faces, the barrels of revolvers crashed on unprotected heads. Oaths, shouts, a scream of pain. Bodies clung one to another, writhing and straining in the darkness.

Neal discovered that he was struggling with Purdy. They went down and rolled over, still fighting, each trying for the moment's advantage that would clinch the victory. The outlaw clung to his revolver, trying desperately for a shot into the belly of the man he hated. Neal dropped his sixshooter, to have two free hands. One of them fastened vicelike on the hairy wrist of the bandit, his arm extended straight to keep the other's elbow from bending. The fingers of Neal's left hand groped for Purdy's throat.

The man's gun flung a bullet into the woodwork of the stall. Another seared Neal's forehead. He felt blood streaming down into his eyes. In the savage battle for mastery the gunman had heaved himself half-free long enough to fire the shot.

Neal had been trying to knock the man out and save his life. He gave up that thought now. One of them had to die. He knew that if his enemy could get that arm free for a fraction of a second, he was lost. His strong fingers closed on Purdy's wind-pipe. The fellow thrashed and strained violently, almost broke loose. With a terrific effort the pistol arm crooked at the elbow, wavered up toward Neal's head.

MacGowan deflected it, drove the barrel of the weapon down against the temple of his foe. His right hand left Purdy's throat and made contact with the fingers of the outlaw clutching the revolver. A moment later a shot rang out. Neal rose from the other's body, breathless, blinded, sick. Purdy lay still, a bullet through his brain.

Hazily there came to Neal the sound of pounding hoofs. The voice of Driskill called his name. He heard himself answer, in a voice he did not recognize as his own.

'Russ and I have got Cad!' Driskill cried. 'You all right?'

'I reckon so. Purdy is dead.'

Miller lit the stable lantern and hung it on a nail.

'Tuck has done lit out,' he said.

'Boys, this wasn't any of my doing,' Clemson whined. 'No need of any of this shootin' a-tall.'

Neal moved inside of the circle of light.

'You're wounded!' Driskill cried. His own face was bruised, his cheek slashed open, and his lips cut.

With his bandanna Neal brushed away the blood pouring down through his eyebrows. 'Yes. Not too bad, I reckon. If you and Russ are all right we'd better look after Tim.'

Tim Owen lay crumpled on the dirt floor beside the dead man who had shot him from the stairs.

'I think poor Tim is gone,' Miller said. The youngster's face was chalk-white. He had never before been in such a packed zone of death. In the mêlée his thumb had been bitten almost to the bone.

Neal knelt beside his rider and felt the young man's heart. Tim opened his eyes and spoke feebly. 'I ain't either dead,' he feebly denied, 'and I don't aim to die for quite a spell of years.'

It might be true, but Neal knew he was badly hurt. He had been shot through the chest. They did what they could for him, after which they carried him to the house and put him on Clemson's bed.

The two dead outlaws they left in the stable. Clemson they carefully secured hand and foot, tying him to a bunk.

Driskill washed Neal's head and bound a clean towel around it.

Briefly the three men consulted as to what was best to do.

'First off, we need a doctor for Tim,' Neal said. 'Russ, you slap a saddle on a fresh horse and get Doc Seneca. He may be headin' for the Gap, or you may have to ride all the way to Sundog. But bring him, wherever he is. If you meet anybody outside spread the news of how things are. The more that know it the better.'

'We don't have to send word to Allan Dunn and his bunch that we are holding Cad,' Driskill mentioned. 'Tuck is hotfootin' it to his camp to tell him.'

'That's right. We may have to stand a siege. For we have to stay here. Tim can't be moved.' Neal turned to the young rustler. 'It's up to you, Russ. No matter whether you kill the bronc. Get Doc here quick as you can.'

Five minutes later Miller was on his way.

Driskill turned to his friend, a wry indomitable grin on his face. 'We're gonna have a right lively time when that b'ilin' of outlaws come stampedin' down here. I reckon mebbe we'd ought to have sent for about three–four doctors.'

Neal found he could not play up to Pete's reckless defiance of fate, not with Tim Owen's life slowly ebbing away.

CHAPTER XXXII

The rustlers offer terms

The cattlemen trapped in the cove found the second day interminable. A few shots were fired, probably to warn them that they were still cut off from escape, but no attempt was made to storm their position. There had been no casualties. Evidently the plan was to starve them into surrender.

Reynolds knew that it was likely to succeed. The remainder of the deer they had shot had been devoured. About half a canteen of water remained, which he had set aside for the wounded. When he looked into the eyes of his men's haggard faces he could see they were near the breaking point.

In the late afternoon a man approached the entrance of the pocket waving a white shirt. Reynolds, Oldfield, and Manson went out to meet him. The envoy was Allan Dunn.

On his harsh sardonic face was a mocking smile. 'Hope you are enjoying yore little trip into the mountains, gents,' he said.

'Talk turkey, Dunn,' advised Reynolds curtly. 'If you've got a proposition to make let's hear it.'

The lank rustler met the cattleman's cold gaze derisively. 'Yeah, I've got one. But I'm making it to the others and not to you. I reckon maybe we ought to clean out yore whole outfit. Some of us think so, but I'm not that thorough.' His gaze shifted to Oldfield. 'If you want to lay down yore arms and march out we'll take you far as the pass. From there you can slink home with yore tails between yore legs.'

'Let's get this straight,' Oldfield answered quietly. 'You're offering to let all of us go?'

'All but two. Cross and Reynolds won't be with you.'

Oldfield shook his head. 'No, Dunn. It has to be all or none of us. We came in together. We'll go out together.'

'If you go out together you'll go out as dead freight,' the rustler retorted callously. 'Cross has got to pay for what he did to Dagwell, and four or five of us have personal accounts to settle with Reynolds. Get this right. We're dictating the terms. Take 'em or leave 'em as they lay.'

'You're making a big mistake,' Oldfield argued. 'Reynolds is a friend of the Governor. His sister is visiting at his house right now. So is the President of the United States for a day or two while he is in Wyoming on this Western trip. You can't get away with any such outrage, Dunn. Inside of three days the militia would be up here combing out the Gap. Army troops from the fort might join them. You fellows wouldn't last as long as a snowball in Hades.'

'Be reasonable, Allan,' urged Manson. 'We've

lost two men already. Doesn't that satisfy you? And don't forget that you personally are in bad enough without making it worse. There's a lot of lawbreaking scored up against you.'

'For instance,' Dunn inquired ironically.

'No need to itemize,' Oldfield replied. 'You know the counts better than we do. The smart thing is for all of us to let bygones be bygones and start afresh.'

'Pity you didn't think of that before you came busting up here to rub out a bunch of us.' Dunn cut off the discussion abruptly. 'I didn't come here to join any debating society. You fellows know where we stand. When you are ready to come out on those terms we'll be waiting at the gate for you.' He backed away into the brush and disappeared over a hill.

The cattlemen walked back into the cove and reported to the others what Dunn had said. All day Reynolds had been thinking of a way to get these men out of the danger into which he had unwillingly led them. Now he made a proposal. He suggested that as soon as darkness fell he and Cross attempt to run the enemy cordon. One or both of them might escape. In any case the others could then surrender under a promise of safe-conduct from the Gap.

'We'd never make it,' Cross objected, 'and if we got out these scalawags would start hunting us soon as the others surrendered.'

Oldfield considered the proposition. 'I don't like it,' he admitted. 'We're all in this together. But maybe this is the best that can be done for all of us. It gives you two a chance and lets the rest of us out.' He added: 'Of course we would stick it here till morning so as to give you as much time for your getaway as we could.'

'Which of us would go first—Reynolds or me?' Cross wanted to know.

Reynolds offered him his choice. Promptly the Bar A B man said that he would lead off. Delavan made a suggestion. He realized that the one making the second attempt had less chance than the other, since if the leader was detected the cordon would be tightened. Why not cast lots for position?

Cross glared at him angrily. 'If you're going too you got a right to butt in,' he snarled. 'If not, you can keep yore mouth buttoned.'

'It's decided, Delavan,' said Reynolds. 'Cross first. I'll follow an hour later.'

Cross took his rifle with him as well as a forty-five. He picked as a starting time the first dark hour before the moon came up and the stars out. Most of the rustlers, he guessed, would at that time be gathered at the camps for supper. It was possible that just then the guard would be thinned down to a minimum.

After he had vanished into the aspens the others waited tensely, hoping not to hear the sound of a shot from outside. Five—ten—fifteen minutes passed.

'Looks like maybe he'll make it,' Manson said, his voice low, as if to keep the far-off enemy from hearing.

'He won't be safe for quite a while yet,' Reynolds responded. 'Worming a way through the sage and brush is a slow business.'

The sound of a shot whipped into the cove and echoed from wall to wall. A cry of warning beat in to the distressed listeners and after it two more explosions.

'I reckon they got Jack,' Delavan said.

Reynolds nodded. There was in him an urgent nervousness to start at once and get the thing over with, but he repressed it sharply. His cold set face showed no more expression than a stone wall.

He waited his hour before he rose to go.

'Luck,' a cowboy said, and Manson added, 'Here's hoping.' Nobody shook hands with him. They all wanted to keep this as casual as they could.

Oldfield picked up the rifle which he thought the Triangle R man had forgotten. Reynolds declined it. 'Makes more noise in the brush,' he explained. 'I'd rather travel light.'

'I guess you're right,' Oldfield agreed. 'In the bushes a Winchester is not a handy weapon to handle.'

Again the men in the cove waited for what seemed to them hours. No gunshot broke the stillness of the night.

'He must of made his getaway,' Christy said.

Oldfield agreed briefly. But he was not at all sure. They might have captured Reynolds without giving him a chance to fire a shot. Yet at least they could hope he had escaped.

CHAPTER XXXIII

Eleanor reaches the front

Drowsily Eleanor came out of sleep, to the murmur of voices. She opened her eyes and saw Doctor Seneca talking with a young man on horseback. The rider showed exasperation, and his words took on a sharper note.

'We got to get a jump on us, doc, or we'll be too late. Cad's men will be swarming all over the place. Don't forget for a minute that hell has broke loose in the Gap.'

'I'll leave a note telling her to wait here till Muir gets to the pass with his posse,' Eleanor heard the doctor say. 'You're right. We don't want a woman getting mixed in anything like this.'

The man on horseback said, 'What in tarnation is she doing up here anyhow?'

Seneca shrugged his shoulders. To explain Eleanor to this simple son of the saddle would take more time than he had. From a pocket he drew a pencil and a prescription pad. 'Cinch up my horse, and I'll write the note,' he told the cowboy.

'Right,' the other answered. 'Let's be hitting the trail.'

Eleanor flung the blanket from her and rose.

'Tell it to me, doctor, as we ride,' she suggested. 'I'm going with you, wherever it is you're starting for.'

The cowpuncher protested. 'Now looky here, Miss. Where we're going—'

The girl cut off his objection with curt decision. 'Doctor Seneca and I have been all over that. Let us not waste time talking.'

'This is Russ Miller,' the doctor explained. 'Neal MacGowan and his boys have been in a terrible fight and one of them is shot up badly. The rustlers are closing in on them and there is bound to be a lot more trouble. My idea is for you to stay here and tell Muir about this. This young man will be back and guide you.'

'Give me that pad and pencil,' Eleanor said, 'and I'll tell Bob Muir to wait for Mr. Miller.'

She scribbled the note, put it on a flat rock, and weighted it down with a stone. At the muscles of her stomach she felt a weak cold sinking. Her legs were shaky. There was a question she had to ask. When she put it into words she heard a tremulous knot in her voice.

'Which of them is hurt?'

'Tim Owen,' answered Miller. 'Miss, I can't take you down into that hell broth. If you was to get hurt—'

She walked to her horse, tightened the cinch, and swung to the saddle. 'I won't get hurt. Please let us start.'

Seneca smiled, with a grimace. 'We'll be going, Russ. She is going to have her way anyhow.'

Miller still hesitated. 'Is yore horse sure-footed, Miss? Breakneck Trail is a pretty tough proposition.'

'He's all right,' she replied impatiently. 'Don't let's waste any time . . . please.'

There was no conversation till they reached the valley below. Along a hill shoulder they passed, and from it dropped to the mouth of a box cañon. Here Eleanor jogged her mount up to join their guide.

'Is Mr. MacGowan all right?' she asked. 'He wasn't hurt in the fight, was he?'

'We all got worked over considerable. A bullet skidded off his head, but he was lucky at that. It bounced off without going through his skull.'

'Tell me the whole story. From the beginning.'

'Why, there's not much to tell. I rode down and told Neal MacGowan about yore brother's party being corked up in a pocket. He figured if he could capture Cad Clemson he could swap him off for the cattlemen, in a way of speaking.' His life against theirs, y'understand. So I led him down to this Lonesome Valley Ranch where Cad hangs out. Everything was going dandy till somebody started shooting. It ended up with two of Cad's men killed, Tim Owen shot up bad, and Cad a prisoner. But a guy called Tuck got away, and o' course he lit out to tell the fellows besieging yore brother's party. By now they'll be headin' for Lonesome Valley like a swarm of bees.'

'To kill Neal MacGowan and his men?'

Miller threw up his hands. 'Lady, I don't know how this is coming out. They'll find two of their party dead in the stable. That won't please them any. But I'll say this: That ranch-house is a regular fort. It won't be easy for them to dig MacGowan and Driskill out. They're a tough pair of customers.'

They came again to a steep trail that had to be taken in single file. Eleanor fell back. She rode in silence the rest of the way, her heart heavy with dread. Bob Muir was coming with a posse. Others would follow. There would be battles and snipings in which more men would lose their lives. Some of them good decent citizens. It was all wrong.

The sun came over a crotch of the hills and flooded Lonesome Valley with a warm bright light. They could see the buildings of the ranch clustered in a draw. In Eleanor's throat a pulse of excitement beat fast. There was no sign of activity outside. Were they in time? Had they arrived before the rustlers?

'Look!'

Doctor Seneca pointed across the valley to a trail dropping down from the rim rock above. On that ledge were eight or ten small moving objects no larger than ants. Eleanor knew they were horsemen. Her heart lifted. The rustlers could not get to the ranch until long after their party.

Miller led them along the ridge to the pine-covered hill above the steading. Through the timber they advanced, dropping down to the valley. A dog in the yard barked furiously at them. In the doorway a man with a rifle waited for them to declare themselves. Their guide flung up a hand and shouted, 'Hi yi, Pete!'

The man with the Winchester turned and called to somebody inside the house. 'Doc Seneca here,' he announced.

A wave of heat foamed up in Eleanor's breast. For Neal MacGowan had joined Driskill. A bloodstained towel was tied around his head, but he came to meet them with the same light rhythmic tread she had loved from their first meeting.

His amazed eyes were on the girl, though his first words were for Miller. 'Russ, take Doc Seneca in to Tim.'

The doctor dismounted wearily and followed the young rustler into the house. Over his shoulder he snapped, 'I'll be doggoned if I spend my life in a saddle riding to patch up men you fellows shoot so fast I can't get any sleep.'

To Eleanor her lover said, 'What are you doing here?'

She answered, a sob in her voice, 'I couldn't stay away, Neal.'

So pathetically weary did she look, hanging to

the saddlehorn with both hands, so slender and young and troubled, that his critical stiffness relaxed. He lifted her to the ground, and she went into his arms as a homing dove does to its nest. For the past twenty hours fear had been riding her hard. Now she had found him alive, and the reaction set in. She broke down and wept, clinging to him as if she could not bear to let him go.

'Oh Neal—Neal!' she cried. 'It's been so dreadful. I was afraid that—I thought—'

He held her close, petting her, kissing her soft disordered hair, laughing at her fears.

Pete Driskill returned from stabling the horses. 'Not wanting to butt in on a happy reunion,' he drawled with some embarrassment, 'I hate to mention that a passel of hurry-up gents are headin' this way to pay us a call.'

Neal looked over the shoulder of the girl. A straggling line of riders were coming down the long ledge trail into the valley. He flung a swift question at Eleanor.

'Did you hear of any relief posses coming into the Gap?'

'Bob Muir was organizing one when we left Sundog. He's probably at the pass now waiting for a guide.'

'Get Miller into the saddle again, Pete. That boy has been on a bronc's back without any rest for a full day and night, but he has to get back to the pass and bring here any posse he finds there.

Tell him to take my Keno.' Neal's voice was brisk and decisive. 'And tell him to get a hump on him or his rustler friends will cut him off before he gets started.'

Driskill saddled while Miller slapped together some bread and meat sandwiches. He would have liked a cup of strong coffee, but there was no time for that. As it was, he ran his departure fine. He had scarcely reached the pines before the first of the outlaws drew up three hundred yards from the house to wait for the others.

'What are we going to do?' Eleanor asked. It was curious, but she was no longer afraid. She and Neal were together. Nothing could hurt them now.

'We're going to hold the fort if we have to do it. But we have another shot in our locker first. I'm going to make it plain to the enemy that if they did manage to break in Cad Clemson would be defunct.'

She looked at him, startled. 'Do you mean you would—?'

'We'll cross that bridge when we come to it.'

He pushed heavy bars into their sockets to bolt the door. Thick shutters had been fastened over the windows. The house walls were of log. Small loopholes had been bored at convenient intervals through which riflemen could fire at an approaching enemy. The ranch-house had been built to stand a siege if necessary.

Neal left Driskill to watch the foe while he and

Eleanor went into the room where Tim Owen was lying. The cowboy grinned at the young woman feebly and apologetically.

She said, 'I've come to nurse you, Tim.'

'That's what he's going to need,' Seneca told her. 'Good nursing will fix him. The bullet went through his shoulder and missed the lung. A piece of luck for him. He'll have considerable fever, but in a month he'll be as good as new.' The doctor grunted a sour admission. 'Never did see the like of these cowpokes. You can't kill them with bullets. I've seen one riddled in six places and then get well.'

'That's fine, doc,' Neal said, tremendously relieved. 'Fix him up good and send the bill to the K-B Ranch.'

MacGowan walked into the next room. Cad Clemson lay tied on a cot. 'You'll be glad to know,' Neal told him, 'that you won't need to worry after the next hour or so. Yore boys are here making us a nice neighborly call. Inside of a reasonable time you'll either be ready for a wooden box or you'll be giving them hell for botching up this job.'

'I could fix this up in two shakes of a cow's tail if you would let me talk with them,' Clemson pleaded. 'No use starting any more shooting. We've always been friends.' His voice fell into an oily persuasive whine. 'I'm a peaceable citizen, not lookin' for any trouble. You an' me can settle this right here, then I can go out and lay the law down to these wild coots outside.'

'If I need you I'll let you know,' Neal answered, his words falling cold as the wind sweeping a glacier. 'You're a hostage, Clemson. Get this one thing in yore head. If that bunch of outlaws ever break in here they will find you dead. I may let you talk with some of them. In that case back my play, no matter what it is. You'll be talking for yore life as well as ours.'

From the front door Pete Driskill shouted back to Neal. 'Guy coming forward making peace signs. I believe it's Allan Dunn.'

MacGowan joined his friend and looked through the peekhole.

CHAPTER XXXIV

A peace treaty discussed

Dunn was moving toward the house, waving a red bandanna handkerchief. He carried no rifle. His revolver belt he had discarded. About sixty yards back of him Neal caught a glint of sunlight from the barrel of a Winchester. It was in the hands of a sharpshooter crouched back of a cottonwood. Two other men were skirting the edge of the valley, evidently with intent to get back of the ranchhouse to the shelter of the stable.

'Want to have a pow-wow with you, Neal,' shouted Dunn.

'Good enough,' MacGowan called back through the peekhole. 'And yore friends sneaking back to get in our rear—what do they want?'

Dunn waved back the two outlaws. 'Stay where you're at, boys,' he told them. 'Don't get so damn anxious.'

'Do we talk through the door or let Allan in?' Driskill asked.

'Let him in, but keep yore eyes on him every second. I don't think he is here to make trouble now.'

Pete unbarred the door. 'Come right in to our hacienda,' he said with a grin. 'Sure swell to have you drap in this lovely mornin'. With so many of yore friends too. We got a nice place here, and we're always pleased to welcome visitors suitably. You an' me haven't had a good visit since we busted up the dance at Peterson's. Lemme see. That musta been six years ago come Christmas. Time sure does fly.'

The lank saturnine rustler did not answer Driskill's ironic cheerfulness in the same spirit. He looked at Pete, then at Neal, and said sourly, 'You fellows have got yourselves in a hell of a tight.'

Neal adopted the light-hearted gaiety of Driskill. It was always a good policy to let the enemy know that your morale was of the best. 'News to us,' he replied. 'We're forted up in a place built for a siege, kindness of Cad Clemson, with plenty of provisions and ammunition. There's a well in the house. And we have our own personal doctor to look after us if any of us catch the measles or any other little sickness. For quite a while I've promised myself a nice vacation. I mean to enjoy this one.'

'What personal doctor?' Dunn demanded.

'Doctor Seneca. He's busy right now, but you'll meet him before you go.'

'Why did you have to come buttin' in on this, Neal?' Dunn wanted to know sourly. 'These raiding cattlemen aren't any friends of you or Pete. They have treated you like you were the scum of the earth. Reynolds and Cross brought them up here to rub out a bunch of us. What business is it of yours that they got in a jam?'

'Don't you see, Allan, that we came to help you fellows as much as them?' Neal said. 'If you massacred Reynolds's men troops would be up here in two days. We want to work out some kind of a truce with you.'

'I hear you killed Folsom. That was a fine way to help us.'

Neal thought it just as well to let him face the full facts at once. 'Folsom and Purdy both. Cad is our prisoner. Not our fault. We had them covered. We told them they were quite safe, that we didn't mean to harm them. Folsom went crazy and started shooting. Wasn't that how Tuck told it to you?'

'The boys won't listen to any such story.'

'Folsom shot down Tim Owen before we fired a shot.'

'Tim dead?'

'No. Wounded in the shoulder. What about Reynolds's men? Are they still holding out?'

'We starved them out. They surrendered this morning.'

Eleanor had been listening at the door of the room where Tim lay. She came down the passage now in the Levis and boots she had bought for the trip.

Dunn stared at her. 'Good God!' he exclaimed.

'Is my brother all right?' she asked.

'How did you get here?' he inquired.

'Never mind that. Answer my question. Is Austin . . . all right?'

'I don't know how he is,' Dunn told her sullenly. 'He wasn't with those who gave up.'

'You mean—?' Her question hung suspended in air.

'He slipped away during the night.'

'Left his friends to save himself?' She added, a flash of anger in her eyes, 'I don't believe it.'

'We haven't heard the whole story yet,' Neal reminded her gently. 'Dunn is holding something back.'

'You can have it, since you ask for it,' the rustler told them doggedly. 'We had the whole bunch, except a couple who had been killed, cooped up in a hill pocket. The boys made them an offer through me, to let the whole clanjamfry go with whole skins—except two. Oldfield turned the offer down. But they had no grub and no water. We had them cold. All we had to do was wait till they gave up.'

'The two exceptions?' Neal asked.

'Cross and Reynolds. After what Cross did to Dave Dagwell we didn't intend to let him go. Reynolds always had ridden us hard as he could. So he was number two.'

Neal began to see light. 'I reckon the besieged men decided that Reynolds and Cross had better try to slip out of the net before the others surrendered.'

'That was the idea.'

'And they made it?'

'Reynolds got away. We shot Cross full of holes. He bumped into two of our boys. There was a fight, and they got him.'

'Where is Reynolds?' Driskill queried.

'Yore guess is as good as mine. Wandering around in the hills somewhere, I'd say.' Explosively he added, 'If he starves it would be all right with me.'

'Do you mean that he is lost?' Eleanor questioned.

'The whole bunch of them were lost before we trapped them.'

To Neal she said in a low voice, greatly worried, 'I'll have to find him.'

'We'll set some of these posses that are pouring into the Gap to combing the hills after him,' Neal promised.

'What posses?' Dunn probed quickly.

Driskill looked at him, apparently surprised. 'What did you expect, Allan? Didn't you know there would be considerable travel of fighting men in here soon as the news got out?'

'Robert Muir is leading one party,' Eleanor put in quickly. 'And others were being outfitted when I left Sundog. The Governor is being kept in touch with the situation by wire and he will call out a company of militia if necessary.'

'To protect us against the raiders,' Dunn said ironically.

'What about the men who surrendered, Allan?' Driskill asked.

'You fellows haven't helped them any, Pete. We figured on throwing them outa the Gap and letting them go. But when Tuck reported on the trouble down here our boys saw red. They're not letting anybody go.' The lank rustler mopped his fore-head with the bandanna he had used as a flag. 'You fellows have put me in a nice hole. I'm under obligations to you both for standing back of me when I had that trouble with Brock. I'll go through with you two all the way. But my crowd will go crazy when they know you got Purdy as well as Folsom.'

'Come in and talk with Cad,' Neal suggested. 'Ask him who started the shooting here.'

He led the way into the room where Clemson lay on the bunk. The outlaws looked at each other with no friendliness. Dunn always had been a rebel against the authority of the older man.

'Looks like they got you where the wool's short, Cad,' jeered Dunn.

Clemson ignored the taunt. His mind was intent on saving himself. 'Now look here, Allan. There's been trouble enough over this business. These pesky cowmen started it, but anyhow we got to fix up a compromise. If we don't there will be war. The Gap will be overrun with soldiers and gunmen. The thing is to stop the shooting before it goes too far. Turn Reynolds's gang loose and get them out of here.'

Dunn was a hardy scoundrel, one who faced peril without fear. He looked down at Clemson contemptuously. There were tiny beads of perspiration on the man's face and his eyes were quick with fear.

'That wasn't how you talked yesterday,' he answered harshly. 'You said to wipe the whole caboodle out.'

'Forget that,' interrupted Neal. 'Today isn't yesterday. Face this thing as it stands now. Cad, tell Allan how the trouble broke here at the ranch.'

Clemson told the story, putting the blame for the shooting on Folsom.

'Got yore story down pat, haven't you?' commented Dunn scornfully.

'He's telling it the way it was,' Neal replied curtly. 'Make up your mind, Dunn. If you want war, get out there and tell yore army to start shooting. But keep this in mind: Help is on the way to us. We can stand you off till it gets here, and if you did break in Cad would be dead.'

'That last would worry me,' Dunn said with a bitter grin. 'But you don't have to sell peace to me, Neal. I'll go out and do my darndest with the boys. They are not going to attack this ranch anyhow with Miss Reynolds in it.'

'After you have told them how the situation is I'd like to come out and talk it over with them. Now is the time to stop this hate that has been boiling up for years. This ought to have knocked some sense into the heads of the smart ones on both sides.'

Dunn agreed that was true. He walked back to join those whom he had been representing. Before he reached the place where they were grouped he saw three men ride across the valley and join them. A yell of triumphant execration came to him. The one in the middle with his hands bound was Austin Reynolds.

CHAPTER XXXV

Aces in the hole

Austin Reynolds looked around on the exultant faces of a dozen men who hated him and he realized that he was doomed. Two of these outlaws he had sent to the penitentiary during his term as sheriff. Another he had wounded while resisting arrest. Several of the rustlers he had temporarily driven out of the country. Because he had been the most energetic of the cattlemen in fighting their foes he was the most hated.

'The boys found him on Wolf Creek,' Fox explained to Dunn. 'We aim to hang him to that big cottonwood.'

'What did you find out about the fight in the stable?' Tuck asked. 'How did Purdy and Clemson come out?'

'Purdy was killed—Folsom too. Cad is a prisoner. I talked with him. He says MacGowan and his boys did not want to do any shooting, but Folsom cut loose and plugged Tim Owen.' Dunn's hard eyes fastened on Tuck. 'Was that the way of it, Fred?'

Tuck nodded. 'Yeah, Folsom started the rookus. I reckon he thought they were going to bump us off.'

A dark-bearded man broke out angrily. 'That ain't the point, Allan. The K-B outfit wasn't in this row till they came bustin' up here looking for trouble. What I say is, they've done found plenty.'

Reynolds put a question to Dunn. 'MacGowan and some of his riders are in that ranch-house holding Cad Clemson a prisoner. Is that how it is?'

Dunn looked at the Triangle R man with bitter resentment. He too had his personal reason for hating Reynolds. But he gave the man a grudging admiration for his intrepid bearing. If it came to the last showdown, he would go to his death with no sign of fear in his impassive face.

'You've got it right,' the lank rustler said. 'MacGowan is roosting right there with two aces in the hole—and another one coming up.'

'What do you mean?' Fox asked. 'He has Cad, but he wouldn't dare touch him, knowing we would wipe him out if he did.'

'Don't fool yourself,' Dunn differed sharply. 'He's not worrying about what we'll do to him. That fellow never did pinch his cards. He plays 'em for all their worth. If we hurt Reynolds or any of his men you can order a coffin for Cad.'

'All right,' Tuck cut in. 'Cad is one ace. You spoke of two more.'

'The second one is that Miss Reynolds is at the ranch with him. She rode in with Doc Seneca just before we got here.'

'My sister!' the prisoner cried. 'You must be

mistaken. She is at Cheyenne visiting the Governor's daughter.'

'She's right there in that house nursing Tim Owen,' Dunn denied doggedly.

His companions stared at him, much disturbed. This was not a woman's war, and they were taken aback at finding one involved. Her presence was a complication. At least a minority of the outlaws would countenance no attack on the house with her in it.

'And the ace just being turned for MacGowan is a posse heading this way led by that Scotch fellow Muir,' Dunn continued, exasperation in his voice. 'Miller has turned on us and is leading it in. There will be several others pouring in after that. If necessary, the Governor will send the militia.'

'Neal has been loadin' you, Allan,' the bearded man said.

Dunn shook his head. 'No, Buck. The game is up. We've got to turn loose our prisoners and fix up a truce with Neal. His idea is that the cowmen have been whipped plenty. From now on they will be reasonable. We'll have to pull in our horns some too. Me, I'm drifting over to Montana.'

'We'll turn them all loose but Reynolds,' Tuck suggested. 'I won't stand for letting him go.'

'Go ahead with yore plan and hang him,' Dunn said, sarcasm heavy in his manner. 'He's the one with the drag at Cheyenne. Maybe the Governor won't do a thing about it.'

'How can we hang him with Cad in that ranch-house?' a man wanted to know irritably. 'I never did like Cad, but we can't throw him down.'

Reynolds said nothing. He felt his case was stronger if he let others argue it for him. Until Dunn came from his conference with Neal MacGowan the ranchman had been a man without hope, but now the despair was blotted out. He believed he would come through alive. At great risk to himself and his men Neal had probably saved him.

The argument went on with acrimony. It was interrupted by the waving of a towel from the ranch-house.

'They want to surrender!' Fox screamed jubilantly.

'Guess again,' Dunn corrected acidly. 'They have found out we've got Reynolds and they want to talk turkey.'

He waved a bandanna in answer to the enemy.

CHAPTER XXXVI

The fort abandoned

Neal made a tour of inspection after Dunn had left, to make sure that none of the enemy were sneaking up on the house. Eleanor went with him. She had an urgent desire to be near him, as if to remain assured that after all her dreadful fear she had really found him alive and safe. It was difficult to keep her hands from rumpling his crisp short hair, from rearranging the bandage round his head, from straying down the sleeve of his coat to the strong warm fingers. She was so wildly in love with him.

'I've been such a prig,' she confessed. 'I measured you by my little conventional yardstick and smugly found that you were wrong, and all the time you were the only one right in all this trouble. Though Austin and his group treated you so badly, you rode in at a fearful risk to try to save them. When I have time to think of it I'll be very very humble. But just now I'm too happy. Except about Austin. Ever since Janet wired me I've been so awfully afraid. I kept thinking—if I didn't get here in time—'

She choked up on that thought and left the conclusion unexpressed. He drew her close and looked down into the mobile face broken with emotion. There was a black smudge on one cheek. Her shirt was dusty and her Levis travel-stained. But he thought he had never seen her so lovely. All her assurance, her impudence, her mocking laughter, had been swept away. Her shy sweet confession stirred in him a wave of joy. They had come together at last after great peril. Nothing could separate them now.

'I'm very happy too,' he told her, 'though maybe I ought not to be until we are out of the woods.'

'If you are still in danger I want to share it with you,' she said, in her low husky voice. 'I hope I won't have to live unless you do. All the way up I kept thinking that.'

His eyes caught fire from the ardent glow of his sweetheart. A drum of happiness began to beat in his breast. Life flowed through him, deep and strong and vital.

The voice of Driskill brought them back from the enchantment of love. 'Three more guys joining our friends outside,' he sang out to them from the front door.

In Clemson's bedroom Neal had found a pair of field glasses. He took them with him to the peek-hole.

'They're right excited about something,' Pete said.

Neal focussed the glasses on the huddle of out-laws. They were packed close in heated argument. One or two in the middle of the group, blocked out by the others, Neal was unable to see plainly.

He handed the glasses to Eleanor. 'Looks to me like one has his hands tied,' he told her. 'Maybe you can make him out.'

She took a long look and lowered the binoculars. The color had washed out of her cheeks. 'It's Austin,' she faltered. 'There's a rope 'round his neck.'

Neal verified what she said. He unfastened the belt from his waist. 'I'll have to go out and talk with the boys,' he said.

'No,' Eleanor protested. 'I'll go. They wouldn't hurt me. I would be quite safe.'

'So will I,' Neal assured her. 'If I go unarmed carrying a peace flag.'

'What makes you so sure of that?' Driskill cut in doubtfully. 'With those two men lying dead in the stable. Someone is liable to go crazy the way Folsom did.'

'I'm the one that ought to go. Austin is my brother, and we all know none of them would shoot a woman.'

'One of them might shoot first, and find out afterward you are a woman. It's a man's job, Eleanor. We can't hide behind you.'

'Let her go too, Neal,' Driskill urged. 'They won't hurt either of you if she is along, and they are a whole lot less likely to rub out Reynolds.

Fact is, they are probably as sick of all this killing as we are. If we give them a reasonable excuse I've a notion they would throw in their hands and quit. Why don't you suggest they bring down here the fellows they have taken prisoner and have a pow-wow? A peace treaty could be fixed up in half an hour. The cattlemen would have to tear down fences around land they don't own and they would have to agree to respect the rights of the little man. If they promised that and stuck to their pledge, all the decent people would quit supporting the outlaws and rustlers. The situation would clear up mighty fast then.'

'I think you're right, Pete,' agreed Neal. 'The time is right to straighten out this thing for good.'

'What say we all three go? They will certinly be flabbergasted to see us all walk out without even a pistol among us. O' course it would be duck soup for them to rush the house and grab us all, but my bet is they would go halfway to settle the jam we're all in.'

'If they didn't think we were giving ourselves up because we were afraid,' Eleanor suggested.

Driskill smiled. 'If they have a lick of sense, and I reckon they have, these guys know that Neal MacGowan isn't scared of anything. Back of these walls we can hold out till help comes. Allan Dunn doesn't have to be told that.'

'It would be a bold move for us to walk out and leave the door open behind us,' Neal admitted.

'Very likely it would work, if they take time to think. Maybe they wouldn't do that. They might come roaring forward like a pack of hungry wolves.'

'So they might,' Driskill assented. 'I reckon it isn't such a bright idea.'

'Let's risk it,' Eleanor said, her eyes starry.

'Yes,' Neal answered, the ring of decision in his voice. 'Get a white towel, Eleanor. I'll tell Doctor Seneca what we are going to do.'

They walked out of the house carrying the towel stretched between Neal and Pete. It was important that nobody have any doubt their mission was peaceful. Taken by surprise, the outlaws watched them approach, uncertain as to the meaning of this move.

Eleanor ran ahead of the men and flung her arms around her brother. He smiled at her grimly, from a face drawn and haggard.

'I didn't expect to see you here,' he said.

'Have they given you anything to eat?' she asked.

'The condemned prisoner ate a hearty breakfast of flapjacks, steak, and coffee.'

'I left Cheyenne just as soon as I heard of the trouble. Janet telegraphed me. I made Doctor Seneca bring me up here with him.' Eleanor looked at the man holding the loose end of the rope that was round her brother's neck and took it from him. He let her have it without protest and she slipped the noose from Austin's throat.

Dunn pointed to the open door of the ranch-house. 'What's to prevent us going in there and freeing Cad?' he asked Neal.

'Nothing. We've decided not to hold the fort. Muir will be here with the first posse soon. That would mean more fighting. We're through with killing and don't want any more of it. If you and yore men will work with us we believe most of the trouble between you and the cattlemen can be straightened out.'

'How?' Dunn asked.

Neal went over the points he had discussed with Driskill. Some of the rustlers jeered at what he said. Others flew into a rage. Neal did not raise his voice nor lose his temper. He made quiet and reasonable answers. Dunn backed his suggestion that the captured cattlemen be brought to Lonesome Valley and freed, after which a workable understanding could be reached. Surprisingly, Cad Clemson took the same view. He wanted to stop the fighting before the posses coming in got mixed up in it.

'The thing to do is bump off Reynolds first,' Buck cried bitterly. 'That fellow put me in the pen for three years and I don't aim to pass up my chance now. After he's taken care of it will be fine to make all the peace talk you like.'

Neal shook his head. 'No, Buck,' he told the black-bearded man. 'It's one of two things. Go on with this war till fifteen or twenty of us are killed, or quit right damn now. You can't do this to Reynolds and have the trouble stop. Maybe he crowded you too hard when he was sheriff. No need to go into that. After all, he was an officer of the law. He did what he was paid to do. Forget it. We've all got to forget a lot if we are going to patch this up and bring about better conditions. Inside of a couple of hours Bob Muir will be coming down into this valley with a bunch of gunmen. Before they get here we must know whether it is to be war or peace. There will be other posses coming after his—and maybe soldiers. You can't win in the end. But you can keep this drive against you from ever getting under way.'

Dunn said: 'I've had a bellyful, Neal, and that goes for most of us. But how do you expect to stop these posses?'

'Fix up a big barbecue for all of us. Bring down into the valley the cattlemen you have taken prisoners. Talk this whole thing over reasonably like businessmen without flying off the handle. Then we'll all sit down to a good feed. When Muir gets here we'll invite him and his men to sit in too.' Neal turned his wide friendly grin on the rustlers. 'I expect you have got a K-B beef here. I'll dedicate it as a peace offering. If you haven't one of mine I reckon Reynolds wouldn't object to finding out what a Triangle R steer, a good fat one with plenty of tallow, tastes like when sacrificed in a good cause.'

Reynolds said dryly that a few hours earlier he had not expected ever to sit down to a chuck-wagon dinner under any circumstances and that he would be glad to donate a beef to so good a picnic.

The trapped men who had been captured were brought down to Lonesome Valley in time for the barbecue. Three of those with whom they had started on the raid had been killed and several not too seriously wounded. They had faced disaster for two days and were elated at a settlement which allowed them to escape safely.

So it happened that when Bob Muir led his posse into Lonesome Valley, prepared for a desperate battle, he found himself instead invited to a love feast. That there were still hatred and bitterness in the hearts of some of those present he knew. But the fact that Neal had induced them to sit down and eat beside the same campfire was in itself a great triumph. Moreover, he knew that if the cattlemen lived up to their agreement, the ill will would gradually die down. The men who wanted to live by preying on others would continue their depredations until at last the law took care of them. But those who had been driven to rustling by the harshness of the stockmen would turn to better ways of life.

CHAPTER XXXVII

'Port after stormie seas'

Neal elected to stay at Lonesome Park as a guest of Cad Clemson to take care of Tim Owen and the other wounded men until they were ready to travel. Before Reynolds set out on the journey back to the Triangle R with Eleanor and Robert Muir he made public acknowledgment of his debt to MacGowan and an apology for the way in which he had been treated by his fellow cattlemen. His manner was stiff and formal, since that was the nature of the man, but Neal understood that the spirit back of the words was not grudging.

Eleanor and Neal said good-bye in public after she had swung to the saddle. He smiled up at her, a gleam of mirth in his eyes.

'When I get back to the K-B there won't be any press of business holding me at the ranch,' he promised. 'I don't want to discover that you are sincerely mine a second time.'

She answered, in a murmur for his ears alone, 'I'll never be that again, for I've lived and died too often with you in the past twenty-four hours.'

Doctor Seneca stayed two days in the park and then left Neal to nurse the convalescents. Cad

Clemson was a suave and smiling host. He realized that his day was done as dictator at Rustlers' Gap. Too many people now knew the way in and out of the place to make it any longer an ideal retreat for bandits. Moreover, he had lost most of his following. The hard-pressed home-steaders who had done some rustling on the side to feed their families no longer would support him. They were relying on the pact of peace signed with the cattlemen to ease the pressure of poverty.

Though Neal knew Cad for a bad lot, he found it amusing to listen to the lame little villain explain himself as an honest man. Clemson had a fund of entertaining stories of his experiences, and in the hours when Neal was not with the patients he enjoyed sitting on the porch and listening to the carefully censored experiences of the old scoundrel. The outlaw knew he was not fooling the owner of the K-B in the least, but it was his theory that if he worked hard enough at white-washing his past, some of his brushwork would stick.

It was two weeks before Neal got back to the K-B with Tim. Before he had been there an hour he saddled a fresh horse and rode across to the Triangle R. Eleanor was in her smartest clothes, and if she was very very humble, as she had promised to be, there was no external evidence of it. She came to meet Neal light-footed and gay, an eager sparkle in her eyes, the light of gifts in them that no other man would ever see.

He held her off from him a moment to look at the face he loved. 'My girl?' he asked.

'For ever and ever,' she told him.

It was a good many minutes later that they came back to connected speech again. Austin was away from home she explained, calling on Janet. 'A school director has so many things to talk over with a new teacher,' she explained, her face crinkling to laughter.

'I can understand that, when the teacher is Janet,' he agreed.

'Once I was afraid you understood too well how pleasant it was to talk things over with her,' she confessed. 'I had to buckle on my armor and go to war. I'm lucky I started before you became the hero of the valley.'

'Now, look here,' he warned. 'I won't have any of that kind of talk.'

'Not after this one time,' she promised. 'But I am very happy because everybody I meet thinks now you are the top man in our district. I don't hear any more about how wild and undependable you are—about how you gamble and make friends of outlaws and fight at any opportunity.' She made a mocking little *moue*. 'I think you could go to Congress if you would acquire the statesman's manner and not tilt your disreputable hat so impudently on one side of your head.'

'I'll have to tilt it a little more if it will keep me from such a fate,' he smiled.

She grew serious. 'I think I fell in love with you for the very recklessness people used to deplore,' she confided. 'When I have you in mind—and that is very often, sir—sometimes a snatch of verse jumps to my mind, written, I believe, by Sir Walter Raleigh the night before he was executed.

> Cowards fear to die,
> But courage stout,
> Rather than live in snuff
> Will be put out.

If you want to know just how I feel about you—'

He did not, along that particular line. It made him feel a little foolish. So he stopped her by the method lovers have known ever since Adam and Eve discovered it in the Garden.

Center Point Large Print
600 Brooks Road / PO Box 1
Thorndike, ME 04986-0001 USA

(207) 568-3717

US & Canada:
1 800 929-9108
www.centerpointlargeprint.com